I0598642

Coven of Desire

WINGS

ELLEN MINT

Wings
ISBN # 978-1-80250-986-1
©Copyright Ellen Mint 2022
Cover Art by Claire Siemaszkiewicz ©Copyright October 2022
Interior text design by Claire Siemaszkiewicz
Totally Bound Publishing

WINGS

Dedication

Thank you to my amazing readers for picking up this series and giving Ink a chance to wow you with his cooking prowess (among other things). Extra big thanks to my review team who help give my books a chance against the algorithm, and especially Fiona for letting me borrow her name.

Last biggest scoop of thanks with a cherry and whipped cream to my editor Anna and TEG for whipping my book into shape. Sometimes there's chains too.

Chapter One

"I'm late!"

My shout, ten seconds after I blearily checked my phone, reverberated off low wooden beams that I was shocked had never beaned my boyfriend. Stumbling on the slick floors in my wool socks, I slid for the closet and grabbed the first shirt I found. It wasn't until I already had my arms through the sleeves that I smelled the musk of man and a hint of wet fur. Even a month later, most of my clothing was scattered between four cardboard boxes I swore I'd unpack once the semester was over.

I began to reach for the top one, hoping to hit summer tees and not sweaters, when my phone's alarm went off again. Damn it, there wasn't time. While half-hopping into my sweatpants, I dashed down Cal's... No, he wanted me to think of it as my hallway, too. The bathroom door was partially open. At my blur, my werewolf boyfriend called out, "Babe!"

"Yes?" I skidded in my tracks and turned to find him in nothing but a nearly see-through pair of gray boxers.

Even with his blond hair smooshed on one side and his eyes drooping after our long night cramming—of both the academic and carnal variety—he was perfect. Cal smiled with his total sunshine grin and my legs began to wobble. He slipped a hand around my waist and pulled me into the bathroom.

"Morning," he whispered before kissing me. "I still love doing that."

I'd had no choice but to take the leap to live-in girlfriend thanks to evil witch hunters, and it'd taken some adjusting. I can't say I'd have been so quick to move in with Cal minus the pitchfork-wielding agents, but he'd been trying his best to make it all work.

Cal picked up the blue toothbrush from the cup, leaving my purple one alone. "Are you ready for the last one?"

"No," I admitted without pause.

He squirted out a huge glob of toothpaste, then stared at me. "You've got this. Or should we"—Cal cocked an eyebrow and full-on smirked—"cram again?"

A laugh escaped my lips even as goosebumps rippled up my legs and arms. It sure as hell was a cramming session with him, even using lube, but I didn't have time. "I can't." I groaned. "I'm already late. Do you know where I left my purse?"

"Maybe downstairs?" He went to town on his incisors with the toothbrush before stopping and turning to me. "How are you late? We've got at least a half hour until exam time."

"Only a half hour?" I repeated, the sarcasm thick. Talking to Cal wasn't getting me to class any faster. "I hate boys."

As I dashed down the stairs, Cal called out, "I have proof you love certain parts of us."

Upon reaching the landing, I was greeted by the sound of pans striking a stove. That could be just one thing. I took a quick look around the living room. The TV was running through a mess of old sitcoms, but no one was watching. No sign of my purse or book. I remembered needing it when the pizza arrived, but wasn't certain where it went after the demon and werewolf ambushed me.

If the latter didn't know, maybe the former would. Dashing down the narrow hallway, I had to cling to the walls to avoid tripping. The last lightbulb had burned out and no one had bothered to replace it. I pushed open the kitchen door with my foot and it swung in on a baking disaster.

Standing in the middle of an egg-and-flour apocalypse was my own personal incubus. Ink's go-to outfit was splattered in white powder and dough while he held a far-too-small bowl in the crook of his arm and stabbed it with a knife. I must have made a sound as he looked up from his concoction and smiled.

Unlike Cal's sweet sunshine, Ink's smile was panty-melting nefarious even when he was covered in flour prints. My mouth dried and I tried to think. Why was I here? I was doing something important, something that didn't involve him swiping the pans off the counter and taking me now.

"I'm late," my mouth supplied to my frozen brain.

"I assume that is not in reference to your moon cycle," Ink said, straight-faced, before smirking. "Unless you're far more devious than I imagined."

"That isn't. I can't even..." I slapped him on the arm with barely any force, not that it mattered. I'd seen him take knives to the chest without reacting. "I wouldn't."

"It was but a jest. Your virtue is pure."

"Ha!" It was hard to think myself virtuous when three men shared my bed, often two or more at a time. "Have you seen my purse?"

"I believe I last viewed it in the galley when I'd bent over your back and pressed your hands to the wood while the wolf—"

"Yes!" I interrupted, my cheeks hitting ten thousand degrees at the reminder of where Ink and Cal had been. "I remember that part. Thanks."

I had turned to find my purse when Ink hefted up a tray. "My bond, before you attend your academic gauntlet..."

I stared at whatever he'd been cooking with dread rising in my stomach. "What is it?" They looked like generic toaster pastries with a smear of chocolate on top, but it couldn't be that simple.

"A sandwich of my own concoction to aid in breaking your fast."

That was what I was terrified of. Still, I picked one up. Ink had been helpful as of late. I couldn't even hazard a guess as to why he suddenly wanted to do the occasional bout of cooking and laundry, even if what he made was usually inedible. And I was never getting that dress back after it floated down the river. But turning him down felt mean. As I raised his sandwich, I realized it was two toaster pastries stuck together. What was in the middle was anyone's guess. Could be more chocolate, mustard or even a thickened soy sauce.

With the tips of my teeth, I nibbled down on the edge, hoping to escape the answer when brown goo clogged my throat. "Peanut butter?" I coughed out. It oozed and dripped off the sides, like he'd heated it between the two pastries.

Ink only smiled wider. "Yes. I am quite ingenious."

"Yep," I agreed.

"Do have a delightful day." He pulled me closer while I stared at the PB and T sandwich. Once the peanut butter cooled, it wasn't too bad, the strawberry in the pastry combining well. I was about to take another test bite, when Ink whispered, "Upon your return, I shall..."

He plunged his teeth against my neck, just to the edge of breaking skin. The pressure rushed through me, filling me with pleasure. Ink pressed the tip of his long nose to the middle of his bite mark. "That is for your inner thigh, and this..." He darted his tongue around the wound, the slick heat causing the same in my panties. "You can decide where you wish it."

I groaned as my entire body lit up with anticipation and my hand clenched, shattering the breakfast sandwich. We both stared when the soggy pastry halves hit the floor. "Sorry," I muttered, struggling to get my breathing under control.

"No matter." Ink popped open the oven and, without gloves, pulled out a bright red tray. "I made three sheets' worth."

"That's...good?" I inched out of the kitchen, leaving Ink to it while hoping Cal wasn't counting on the mega-box of toaster pastries to fuel his wolf metabolism. An impertinent *brring* chirped from my phone and I glared at it.

"Yes, I know. I'm working on it!" I shouted at my inanimate object while walking into what should have been the dining room. A man dressed for a punk concert in the nineties hovered next to where every book in the house had been scattered across the long dining table. As quite a few were nursing textbooks, the old wood was bowing in the middle.

"Daniel? Have you seen my purse?"

11

"Hm?" Slowly, the book lowered, revealing my ghost from his cheekbones up. Not that I was complaining—they were fantastic. His deep umber eyes flared blue a moment and he snapped the book shut.

I reared back in shock. "You can do that now?" Last I remembered, the best he could do was push a page and maybe the cover.

Daniel dropped the book where it landed on knowledge mountain and picked up another. "Yes, I found I could move the book much in the way I sit."

"I assume you mean using muscle memory and not that you close it with your butt."

The air froze at the serious glare buffeting from Daniel's face. I swallowed haphazardly, the peanut butter still lodged at the hollow of my throat. *Did I say something wrong?* He'd been waffling between a debilitating state of sadness followed by manic bursts of certainty. I couldn't handle pushing him back to the dark side again.

Slowly, Daniel scratched his chin and cocked his head, causing the single blue stripe of hair to fall to the side. "Is that something you'd like to see?" he asked with dead certainty.

"Ah..." I was about to laugh it off, when I remembered my werewolf boyfriend who was into leashes and the demon that'd do literally anything. What I found hot seemed to shift by the day. "I'll get back to you on that. In the meantime, I need my purse."

"Under the table," he said, gesturing to exactly where Ink had said it was. As I bent over to pick it up, Daniel immersed himself in yet another book. I reached inside to find my spell book safe and sound. Running my finger down the spine calmed me. Ever since I had learned that a witch losing her book caused her to go mad, I'd taken to sleeping with it under my pillow. Only the dual exhausting talents of Cal and Ink could distract me from my mortal dread.

"Did you read all of those?" I asked, pointing to his stack. There had to be a good three thousand pages there.

"Oh no," he said with a laugh. "I read the whole table. Which reminds me, I have a list of new books I'll require." Daniel gestured to an old tablet Cal let him use. He couldn't pick it up, but with his ghostly powers he could use the apps and leave lots of lists.

"I'll have to look later," I said, trying to work around the book peaks to escape.

"I also discovered another three potential protection spells for the house."

"And how many of them will banish a demon?" I asked.

He frowned. Their whole ghost and incubus bromance had lasted a few days after my rescue, then it was right back to openly hating each other. "To my knowledge, none. If you'd take a look?"

"I really have to run. Last day of exams."

"That was today? Hm, I thought they'd already occurred. Or were going to…" The unsleeping ghost stared back at the dining room window as if it could act like a calendar.

"Nope. Happening in an hour. I've got to bolt."

"Why are you not going with your wolf?"

I heard him but didn't want to answer. 'Because' was a cheap response, but also the best I could give. If it were the usual lecture day, of course I'd go with Cal, even if he'd wait until the last second to leave. But the only way I could keep the letters on the page from dancing the dyslexia steps was if I had a half hour to myself to calm down. Sitting next to Cal this close to a full moon would make my brain more stupid.

As I approached the front door, I called out, "Bye," to the house and opened it. A very small man in a bowtie stood outside holding an envelope. I gasped in surprise and he opened his mouth.

"For Lady—"

Before he could speak, a demon's claw latched around his shoulders and hefted him off the ground. I reached over to stop Ink from damaging him, but a naked arm wrapped around my stomach and pulled me deeper into the house. "What's going on?" Cal shouted behind my ear, his words garbled from the toothbrush still in his mouth.

"They seem to have sent a spy gnome. What do they have on you? Kidnapped your gnome wife? Threatened your fox? Out with it?"

"Layla?" Daniel rushed to my side. My three guys were now standing guard against a two-foot-tall man armed with a letter. "Gnomes are often indebted to powerful magic users."

Ink groaned and glared back over his shoulder. "Shall you read to us from the Compendium of Wikis next? We all know what gnomes are. And this one has come bearing a piece of parchment. A written threat, perhaps?"

"It's a note, you demented fucktoy," the gnome snarled, his little legs kicking in the air.

"A likely... Ah, it is a note addressed to Layla. Wolf?" Rather than pass it to me, he handed it to Cal who stepped even further back while taking me along.

He breathed in the scent of the envelope. "I don't smell the sewers, but there's obvious magic."

"No shit," the gnome responded. "It's from..."

"Allow me." Daniel was the next one to excise the letter, somehow pulling it not only from Cal's fingers, but flipping open the flap and lifting the paper free. We all watched him carefully unfold the paper.

Ink pulled the gnome closer. "If it is coated in a ghost purging powder, I will buy you a keg."

Daniel didn't respond to that, his focus on the letter.

"Well," Cal snapped. "What's it say?"

"It's a letter for Layla."

All three jerked to attention at once, as if certain it had to be a sign the witch hunters were on my trail. Daniel glanced down to the bottom and sighed, "From a Valerie. Were any of the hunters known as Valerie?"

"Val... That's the witch that saved me." I was about to rip the letter from his ethereal fingers to read myself, when Ink grabbed it first.

Where is the gnome? I stared around in a panic to find the small man scurrying down the stoop as fast as possible.

"'To Lady Layla, so on and so forth. I have engaged in much research...' Humans do like to prattle...oh. Oh, great." Ink's interpretation of the letter smashed to a halt and he raised his head to stare at the sky.

"What?" I tried to look closer, but Cal had ahold of my waist and he wasn't about to let me get near it just in case.

With a sigh that rattled the windows, Ink said, "It is a potion to bring back the dead."

"Really?" I gasped, tears springing to my eyes as I turned to Daniel. His mouth hung open as if he too couldn't believe it. We'd been hunting for a month, him for all hours, day and night, and had found nothing. If it was true that I could bring him back, he could touch, feel, live...

"What does it need? What do I have to do?" My excitement hit a peak, then crashed hard as Ink stared at me not in exhaustion but a distressing concern. I gulped and asked, "Don't tell me it'll cost me an arm and a leg?"

"Not quite so macabre, lest you happen to be hiding a horn I am somehow unaware of?"

A horn? I wrenched the letter away from Ink who stared in surprise that I'd dare. Damn thing was addressed to me after all. I skipped past the preamble from the witch who'd saved me from the hunters to the helpful bullet points.

Blood of a demon
Piece between realms
Skin of a unicorn
Feather of an angel
Bone of the dead

Boil in a cauldron or available kettle for thirty minutes, then recite the intended's name while pouring the potion out.

That was it. Laid out like a recipe, it felt easy, doable. I glanced to Daniel and hope shone in his eyes. Reaching over, I placed my hand above his. He took control, holding mine as we both grinned like two idiots who won a chocolate factory. Soon, he'd be able to hold me for real.

"We can do this," I whispered to him, trying to seal the promise I made.

"Ah, yes." Ink peered over my shoulder at the list he'd already read. "Only requires the blood and brains of two celestials and a piece of the void to seal it together. A light shopping list. Perhaps your interconnected webs have an all demon and angel body part store?"

They never said it would be easy. "You're a demon..." I began to my incubus.

"Even ignoring the technicality, I am not a demon. My blood is not special enough for this spell."

"I pray I don't expire twice from the lack of surprise," Daniel cut in.

Ink's lips cut apart into a toothy grin aimed at the ghost. "Would be much easier to simply acquire a bowl of salt and a torch."

I was about to cut in, when my phone gave its final warning. All of this demons and angels mess would have to wait. My other life needed me. "We'll figure all of this out later. I've got to get to the test." I started to fold the letter up, but Daniel held his hands out for it.

For a moment, I hesitated. Not only was it addressed to me, it was also a private letter between witches. But it was his life, literally, in my hands. I handed him the paper, which he managed to keep floating a millimeter above his palms while he stared at it.

Checking my purse once more to make certain my book hadn't fallen out, I tugged open the front door. "And, if you wouldn't mind, can you dial back the 'big scary bodyguard' routine? Not everyone in the world is trying to kill me."

"Are you certain of that, my bond?" the one who'd assaulted the gnome asked without pause.

I glared at Ink, then caught a quick blown kiss from Cal. Daniel broke from the letter to give me one last smile before I slipped out of the house. I couldn't blame them for being so overprotective, but it'd been a month since I had escaped the hunters. At some point, I had to return to normal life.

"Wait!" Cal dashed to my side. It was sweet that he didn't want to say goodbye, but I really had to... He reached up and tugged my bonnet off my hair. "Didn't think you wanted to leave the house with this on."

A jab of embarrassment jolted through me. I had forgotten I even had it on. That he'd cared enough to tell me and it didn't faze him warmed my heart. I pulled him close for a quick peck and whispered, "Thank you."

"When will you return?" It was Daniel who spoke, still transfixed by the letter.

"Once this test is done, we can get to work on figuring out that potion."

"Ah, Dana's party," Cal interrupted.

I winced at forgetting my friend's 'we're free' bash. I'd been so busy lately, the only time I spent with her or Fariah was during deathly quiet studying. "After that," I promised Daniel. "Then we'll bring you back to life."

He smiled so sweetly that I ached to kiss him. It was Ink who sighed dramatically and turned. "I shall fetch the lightning rods and pitchforks then."

I really had to go. With one arm around my purse, I stepped out of the door to the walkway lined with untrimmed bushes and tried to force my brain to think about gram-negative bacteria. What would it feel like to hold him? To touch warm skin instead of cool air? To pull off his jean jacket and lift the old band shirt to touch his body below? To feel his lips on mine?

I was electrified, certain I could take on the world. *Pass my finals, bring back the dead, stop whatever evil Mr. White is, end the witch hunters once and for all.* I was unstoppable.

The bushes rustled and an arm bigger than a fencepost shot out. It wrapped around my throat and pulled me back, tightening so fast I couldn't even scream.

Chapter Two

"Squeal." The stench of onions and copper splattered against my cheek with that single word. He tightened his grip, pressing his iron forearm into my trachea until the bone scraped my spine.

"You're gonna scream for me. Now!" The bastard locked his hand around the side of my head, crushing my ear. A metal band around his wrist cut into my chin, but I refused to give in.

He let go for a second, no doubt assuming I'd cry for help, but I whispered under my breath and clung to his skin. He laughed, knowing I had as much chance to pull a truck out of a lake as I would removing him. But that wasn't the plan.

"You're gonna die, anyway. Scream and I'll make it quick."

Power rushed through me as I focused the spell. He loosened one last time to get me to scream for his entertainment. With a single gasp of air, I shouted "No!" I unleashed flames across the entirety of his arms, the fire licking against the muddled red and pink flesh. But it wasn't turning black. He wasn't falling away and screaming.

No. He started to laugh.

"That tickles, green skin. Wanna see what I can do?"

Shit! He dug his hands into my face, filthy nails piercing the skin. The bastard pinched my head between his palms. "I'm gonna snap your neck and toss your body on his front porch."

Without thought, I clawed at his flesh. My nails struck, bending and breaking against the skin, but he wouldn't let go and just kept laughing manically. I tried to twist, hoping it'd throw him off balance, but there was nothing I could do against his force.

"That's not friendly, stranger."

Oh, thank god! Tears sprang to my eyes at my incubus speaking behind me. The grip on my head opened and I spun around while kicking backward as hard as possible. I didn't know what it connected with, but my entire heel throbbed as I stumbled away from the widest man I'd ever seen. His shoulders were so far apart they needed two zip codes. The muscles on his sledgehammer neck were thicker than ship ropes and bulged against the slender hand clasped around them. Ink could barely reach with his claws extended, though all five were pierced so deep into the skin red blood dribbled out.

My attacker's face wouldn't look out of place in a Neanderthal exhibit. That gnome could have sheltered from the rain under his brow. His lips were sunken and flat, while the nose was wide from the long bridge to the stubby tip. But what flared was the shock of red hair, shaved on both sides so a single long strip tumbled from the middle. He looked like a caveman Viking plucked from the ice...and he had a grip on Ink.

"Stop!" I shouted, fumbling in my purse for a way to make him stop.

"Perhaps, my bond, it would be in your best interest to—"

The fucker hauled back his fist the size of my head and plowed it into Ink's stomach. For a brief moment, pain flashed in his once-cocky eyes.

That bastard! I reared back, ready to smash my spell book into him, when a howl ripped apart the suburban morning. We all turned as a massive gray wolf launched off the porch and straight onto the man. Anyone else would have buckled from Cal's werewolf weight and his jaws and claws hacking away. But the giant bastard wrapped his arms around Cal and the two fell to the ground.

He began to throttle Cal's chest with massive punches. "Nice. To. See. You." He punctuated each word with a fist. "Brother!"

Brother? Fuck! I reached into my purse, slipping past my spell book for the only weapon I knew that could stop one of Cal's rampaging kin. "Ink!" I shouted to my struggling demon just as I held up the bottle.

He nodded and dug both hands into the monster's head, pulling it back. "Look away!" I ordered as I unleashed the full bottle of pepper spray straight into his eyes. Cal whimpered from the onslaught, Ink turned away but that unstoppable monster stared up at me as if he enjoyed it.

"Girly thinks she's got balls now," he taunted even as his eyes burned redder than tomatoes and tears gushed down his cheeks. His hand sprung out for me, which was when Cal locked his jaws onto his arm.

There was no escaping the bite force of a werewolf. Cal shook his head, yanking the man off his feet. As he fell, a pop wrenched his arm out of the socket. He shook again, snarling as he fought to drag the bastard away from me. I knew a spell to keep him pinned, if I could just…

Ink threw his arms around me, knocking my marker to the ground to put himself between me and the asshole. "What are you doing? I can help!"

"By becoming collateral. Remain away from the monster's claws and fangs."

"Cal wouldn't hurt me," I insisted, feeling every strain from Cal as he struggled in the fight.

"I know," Ink declared as if the matter was finished.

The flailing man suddenly turned and reached behind himself. "He has a knife!" I cried. The glint swept through the air when Cal dodged away.

"Let's finish this, meat." He staggered to his feet even though blood gushed from the open wound on his arm. He obviously could barely see from the pepper in his eyes, but nothing seemed to stop him.

This was going to take all three of us. My fire didn't stop him, but maybe twisting his intestines into a bow would do the trick. I flared my hand out, expecting Ink to rush him, when Cal stepped back and the wolf melted away.

Naked, he rose to his human legs, his entire face as red as his eyes. "Get out of here, Eric. You have no standing."

"Funny. I'd have said the same about you, traitorous coward, until you started staking the claim for yourself." Eric tossed the knife back and forth while he spoke, his leg twitching as he went.

"Get out!" Cal repeated, the full force of the wolf behind his words.

Eric bent back a moment, as if he had to obey, but he laughed and shook it off. "You're a worthless scrap of gristle and bone. Even our dear father knew. When your bitch stole you away, do you know what he did? He laughed."

"I don't care what the fuck he did. He's dead!"

The shoulders on Eric tightened, veins bulging in his arm from how hard he gripped the knife. But he didn't rush for Cal. He seemed to be rooted by whatever order Cal had barked.

"Stay away from the home, you hear me? Stay away or I'll..." Eric twisted around and he smiled right at me. "I'll take her from you just as you did Father."

"I'll kill you first!" Cal thundered, rushing for him, but Eric drew the knife out, freezing him in his tracks.

"You better be sure before you try, meat." His callous chuckle rumbled as he turned away from his fuming brother and began to walk toward us.

Ink swept his wings around me and the world shifted. In one second, I went from the pathway to the garden.

"Cute trick," Eric said from the fence's gate. "But if you don't stay away, there ain't no demons that can protect her." Even with his blood splattering to the sidewalk, Eric calmly shut the gate and walked to his massive truck, whistling. The roar of the engine deafened the entire neighborhood.

As the giant red vehicle drove past, he shouted, "Witch fucker!" I didn't see the knife fly out of the window until Ink held it in his hand, the blade still vibrating.

That'd come straight for me. Ink merely inspected the handle and took a quick whiff before wincing. "Smells of wet hound." He tossed the knife into the garden and I broke from him for Cal.

"Are you okay?" he asked me even while I spotted a bruise sprouting across his ribs and back around his lats.

"I'm fine," I insisted through hysterical tears. I had nearly died five minutes after breakfast, but that was normal for me. I whispered my healing spell, trying to help him. He barely reacted even as the magic wiped away the pain. Cal had one hand wrapped around my waist while he stared pure murder in the direction of the woods.

Out there lay the compound where Cal had been born, a horrific off-the-grid torture shack that housed a cult of werewolves. I'd thought that after he'd killed the alpha, his father, that'd be the end of it. But he'd been watching them late at night from afar, keeping tabs on the inner turmoil and refusing to talk to me about it.

"You've broken your word," Ink spoke from behind both of us. I jumped at the voice, my heart yet racing, and my incubus placed a calming hand on my shoulder. I assumed he blamed me for failing to keep safe, but he looked to Cal instead.

"I know." Those two words spat from Cal's lips as if he'd been fighting a losing battle.

"What are you...what's he mean?" I wasn't sure which one I was talking to—both really. "Cal?" My boyfriend shuddered, his head so low I couldn't read his face. "Ink?" He was even worse. Oh, he looked me in the eye, but his expression was stone.

"That was him?" Daniel asked. He walked through the door and stood under the shadows of the porch, his face a drab spotlight from the library's fluorescent lighting.

"Even Daniel knows what that was about?" We'd been over this, a lot. In order for our complicated relationship to work he had to tell me shit, not run off into the woods to solve it himself.

"It's the pack," Cal whispered, barely suppressing a combination of tears and rage. Pins and needles broke out across my skin—the animal part of my brain wanting to scamper away from the voice. Instead, I reached over to caress the wolf's head. "I didn't know how to explain all of this."

"Before or after a caveman thug ripped my throat out?"

Cal jerked at the thought, but it was Ink who wrapped his arms around me. "That would not have occurred, my bond."

"Why didn't you tell me? If he's telling you all of his secrets." I'd been abandoned by the three men I thought I could count on for anything. But a current of rage snapped through me from my attacker getting away. How did he shake off my fire? Was he more than just a werewolf?

Ink blanched for a moment, as if he could feel shame for his actions. But he shook it off and smiled. "The politics of dogs and where their bones are buried are rarely my concern."

"It's Ophelia," Cal whispered.

Who?

He rubbed his shoulder haphazardly. "Mark's mother. She approached me one night. I had no idea she'd do it."

"Approached you where?" I asked.

Cal's lips tightened and I feared he'd run off instead of telling me. He risked looking up into my eyes and admitted, "In the woods. She asked me to take over the pack...the cult. I refused, flat out."

"But you kept going back there, you kept watching them."

"You wouldn't under—"

I glared hard at him and Cal gulped. "Werewolf packs, they aren't like real wolf ones. We aren't all family."

26

"From what I've observed, I'd say your family shares much in common with the Julio-Claudian family dynasty," Ink mused to our confusion.

"He means Roman emperors like Caligula and Nero who'd, you know," Daniel trailed off.

Cal snorted hard. "They'd fit right in, for sure. I had hoped with the death of…him, the pack would dissolve or another would swoop in to take over the territory. Anything but this."

"What? What's happening?"

Ink snickered. "What always occurs when humans try to topple the structures they once worshiped—a power vacuum."

"You mean that…that massive asshole is trying to take control?"

"He has," Cal said. "With Eli…with the three of us refusing, he took his opportunity. I didn't think it possible, no right-thinking wolf would follow him given—"

"No offense, but the brainwashed are rarely known for thinking rightly under the best of circumstances," Daniel cut in.

Cal kept cupping his hands tighter, claws extending out then retreating. He stared at the shadow at his feet as if he couldn't believe it was still human.

"Is that what you were doing out there? Trying to save them?"

"Fuck the rest of them. Most are the same as Lucien, as Eric. Abusive assholes more than happy to put up with the occasional punch from the alpha as long as they get to punch those lower than them. The entire thing's rotten."

"Then why?"

His lips parted as if he wanted to confess, but Cal gasped and in a breathy voice he said, "I don't know. I just felt like I should. Are you angry with me?"

The question completely disarmed me. Yes, he was keeping shit to himself again. Mark's mother, the one so brainwashed she'd have sacrificed her own son, had approached Cal and he hadn't told me. How long had he been carrying this? Acting like his life was normal, going to work, class, protecting me from yet another monster I'd stumbled into? And the whole time, the flames of his past blazed higher and higher, threatening to take out everything in his world.

"No," I whispered, folding around him.

All three of them gasped in surprise. Ink placed a hand to my forehead. "Hm, the brain fever is undetectable, but I fear she could be suffering from ear worms."

"I do not have... Wait, are those a thing?"

He shrugged, but smiled wickedly as I did my best to not think about maggots crawling down my ear canal. "You're not alone in this. You don't have to take on the entire pack by yourself."

"But..."

"Let me help you, please?" I cupped his cheeks, raising his head so he had no choice but to look at me.

I feared he'd turn his eyes away, shrug me off, insist he worked best alone. But Cal placed his hand behind mine and entwined our fingers together. "Okay."

Brushing back his hair, I pulled Cal close to kiss him, when my phone screamed—literally. The sound sent me leaping into the air. Cal crushed me in his arms and Ink excised my phone.

"Your confidant Dana appears to be concerned about your whereabouts," he reported while twisting around the cracked screen.

I ripped my phone away, grumbling to myself, "Very funny, Dana, changing my phone ring to scare the shit out of me."

"She's right, though, babe. We need to get to class." Cal kissed me on the forehead, then ran back inside where he had hopefully left his clothing. If he took the test completely naked, his anatomy would put the diagrams to shame.

I twisted around my phone, trying to chase a calm I knew was impossible. My heart was still racing, and my mind churning with fear for everyone I loved with a good dose of anger too. As I did, my screen glitched and a song began to play. Not just any random one, but the only recording I had of my mother singing to me.

I'd thought she was dead. I'd clung to this foreign lullaby like my solitary branch when I dangled off the cliff. Except it wasn't a song, but a spell from a woman who had never told me what she was, what I was. She wasn't lying in her grave. She'd abandoned me, faked her death, and I'd never learn why I wasn't good enough for her.

"Let's go!" Cal called, ripping me away. I forced a smile and stuffed my phone in my pocket. He dashed to the driver side of his truck while I cracked open the passenger. When we both got in, he reached over to hold my hand. "You ready for this?"

"Yep," I said through gritted teeth.

Not-dead mom, murderous gigantic werewolf, bringing back the dead, hiding from witch hunters — nowhere in there was room for microbial bacteria. "I'm so fucked."

Chapter Three

Where is he?

A burst of fresh grass and baking blacktop rolled across the abandoned volleyball sand and tugged back my hair. I breathed in the return of summer to the park, but my heart churned with the frost of a factory floor in late November. A werewolf cult prowled the woods encircling the city, baying for mine and Cal's blood. Deep underground, an entire secret organization of witch hunters plotted to destroy not only me but everyone I loved. And even worse...

The songbird's chirps sharpened to a sour note, the fresh air rotted to a metallic sting and the sky darkened as if the whole of the world were about to be swallowed by the space in-between.

"What's got you so bothered?"

I shivered. My eyes stung with unshed tears so I blinked them. The ominous warnings vanished, revealing a pleasant early May afternoon in one of the city's better parks.

"Hm?" I asked, finally facing Dana, who held two cheap beers. She passed one to me and I popped it open, despite hating beer. It poured down my throat like burned bread, but I kept drinking it.

"You been staring at that car in the lot like you know it. Don't tell me it's an ex's."

I barely looked back, seeing the car for the first time. "No, I don't have a clue."

"No kidding. Here." Dana raised her beer can high and I clinked mine against it. "To another semester down the drain." She tipped hers back like a pro while I couldn't pretend to nurse it any longer. Nearly the entire class had turned out for this fourth semester sendoff. Most were arranging the tables, laying out some of the weirdest salads I'd ever seen.

The three guys in the class guarded the solitary grill, Scott and Jared offering advice on when best to turn a hot dog while Cal manned the spatula. I didn't know how he did it. Not grilling—a trained guinea pig could handle that. He was smiling and laughing along with his friends as if he hadn't been attacked by his eldest brother six hours earlier.

"You're staring," Dana said, a sly smile rising above the lip of her can.

"So?" I hadn't been, but now I did. It hurt how hot Cal was. Strong shoulders, narrow hips, a jawline built for striking matches but eyes that insisted he'd rather cuddle on the couch. Best of all was that little dimple in the middle of his chin—it pointed straight up to his blinding smile.

Fariah approached the grill and asked for something. Cal smiled and scooped a burger onto her plate, then Jared snatched up the tongs and plopped a hot dog beside it. She frowned, but walked away, leaving the three boys to resume standing around the fire.

"Dana, Layla," she greeted us while coming to a stop and extending her plate out.

Dana growled, snatched up the hot dog and crammed it in her mouth. Crumbs flew as she cursed at Jared while Fariah delicately added a pristine lettuce leaf to her bun. "Could you stop? I'd rather not waste my time with him," Fariah interrupted. "What else were you speaking of?"

That same dangerous smile returned and Dana elbowed me. "Layla practically panting over Calvin Rollin there."

"I'm allowed to pant. He's got a lot worth panting over." I tried to whisper to myself, but Dana could smell blood in the water.

"Are you finally gonna give us the details? Thick, right? Looks meaty."

Cal's could rival a baseball bat in width...and I really shouldn't tell my friends that. Luckily, I had Fariah on my side. She grimaced. "Please don't answer her."

"Oh, just 'cause you don't care." Dana tried to buzz her away, her interest piqued, but I shook my head.

"That's private."

"Uh huh, and now you got that huge house to get all 'private' in."

I stiffened at the question Dana so badly wanted to ask me. More like lecture me about. She had a few years on me which had made her decide she needed to be my stand-in big sister.

"I mean, must be nice waking to that every day." She waved to Cal, who was juggling the various jars of barbecue sauce to the jeers of Scott and Jared. *He can do that?* Every time he caught, then hefted a glass bottle into the air, his biceps bulged.

"Then again, you work together, go to school together, live together. You must be getting sick of each other."

"No," I admitted, as surprised as Dana. Granted, it'd only been a month since I'd moved in with him. But I wouldn't trade it for anything.

"Young love." She clasped her hands together and sighed. "So starry-eyed and delusional."

"I'm twenty-five. That's not young."

"You're a baby."

"You're twenty-eight," I countered back before watching her frown. "Sorry, twenty-nine." I'd missed her birthday party due to a demon and wolf emergency, but we'd made it up the next day. A cold draft blew between us and Dana stepped back beside Fariah.

I didn't mean to keep missing things. But with the fate of humankind as well as my nursing degree resting on my shoulders, something had to fall by the wayside. That something kept being my friends.

Maybe I should invite them over more, not for studying, but to hang out without threat of monster attack. Cal won't mind. Though I'll have to tell Daniel to hide in the attic. Ink will do whatever he wants. Controlling him is like trying to herd a...

"Ink?"

"—Angelo's with me for the summer. She swears it'll stick this time but..." Dana paused and turned to me as I spotted a man in crimson and black ducking behind some bushes. "Layls. You good?"

"What?"

"You said 'ink,' then paled," Fariah chimed in. A cold wind from the north struck, tugging back her headscarf. Fariah slapped a hand to it while I rocked back on my feet.

"I don't know why I did that," I lied. Maybe I'd imagined it, or someone in the same outfit was wandering through the park. If Ink had walked into the bushes, he wasn't coming out. That wasn't like him. Then again, he hadn't been acting like himself lately. He was being helpful, sometimes without asking.

A hand clamped onto my shoulder. I reached back, slamming my palm to the elbow to break it, when I realized it was Dana holding me. "I do," she said solemnly.

"You...do?"

"I'll have to set up a call for Angelo with my sister, but after that, I'm yours for the day."

"What?"

"First Sunday in May," Dana said and my heart plummeted. *Mother's Day. Fuck!* The tears came before I had a chance to stop them. I ducked my head down and clasped my hand over my chest.

"Ah, Layls, I'm sorry. I didn't mean —"

"It's okay. I'm...I'm okay. Just, forgot, somehow." The world didn't make it easy. Every damn store dangled giant 'Don't forget your mother' signs in front of me. It was hard to forget when I'd thought she lay six feet under — harder now that I knew the truth. "I should...get some air. Better air than this."

I wasn't making a lick of sense, but I had to get away before I blurted everything out. Not just about my mother being alive, but how I was a witch, that I had a ghost in my dining room and an incubus wherever he wanted to go. They'd only worry more, or worse, think I was insane.

"Are you certain?" Fariah asked, her perfect eyebrow curled above her cat-eye sunglasses.

All I could do was nod and walk away from my friends, my classmates — the humans. Cal watched, and

I didn't look back to check. It was as if I always knew when his eyes were on me.

"Gonna tell me about her?"

"No."

"Come on! I heard you two were..." Dana and Fariah's conversation faded as I wandered toward the swings. Pieces of glass lay at the end of the slide while the wind twisted the one broken swing so it spun in a circle. I'd spent a lot of time at playgrounds like this after my mom had died. After she had run. It didn't matter how rundown they were, how many splinters or cuts they gave me — I had to get out of the sardine room in the cardboard trailer.

I lowered myself to the swing, making certain it wouldn't snap under my weight. Rather than push off, I clung to the rusting chains. How many hours had I sat on a swing like this pleading with the universe to give her back? I only wanted to see her again, to tell her that...that I was sorry. If I hadn't been such a spoiled brat begging her for cookies, she wouldn't have gone out that night. She wouldn't have...

Yes, she would have. If not that night, the next or the one after. It wasn't fate that had taken my mother, but choice. Why did I keep returning to being nine years old whenever I thought of her? I shouldn't be feeling grief, only anger.

"Do you require a push?"

I wiped at my eyes and turned as two hell-warm hands landed on my back.

"That is what elder adults do in these situations, yes?" Ink asked. He did more than push. He pulled me back and gave me a good shove into the air. I watched my feet sweep up, then fall back down as gravity took hold. He was there still, ready to give another push until I got more air. Higher and higher I rose, the bar squeaking and bouncing off the ground with each swing. What would happen if I fell off?

Cal would run to my side. Broken leg, scraped knee, glass embedded in my ribs—he'd be there. He'd probably scoop me up into his arms to take me to the ER even though I could heal myself. But what about Ink? What would he do if I fell?

"Why are you here?" I asked.

"After that rather impertinent display of machismo this morning, I believed it in your best interests I remain close." He didn't miss a beat with his pushing. I tipped back, my fingers digging into the chains, to look at him. Nothing had changed. He was the same nonchalant, mischievously handsome sex demon I'd met on my birthday. His supple lips were perched in a near smirk as if he were thinking of something nefarious or a past sexual conquest. Orange and red flickered in his eyes, the fire never far. And he'd managed to undo nearly all the buttons on his shirt. The lapels flapped in the wind.

"Your best interests too," I said. If I died, he went back to hell. We were literally bonded by chains of magic that he had forged himself. I didn't know it then, I didn't really understand it now, but he had chosen this—as if he wanted our fates tied.

Ink didn't respond, a silence falling between us that wasn't uncomfortable. He slowed in his pushing, my arc drooping with each pass. Instead of pressing to my back, his hands found their way to swoop around my hips. Ink held the swing so my back pressed tight to his chest. My legs dangled off the ground, but I knew I wouldn't fall.

With his chin, he pressed my hair to the side and whispered in my ear, "The orientation of your suspension is giving me ideas."

I chuckled and glanced back at him. "What doesn't give you ideas?"

"Very small rocks," Ink answered honestly.

I reached back, ruffling through his shoulder-length hair until I held the nape of his neck. "Anything else?"

He stared at the horizon as if weighing the answer with his whole heart. A wicked smile rose and he dipped down. "No." Ink bent over, kissing me upside down. Heat scorched across my lips as he pulled the swing further and further back. Gravity meant nothing in his arms, my heart flying and feet dangling as I held onto the back of his neck with both hands.

Ink broke a moment, but not before taunting me with his tongue. "You've a grip of such strength not even a manticore could sunder it."

"Maybe I don't want to you push me away."

He groaned and shook his head. "While I despise such naked allegory..." His voice slipped to the silky whiskey of the incubus. "I'll suffer so for your naked anatomy."

That was terrible, and I chastised him with a kiss. The world jumped as he hefted me higher, hooking a hand to the bottom of the swing. He swept his fingers between my legs, tenderly thrumming against my thighs to get them open. I couldn't stop myself from parting them, Ink knowing exactly where to press his luck and knuckle. I gasped at the touch, stars catching in my eyes. It was the perfect opportunity for my incubus to shove his tongue in, but he toyed with my lips instead—alternating between sucking on and nipping them.

"Okay," I admitted, "there are perks to the swing."

"My bond," he chuckled, "we've only begun." He reached down, ready to rip my shirt off.

"What the fuck?"

The pink haze of sex forever trailing Ink snapped to the sharp reality that I was in a public park with my entire class a handful of yards away. Numb, I rotated to find Dana standing next to a fallen plate of beans. She shook with righteous fury, her snarl frozen as if she'd succumbed to lock jaw.

"Excuse me, we're using this right now," Ink said and turned from her, but I full-on winced and leaped out of the swing. He sighed and threw his hands up in exhaustion, but I had bigger problems.

"You..." Dana dashed across the sandpit to shove her finger in my face, before she rebounded on Ink. "You!"

"Yes, it is I, the wolf in ewe clothing," he huffed.

"Layla, Cal...what the fuck?" Dana was broken.

I reached over to Ink, holding his shoulders so he'd lean closer. But Dana turned more apoplectic at the touch so I let him go. "You should get out of here," I said to him.

"Why?" Ink chuffed, folding his arms like an immovable statue. "It's my understanding all are free to behave in this country as they wish."

I did not need this right now. "Please," I begged, certain there was a fifty-fifty chance of it working.

To my relief, Ink relented. "Very well, but I shall avail myself of the salad of ambrosia before leaving." He took a step to the side, before turning, taking my hand and kissing it. "My bond," he purred, shooting a glare Dana's way, then he finally sauntered off like a pleased tomcat.

Dana burned a metaphorical path in his wake, waiting until Ink finally walked up to the food table before she swung to me. "What the shit, Layls? What are you doing with *him*? Kissing him! Cal is right there! You're living together!"

"I..." All of that was true and I didn't know what to do other than nod along.

Dana grabbed me by the shoulders and shook me back and forth. "Stop this right now. Whatever weird games you're playing, end it. Break it off with smirking and dangerous over there."

"That's easier said than done," I admitted.

"Are. You. Out. Of. Your. Mind?" Dana shook me even harder as if that might rattle sense into me. "Cal is...and you just...what are you thinking?" The man in question raced across the grass in pursuit of a Frisbee. At the last second, he leaped into the air and caught it before falling to his feet and tossing it back.

"That! You have all of that at home and yet you... Tell him, you have to tell him. Tell Cal or —"

"Tell me what?" Those wolf ears had picked up on Dana's rant, which she couldn't have predicted. Her entire face turned burgundy and she gawped from me to Cal, who was striding over to join us. He looked to Dana, who fought an internal battle on which friend to betray, then to me trapped in her clutches. "Babe?"

"Nothing!" Dana sputtered, but I told the truth.

"She saw me kissing Ink," I said.

"Oh." He crinkled his eyes in confusion. "Why do I need to know that?"

Dana pushed me to the side to round her wrath on the other person making no sense. "Why? He's another guy. Who's not you."

"I know. Thank god for that," Cal said with a chuckle. He reached over and took my hand, the same one Ink had kissed before walking away. "What's Ink doing here?"

"I didn't ask him to come. He invited himself."

"Hm..." Cal pursed his lips at the idea. No doubt he was thinking of this morning too.

"What the hell is wrong with both of you? Did I step into the Twilight Zone?" Dana couldn't stop spinning around as if she'd find Rod Serling or a disembodied eyeball.

Cal laid his arm over my shoulder, tucking me tight to his side. "You didn't tell her?"

All I could do was shrug. They knew Cal even without knowing his secret. But Ink... How did I explain all of that without revealing the truth? Werewolf, demon, witch. It'd send them running.

With a set to his voice, Cal declared, "Layla's with both of us."

"Together? At the same time!" Dana squeaked. "Wait, at the same time?"

"Uh..." My face burned red hot and I tried to bury myself in Cal's hold. He nearly remained steadfast, but I saw the prideful grin rising. He could hold his own against an incubus in bed.

"Are you..." Dana fell silent. I girded myself for a thousand embarrassing questions about both of them in bed. "How greedy can you get?"

The cold hatred in her voice froze me to the bone. I stared at my friend, finding disgust. She sneered and shook her head back and forth. "I can't believe you."

"What?" For the first time in six months, a pit opened in my stomach that had nothing to do with witchcraft. "I'm not doing anything wrong," I cried out, flinching at the pathetic tone.

Dana snorted and jabbed a finger at me. "This, all of this is wrong."

"Hey." Cal tried to step in, but Dana pushed him back.

She spun in a circle, looking shocked as all get out, before dashing away. "You're a selfish shit, Layla!"

Pain struck my chest. I could only stare at my feet. All this time, I feared I'd lose my friends because of my magic, because of the monsters leeching into my life. I never thought it'd be the rare moments of love that would send them fleeing.

"Ignore her," Cal insisted, holding me tighter. "She'll get over it soon enough."

Numb, I pulled out my phone to stare at the lock screen image of Dana and me at the beach. I wanted to believe Cal, but I'd never seen such raw hatred in her eyes. "What if she doesn't get over it?" I whispered to myself.

"I don't know why she wouldn't," he said dismissively before he found me, fists bunched, eyes screwed up and lips pressed tight.

"Babe, oh, come on." Cal tried to soothe me. His touch set off the tears I'd fought like hell to keep at bay. Through my bleary rain, I watched Dana talk to Fariah and the both of them walk away. Like my mom had.

"She was just shocked. I mean, can you blame her? Ink's hard to take in small doses. One of his tattoos should be a warning label, or a skull and crossbones, at least."

"They'll all know soon enough. Everyone in the class. How do you think they'll take it?"

The clean-cut, handsome blond stared across the lawn like a man in a Jeep commercial. Pity, that was what Cal would get. People would assume he was so ensnared by my wicked ways he'd agree to anything I asked. *Way to represent there, Layla.*

"Who cares?" He shrugged it off. Cal wouldn't have to worry about being called Jezebel behind his back. "We know, we've got it all figured out and we're happy. Only thing that matters." Cal swept his arms around me, trying to pluck me onto my tiptoes for a hug, but I turned into a lead weight.

"What about your mom?"

He froze half hunched-over, his ass sticking out.

"Did you tell her?" I pressed.

"Um, that's...that's different." He didn't slip away, to my shock, but stood up, pulling me to him. Cal nestled his chin on top of my head as he turned me away from the rising scorn.

"Because you don't want her to know you're in a relationship that's loose with the monogamy part?"

"Because it was hard enough getting her over the witch part. I add in that there's also a demon and ghost and... Look, my mom's more accepting than most, but even she has her limits. I think a denizen of hell living in my kitchen is a stretch."

He hadn't told her because Ink wasn't meant to last. That was how this had all begun. Ink was a temporary solution, and Cal was supposed to be forever. I'd forgotten all about that when I'd held my incubus in my arms, his body dying to save me.

"Cal, I...I should tell you—"

"Did you read another memory of mine?" At least he didn't sound accusatory, but he'd been asking so often I was growing tired.

I shook my head and buried my face on his shoulder. "What if...what would you do if I said that I think I want Ink to be a bit more permanent?" After everything—the wolves, the secrets, the kidnappings— would it be my stupid heart falling for the damn demon who was incapable of love that did us in?

"Layla." He cupped the back of my head, the two of us swaying together in a strange dance. I wouldn't come out of my cocoon, terrified that if I looked into his eyes, he'd end it. "Beloved," Cal whispered, shaking me free. "It doesn't change a thing."

"But you'd said, I'd said that Ink was…and I don't know when he stopped being. Everything's a mess. I know you didn't plan for this arrangement to last forever."

He laughed and brushed the hair from my face. "Babe, please stop. I don't care about Ink being in the relationship. Grinding up all my protein bars and deep-frying them, however…" Cal clenched a fist, as if he could actually threaten the demon. "All I care about is you. Happy, safe." He flinched hard and turned away, regret stinging his words. "It's a good thing the demon's around for that."

"You're not upset? Or even surprised?"

"Truth be told, I figured the demon was sticking 'round about the time you wanted to bring Daniel back to life."

My cheeks turned red at the reminder. It wasn't just Ink, but Daniel too. Though, there was nothing saying that if Daniel got his body back he'd want to stay with me. For now, he was as trapped in Ink. Only Cal could leave the second he wanted, and he held me tighter than before.

I hugged him back, clinging to his enviable shoulders and wishing we were back home in bed. But another problem waited there in the form of a giant red wolf. "Are you going to tell me about your brother?"

"Moon's sake, you do leap from one crisis to another," Cal gasped. That open, understanding boyfriend walled himself away in an instant. His hands slipped off me and Cal stumbled back.

"I don't understand. If he's the eldest, which…I mean, I know living in the woods is a hard life, but that guy looked like a hard-worn forty."

"It's complicated."

"That's all you keep saying. It's complicated. Explain the complications. He's the eldest but not heir to the death cult in the woods?"

Cal slammed his hand to my mouth so fast his finger knocked against a tooth. He spun his head around almost like an owl, staring at every face that didn't give two shits about us. "Not here."

"Then where? When?"

"Not here!" he thundered, before wincing. "I mean…" Cal kept glancing over his shoulder as if he expected to find someone standing there. Someone giant. "We should get back to the party. Keep pretending everything's normal. Who knows who out there is a…hunter."

He'd been arguing and fighting to keep me safe from the witch hunters, but from how fast Cal threw on a smile, I knew that wasn't his real concern. How long had he feared the cult finding him, coming for him? And one of the worst had just appeared on his doorstep. He kept clasping his hands behind his back and pushing on his spine. The farther his smile strained, the more it hurt me to watch.

"Cal?" I held out my hand, uncertain if touching him in that mood was smart.

It was he who leaned into me. He brushed his cheek over the top of my head. "Tonight at home. I imagine our demon and ghost have found some way to keep the wolf at bay. I promise."

I didn't care about Eric. All my concern was on Cal's manic state. He bent down and kissed me. I returned the panicked touch, wishing I could transfer some calm to him.

"Hey, Rollin!" Scott called, waving the Frisbee.

"Coming." Cal rushed off to join them, easily falling into the false image of being one of the guys. How badly was he cracking on the inside?

Chapter Four

My festive mood went straight down the toilet. I would have left the party entirely if Cal weren't coordinating a beer run with Scott, Jared and Jared's still lame foot. That was why I preferred to drive myself — no concern about being stranded because my boyfriend was too damn nice for his own good.

Rather than running through the grass, or rolling, in the case of the very drunk future nurses of America, I sat facing out toward the busy street. A fence and twenty feet of weeded ground kept the park away from the cars. Yet it felt unnerving to face idyllic meadows and frolicking college students one way, and smoke-belching death carriages in a cement world on the other, as if this world were only a hiccup away from inverting.

I glared at the half-finished beer at my side. Whatever was in this discount shit was getting to me.

"One of them's going to break a leg."

I didn't jump, which should have been the first sign I was slowly losing my mind. Instead, I calmly turned my head to Daniel, who was watching the best and brightest in healthcare jump off the top of the slide as far as possible. "Good thing we all know first aid."

"I'm concerned if this is what nurses get up to in their spare time."

I laughed at that. "You should see what the medical students do. I'm not sure when I'll be home. I'm waiting on...Cal."

"He left you all alone?"

"I'm hardly alone." I waved a hand back to said students, though there wasn't a lot they could do against a giant werewolf. "Besides, I don't go out unarmed." I hefted up my spell book, the weight in my hands calming the flash of panic. I hadn't realized I was alone until Daniel pointed it out. For all my bravado, I couldn't forget that my magic did nothing against Eric. I needed something stronger.

"I was hoping to speak to you. Well, to have a look at your book. But I'll take any opportunity to be with you." He smiled with the full force of his Bruce Lee cheekbones and punk swagger. If I weren't digging myself into a depression spiral, I'd have swooned. I nearly passed him the book, before remembering there were a herd of people around who couldn't see him. But they'd certainly see the book floating in midair.

Instead, I turned, falling into his lap—if he had one—and opened the pages. "What are you looking for?"

"That reference to the other realms in the potion list. I've seen it before, I think."

I placed my hand above the book, but it was Daniel who turned the pages. If anyone got too close, I could snap it shut. As he peered closer, my shoulder chilled and shivers danced down my back.

He looked over at me a moment. "Are you cold?"

"It's okay," I said, not wanting him to leave.

"Here." He did something strange. He leaned back from me and tugged on his jacket. The edges crumpled in his hands, but they wouldn't move off his ghostly form. It was as if his clothing was sewn to his body like an old doll. Daniel frowned. He tried pulling on the neck, then the cuffs.

"What are you doing?" I asked, a laugh in my voice.

He blinked rapidly, and blue light warped from the edges of his brown eyes. "Just...trying to make you smile. The old 'pretending to give you my coat but I can't because I'm dead' routine. You looked so lost up here."

"I..." *am lost*. Shaking away the thought, I leaned closer to him. If he were alive, my head would rest on his shoulder. "I'm glad you're here."

"Of all the flowers in all the fields, none bloom as sweet as the words from your lips." Daniel slipped his hand into the one I used for balance on the ground, so he held me up.

"I don't know where that's from," I whispered, turning to look into his endless eyes.

He smiled and shrugged. "I made it up for you," Daniel whispered seductively, his lips so close a chill raced across mine.

I parted my mouth, prepared to lean forward.

"Lords and ladies of the veldt! Fear not, for I come to you in your darkest hour."

Whatever that was carried across not only the busy highway, but the park as well. We both turned to find a bald black man standing before an abandoned Pizza Hut. But what stood out even more than his speech was...

"Why's he in a dress?" Daniel asked.

It was hard to say it was a dress at this distance — it could be a white robe. Either way, it caused everyone to dash to the other side of the street or turn around even as he beckoned for them.

"I require your attention before the worlds come to an end. Have any of you suffered from a tear between realms?"

That drew my attention, before the man kept on. "Perhaps you have seen he who wears a crown and sits upon the throne of crushed dreams and bones?"

"He's nuts, got it," Daniel summed up.

"But he mentioned..." I began, before dimming at the slow look he gave me as if I too had gone mad. Screaming at the top of his lungs at cars, talking about the end times. *Not gonna win this argument, Layla.* "Yeah, crazy."

The man calmly walked up the sidewalk, his hands parted like he was carrying two stone tablets of wisdom. His next speech was drowned out by the eruption of horns from the fool stepping into the street. Cars slammed on brakes, the squealing covering his requests for help.

"Maybe it's in the other book I found on witchcraft," Daniel said, drawing me from the oncoming wreckage.

"Where? In Cal's house? Why does he have a book on witchcraft?"

Daniel shrugged. "Take it up with your canine. I'll check there." His hand slipped out of mine and he began to stand before turning to me. "If you're not home before dark, I'm sending the demon to fetch you."

"Ink will love that."

"I don't care. You're all that matters." With that, he faded from view, vanishing back to the second piece of his bone we kept on a mantle in the house. I pulled in a breath, feeling stifled from their overprotective schtick while also grateful that three impossible and sometimes wonderful men were so concerned. I rose to my feet, prepared to throw away the last of my garbage, when I caught the strange man striding into the middle of the road.

The stopped cars had formed a near circle around him to avoid crushing his body. All four had their headlights on despite it still being sunny, casting a halo around him. He raised his hands at the blaring of the horns…and massive white wings popped from his back.

I dropped my plate and ran for the fence. Before I could get across the field of weeds, the man flew straight up into the sky. I didn't know how long I clung to the chain-link staring where his black and white form had faded to nothing among the blue. Everything shifted when a hand glanced against my back.

"Babe," Cal asked, staring along with me. "What'd I miss?"

"I just saw an angel."

Chapter Five

On the drive home, all I wanted to do was fall into bed and pretend this day hadn't happened. But when Cal put the truck into park, I glared where the monster wolf's vehicle had been. The only reminder was an oil stain on the pavement, and a rising pain in my shoulder if I moved too fast.

Cal stared too, nearly hyperventilating. I ran my fingers over his knee and he stilled. The whirr of lawnmowers filled the air, silence ticking faster with neither of us willing to make the first move.

"You're gonna have to talk about it," I said.

"I know." He pulled his keys out of the ignition and dropped them in his lap. "Can I ask you something? All that magic stuff you're connected with, have you ever seen a warning about never speaking someone's name?"

I frowned at the question not about the red wolf. "There's a lot about the importance of names, but I've never seen anything about not speaking your name out loud." If there was a magic rule against it, I'd broken it the second I met Ink.

Cal groaned, his head falling to the side as if his neck gave out. "It's not that I don't want to talk about it."

I stared at him and he winced.

"Some of it is I don't want to talk about it. But a lot is just...fear. What if all of this — the past twenty years of my life, what if I made it up? And if I talk about the cult, the...vile shit he'd do, it all becomes real again."

"Cal." I held his hand. His fingers were freezing cold. Slowly, he clenched them around mine and turned, a smile that ran through hell rising.

"Where's your book?"

"Holy shit!" I leaped in my seat, the belt retracting against my chest until I sputtered. Pain seared up my sternum, but I barely had time to soothe it before Daniel plucked my book out of my bag and vanished out the door. He vanished, and my book stayed in the cab. I opened the latch as he stuck his head in, looking a touch more sheepish.

He glanced up at me then dashed away with my book in hand. The second it was out of my presence, a disquieting void rose in my stomach. I knew what that was now and it made me unbuckle my seat belt and chase after him.

"I told you it was rosemary!" Daniel called to Ink, holding the book out to the demon who couldn't read it.

Ink was wearing an apron. The image of my unholy, erotic, mischievous incubus in a plain white apron caused my jaw to slam shut. My teeth rattled, but I couldn't stop boggling at the sight.

He inspected the book, which again he couldn't read, then hefted a huge bouquet of fresh rosemary from a satchel on his back. "So you are not an entire waste of energy. Though Layla's toys cry out otherwise."

Daniel glowered even as he gestured to a spot on the ground where Ink dutifully placed a sprig of rosemary. *What was going on?* As he stood up, hair askew from the wafting branches speckled with leaves, Ink crossed his hands over his chest, looking like a stern chef about to paddle his sous chef with a wooden spoon.

In a flash, he stood by my side, skirting his fingers down my arm while whispering in my ear. "You approve of my subservient attire. I admit, I prefer the nipple rings and leather chastity belts to this pedestrian flap of canvas. But if you wish me to sup upon your amused bush in such a getup, I'm happy to bring the sauce."

The sound of the truck door closing told me Cal had joined whatever this was, but I couldn't escape the wanton hunger burning in Ink's eyes. He would drop whatever this seasoning of the house was with Daniel and whisk me off to the kitchen for some joy of cooking. "Why are you wearing that?" The exhaustion managed to beat out the lust.

A flash of disappointment crossed Ink's face, but he shook it off with a smile while drawing a hand down the apron. "To protect my clothing, of course. Incidentally, you require a sturdier cauldron."

"I need... What did you do to my kitchen?" Cal strained up on his toes as if he could see through the house, but collapsed at Ink's assuring pat.

"It was all the ghost's idea. I daresay either he's stumbled upon a protection spell for us all, or gone fully mad. One of six and all that."

Daniel flapped his hands, gesturing to the ground beside a dug-up begonia bush. "Excuse me, my bond." Ink bowed and walked away.

"I saw an angel," I shouted, unable to keep the exciting news in. I'd been fighting like crazy to keep the bombshell bottled up, but after the morning we could all use good news.

The book drooped and Daniel stared at me. Ink glanced over his shoulder and laughed. "Do you yet have your sight?"

"Uh…" I waved my hand in front of my eyes. "Yes."

"Has your mind burned inside your skull until ash tumbles down your nasal passages?"

"No." *What is he going on about?*

"Then you have not seen an angel." Ink dropped a sprig of rosemary to the ground, then trailed Daniel to the back garden. I followed them as Ink pedantically explained, "Celestials are impossible for a mortal to view. Most explode on the spot. The few that can manage shriek gibberish about twenty heads, or lions and goats, or giant spinning wheels of flames. I assume this is while their brains are bubbling into a boiling goo before they explode into dust."

"But…this guy had wings."

Ink stared at me and shrugged his shoulders. Black wings of deepest shadow burst from his back. "Many of us are so blessed."

"Oh yeah, well, his were white." The whiny stupidity hit me the moment I said it. There were basilisks and sirens and god knew what else walking around. A man with wings of white feathers could be anything. Why couldn't he be an angel?

"What if he was hiding his true form? That can happen."

Ink chuckled. "It can? I've never known a celestial to care if a few of their nosy creations have their heads pop off."

He sounded so certain. Even Daniel wouldn't meet my gaze. Had he already read about what angels really were? Of course he had—they were his only way to salvation. He was probably fighting back a laugh at my stupidity. "Oh," was all I said, trying to not crumble.

"Reviving this corpse's 'rigor mortis' can be a problem for the morrow," Ink said. That caused Daniel to glare and Cal to barely hide a chuckle. "For now, we must prepare ourselves against your fraternal black sheep."

"What is he, Cal? We're all here, we all…we need to know."

He gulped, but nodded slowly.

"What size of elk was he regularly consuming to grow so gigantic?"

"That doesn't really help," I interjected, though I too wondered. Werewolves were blessed with an athletic model metabolism, but Cal was half the size of Eric despite coming from the same father.

"Perhaps his mother was seven feet tall and built like a rhino," Daniel added with a laugh. He and Ink were enjoying themselves with the whole thought but Cal…he looked like he wanted to throw up.

"This isn't helping!" I shouted, my fuse ground to dust after today. "There's some maniac, 'roided-up werewolf out there who wants to kill me because his dick is the size of a gherkin."

"My bond, fret not. This shall protect you once we've finished." Ink swept his hands around me, pulling me into an embrace. Instead of brimstone and sex, my incubus smelled like roast pork. I shook my head, but he took my chin and held my gaze so I couldn't escape his smile.

"It's not steroids."

We all turned to Cal, who clawed up his arm as he glared to his feet. "It's a...a condition of werewolves. It's why he shouldn't even be in the running as an alpha. No one follows a Moon-Bound."

"Forgive my inability to muster a care for the ins and outs of werewolf civilization, but are you not all bound to the moon's whims?"

Ink shouldn't have asked like that, but I wondered the same and looked to Cal. He shook his heavy head. "Not like that we aren't. Moon-Bounds are...they have some condition, genetic. They can't control their shift like real werewolves. They can only change from human to wolf when the moon rises. Have to change. Makes them unpredictable, a liability to the whole pack. The bastard lost his shit when he learned his firstborn was Moon-Bound. If Mark hadn't been normal...well, maybe the rest of the pack would have ripped Lucien's throat out and no one else would have suffered."

I couldn't take his careful smile through the tears and clung to Cal. "Don't...don't say that."

"It's true. Most Moon-Bounds are pushed out into the wild, left to fend for themselves as a pup and baby."

Jesus Christ!

"How Spartan of them," Ink said as if he approved, or found the idea funny. I stared in shock at him and he shrugged. "Better people have done worse to their lessers."

"Eric wasn't in the pack. He wasn't his father's son. He had no parents. The bastard ignored him, favoring

Mark, then me as his successors. But he never kicked Eric out either. He found a use for him."

"Muscle," Daniel guessed.

Cal nodded. "The condition also makes werewolves grow huge—double, maybe triple muscling. Eric served better as the bastard's enforcer. He loved beating the shit out of anyone smaller than him. Like father, like ostracized son."

Oh god. The way the three brothers clung together, I didn't even think that the first would have beaten up his siblings. But if he wasn't treated like a half-brother, then what reason would he have to not make their lives hell at their father's command? I wrapped myself around Cal. The whole of his body was wound tighter than a rubber band. "Sweetheart," I whispered, pushing my face flush to his cheek so he could feel the tears I cried for him.

Cal couldn't unknot, his fists locked for a fight, but he kept an arm around me. No wonder he never wanted to talk about the red wolf. Eric sounded like more of a nightmare than his abusive father.

"We discounted him, assumed he'd be the first turned on once the bastard fell."

"Foolish."

"Ink!" I snapped.

"No, he's right. I don't know what Mark was thinking. I just…I don't want to have anything to do with that shit."

"Yet the wolf is banging on your door demanding entrance." Ink stared him down and Cal finally lifted his head to meet the eyes on fire.

Suddenly, his hand clamped around me, a growl rumbling in his chest. "He's not touching her again."

"Which is no concern once we complete this. Demon?" Daniel jerked his chin to a final spot for the rosemary. Ink sneered, but dropped the herb down before he pulled a bottle of red and silver liquid from his apron pocket.

"My bond, if you'd be so kind?" He passed me the bottle.

I held on to it, uncertain what he wanted. "Do I drink this? What is this? Where did you get it from?"

"A passage in your spell book made reference to a potion. I tasked the demon with brewing it through the day," Daniel surmised before slamming my book shut.

I glanced over to Ink. Had he really spent the day doing what Daniel of all people told him to? "Are you sick?" I sputtered, placing my hand to his forehead without thought. An unnatural heat rolled across my skin, but that was normal for the sex demon.

Pulling my hand down, Ink sighed. "It was a simple distillation of tinctures. Hardly such an undertaking for one so skilled."

"In brewing?"

"In everything." There was the smirk I expected. He clamped a hand around my waist and pulled me close. "All you need do is whisper the final words. Ghost? The one thing you're good for, if you please."

Daniel rolled his eyes, but he brushed against the right side of my cheek while Ink held the left. His cool touch chased away the summer heat as he spoke what sounded like gibberish, but I repeated every single syllable and the flask glowed crimson.

"Pour it upon the ground, and the land should be sealed," Ink announced.

I popped open the cork and the stench of burned radishes rose from the top. Turning my head, I tipped the bottle over, the red liquid slowly oozing out. As it fell, the ring of rosemary lit up, illuminating in a path around the house.

I slipped the cork back into the empty bottle and stared. "How long will this take?"

"Not very? A few minutes for full effect, I believe," Daniel explained.

A faint humming echoed in my ear, like a choir practicing harmonies in the distance. Magic. The harmony grew louder and I asked above it, "What exactly did we do?"

"Banished any werewolves from the premises."

Bright red lashed from the ground, smashing into Cal and hurtling him into the air. He only cried out an *oomph* before he flew across his backyard. I turned, about to run after to catch him. He didn't have time to fall, his body crashing into the branches of his neighbor's tree and sticking.

"Cal!"

"I dare say it worked better than expected," Ink declared.

Glaring at the two, I ran through the thorny bushes and climbed the small brick wall while calling to Cal. "Are you all right?"

"Yeah. Ouch. Is that bleeding?" The branches shuddered above me. Ripped buds rained off the tree as he tried to find a way down without taking the fast way.

"What the hell were you two thinking?" I spun on the fools. Ink was gazing up at his handiwork while Daniel ran through the book again. Flattening myself against the trunk, I tried to hold a hand up to Cal. "You can't wholesale banish werewolves."

"Whyever not? A werewolf is a threat. Ergo, remove the threat by any means necessary."

Cal cinched his fingers around mine and I pulled. More branches cracked, twigs tumbling down and sticking in my hair, but he began to move down. "Because!" was all I could shout at the two, the rest of my focus on Cal. He stumbled, nearly falling on top of me. The back of my heel scraped over the brick wall and I almost shouted in his face instead of the idiots responsible.

"Your cheeks..." I drew my thumbs under a mess of cuts to his pale skin.

He winced, leaves and buds sticking out of his blond hair. I pulled him to me. When our foreheads touched, I whispered my healing spell.

"I'm okay, really," Cal argued, before the magical morphine chased his pain away. When I opened my eyes, the red marks had vanished, and I turned my wrath on the one who should have known better, and the one that had goaded him on.

"This is his home. You can't just chuck him into the trees. Where's he supposed to live?"

"My bond." Ink swept across the lawn and took me into his arms. He tugged me back over the wall, where Cal couldn't walk. "We anticipated such an eventuality and constructed a wonderful guest house at the edge of the manor." With a delighted wave, Ink drew attention to a plastic igloo sitting right outside the fence.

"A doghouse!"

"There is a padded blanket inside and twin bowls for all his needs."

"No!" I tossed away Ink's concerned hands and marched for the house. "He is not living in a doghouse."

"It is only temporary," Ink interjected. "He need merely remain outside until we can either remove the red wolf's head or he's grown too feeble to threaten you."

"Are you fucking kidding me." I stared up at the spell, spotting a haze of opalescence shining in the air, like the entire house was surrounded by a thin soap bubble. How did I get rid of this? I looked to Daniel and held out my hand. "Give me my book."

He hesitated, then looked to Ink. "We read through all the various options and this seemed to be the best one."

I wrenched my book away from his cold, dead hands and flung it open. It landed on a spell to chase away hemorrhoids, but my point was made. "It's not happening."

"Wait," my poor banished werewolf called to me. "Maybe it's for the best?"

I paused in hunting for their spell to stare at Cal. He couldn't be serious. "A doghouse?"

He groaned, telling me at least he wasn't out of his mind. "I'm not sleeping in that. I don't think I'd even fit."

"You'd be surprised. It has greater space on the interior."

We both ignored Ink, Cal staring from behind the invisible fence. Pain clung to his face as he clasped his hands together. "If it'll keep you safe, Layla, then I'll find somewhere else."

Where? A motel? Scott's couch? Living in the woods until the threat of the cult drove him mad?

I shifted my foot and felt the hum of magic. Right beside my toe was the rosemary. Of course! Staring at Cal, Ink, and Daniel, I said, "He stays," and kicked the rosemary away. With the circle broken, the shield bubble collapsed. Even still, Cal was careful, swinging a finger out into thin air to make certain.

"My bond —"

"Layla, this is the only way —"

Ignoring them both, I caught Cal's eye. Even facing a life in a tiny plastic doghouse, he too looked wary at my decision. But I didn't care. Eric wasn't the only threat out there, and if the worse I feared was coming, then I needed all my boys under one roof.

Taking Cal's hand, I pulled him across the garden to the back door. Before opening it, I declared, "He stays. And if any of you argue with me, you sleep in the doghouse."

Chapter Six

Is this gibberish?

I hefted my spell book off the cement floor and raised it to my eyes. Even close up, the letters wiggled, words rising and vanishing from incoherent sentences. It didn't help that whatever witch wrote this down hadn't been a stickler for penmanship or grammar.

This was supposed to be my break. I told myself once the semester was over, I could put all my witch and wolf mess on the back burner for a week and take a vacation. It'd be a vacation where I still worked retail thirty-nine hours a week, but compared to my current situation, that was lying on a beach. I glared at my book and twisted it to the side. When I'd asked it for a spell of protection against werewolves, this was what it found, but my broken brain couldn't read it.

"Why won't you make sense?" I snarled, preparing to chuck it at the wall. An instant warning clanged through my nerves that it would be in my best interest to not do what I wanted.

"If you don't want to be thrown, maybe you should help me for once." I was seriously tempted to try ripping a few pages to see what happened. Either I'd go blissfully mad or it'd finally make good on its vague threats.

"You down here with someone?" Cal's voice echoed down the unfinished stairs, finding me hunched over my energy drink and scattered sidewalk chalk. He eased down the steps, the bare bulb striking his naked shoulders and twelve-pack. A small part of my brain wondered why he was shirtless, but the rest drooled.

"N-n-no. Just me and my..." I raised up my spell book as if that would explain my talking to inanimate objects.

"I didn't know anyone came down here." He stopped at the bottom of the stairs and nervously hooked his thumbs in the waistband of a pair of gray sweatpants. Oh right, nightfall.

I picked up my mess, frowning at how far the chalk had rolled. "Sometimes, not often. When I want to practice a ward. Figured if it went wrong and caught fire I could put it out down here...without burning down the curtains. Again." Nervously, I scuffed the chalk circle away with my foot, coating the sole in pastel pink. "You probably need to do your thing. I should get out of your hair."

Cal frowned at the mess in my hands. I moved to slip past him, but he caught my arm. "There's no reason for you to keep lugging all of that back upstairs."

"I...I don't want it to get in the way." I stared at my random garbage then caught his eye.

Carefully, Cal picked out the chalk and markers while knowing to leave my book behind. He spun around in his basement, unfinished save a cement floor and a chain dangling from the ceiling. "Ah." From behind the stairs, he pulled out an old box and set my stash on top.

"If it's in your way…" I began, itching to pull my mess from him, but Cal chuckled.

"I'm big, but I'm not that big."

He meant his wolf, but my eyes went straight to his crotch and I swallowed. "Are you sure about that?"

Cal turned red, though his smile widened. "You don't have to keep putting your things away like that. Stuffing 'em in the boxes, or hiding it in bags. You live here too."

Because a crazy secret society of witch hunters maybe knew the location of my apartment. "Sort of," I said and he stared harder. "I mean, you didn't have much choice. It was move in or, I don't know, let Ink barricade my place until the landlord had me evicted. I'm grateful for all you've done. I just don't want to be an inconvenience."

I didn't realize I'd dropped my gaze until I felt his hand. Cal guided his fingers between mine and pulled me across the floor to his arms. "Do you really think you're an inconvenience?"

"There's an incubus in your kitchen and a ghost in your dining room. Add a vampire in the attic and a sea monster in the bathroom, and I think we'll have a full set."

He kissed my forehead, then cupped under my chin. "There's an incubus in *our* kitchen. Probably filling the toaster with cheese for the tenth time, but that's a problem for tomorrow. I want you here."

"I mean, eventually…maybe, but it was so rushed."

Cal stiffened and his tender voice sharpened. "Do you want to be here?"

"Yes," I said, so quickly it surprised even me. "I love being able to wake up with you without one of us having to figure out how to get the other home. And falling asleep on your chest without worrying Ink will pop in and ask for a threesome."

"He did that two nights ago," Cal said with a soft chuckle.

"But he didn't have to pop to do it. I'm sorry for being weird. I guess I'm worried you were being nice under duress."

He pulled me closer, his hands crossing behind the small of my back. I hugged the nape of his neck, straining on my toes to look in his eyes. Cal kissed the tip of my nose before asking, "Is that why you fought so hard with Ink and Dan?"

I bridled at the reminder of the ones I was at odds with. "Those two idiots. What is up with them?"

Cal shrugged.

"Daniel's got an entire stack of books, some I've never seen before, in his fort. And Ink... He's being helpful. Weirdly helpful."

"He hasn't seemed that different."

"The cooking."

Cal blanched at the reminder we still had an incubus-prepared dinner waiting for us. Gluttonous medieval aristocrats had nothing on the rich and fattening meals of a focused demon. If anyone could turn an oven to sin, it was Ink.

"He was wearing an apron. Why?"

Cal leaned closer, his hot breath filling my ear. "Maybe because the lady of the house's eyes boggle when the men dash around the kitchen?"

That was just him and he hadn't been in a full apron but wore a kitchen towel on his hip that constantly drew my eye to his cock. I clenched my toes at the memory of Cal frying up a mess of eggs with only that towel and his boxer briefs on. Cal, obviously knowing he'd hit pay dirt, caressed his hand around the curve of my ass. He pinched as he drew his teeth to the edge of my jaw.

The bite was playful, but heat bubbled between my eyes and I caught Cal's nostrils flaring. It was hard to hide getting turned on with a werewolf boyfriend, impossible with an incubus. The thought of Ink drew me back to reality. "I don't know if he was trying to help or…kick you out. Whatever it is, it's not happening."

"While I appreciate being able to" — Cal gazed down at my chest, seductively hidden behind black cotton, and used his biceps to squish my breasts — "look upon your bountiful bosoms."

"Jesus, that's terrible," I snickered.

He laughed too and stared at me. In an instant, the jokester died. "I would have stayed out there if it kept you safe."

"But it wouldn't. Ignoring the fact that I'd have to leave for work, or…they were gonna keep me trapped in here, weren't they? Until you or Ink stopped Eric. For fuck's sake…"

"For knowing your every desire, the incubus has a terrible time understanding you," Cal said tenderly. At least he had enough sense to know I'd have broken free of their attempted prison. "Though I can't blame them for trying."

We were all a mess after my kidnapping. I refused to go anywhere near the part of town where Animal Control had gotten me. And the one time I'd tried to take a bath, I'd slipped under the water and panicked

Ellen Mint

so hard, Cal had kicked down his door to pull me free. They weren't much better. Daniel had become a silent guardian, often standing outside of doors, watching and waiting to run to the others. Cal checked on me constantly, even if he knew I was with Dana and Fariah, at work, in the middle of the same class.

But the worst one was Ink. He didn't just face a future of being yanked back to hell. In order to save me, he became mortal, knew the pain of humanity and nearly died in my arms. Every time I tried to get him to talk about it, he'd refuse in the name of wasabi cupcakes or bacon bread. How did one get a two-thousand-year-old sort-of demon to therapy?

"I doubt the spell would have done much to slow him down."

"It worked a treat on me." Cal rolled his shoulder, which must have still been stiff even after my healing spell.

I reached over to massage it. "I mean, given what Eric is and all."

"What he is?" Cal asked.

"His...mutation. Being Moon-Bound. That must make a werewolf immune to magic?"

Slowly, he shook his head back and forth. "I've never heard of that."

"But when I used my magic on him, my fire, it did nothing. He said it tickled." It was why I didn't even float the idea of making a protection potion like the one keeping Samuke at bay. It also wouldn't have stopped an entire vengeful werewolf pack until I brewed up one for every member. And that shit tasted like wet garbage stuffed in a dead fish.

"No werewolf is immune to magic. Could have been bravado. He once took a gunshot to the leg and walked it off."

"Jesus." A massive neanderthal wolf who was also damn near unstoppable wanted me dead. Great. Cal too glared through space, his breathing shallow. I took his face in my hands and centered him. "What you all went through...I can't imagine."

"I don't want pity for it. I don't want to be that guy who grew up in a cult. I don't want to think about him or any of the rest ever again." Cal didn't walk away or start pacing. He met me eye to eye and squeezed tighter to my body.

I could heal his body, but there were no spells in my book to heal a fucked-up childhood. I'd looked. All I could do was ask, "What do you want?"

His ice-blue eyes sharpened and Cal licked the edge of his fang as he stared down me. A snort spurted from his nose like a charging bull. "You," he declared and hauled me off my feet. I started to yelp in surprise, but his lips were on mine. Cal kissed with a ferocity normally saved for a full moon.

He bucked his hips with such force, I nearly leaped out of his arms. Fearing I would fall, I reached out and caught the beam running across the low ceiling. I hung off of that, my legs knotted around the middle of Cal's chest while he drew his nails under my shirt and spread the whole of his hand up my back. Even straining, Cal couldn't reach to kiss me. I watched his eyes blazing as he kneaded his palms under my breasts. He hefted the weight of them high, moaning at how my nipples were nearly out of reach.

Every jostle in his arms caused my thighs to cling tighter and press my soaked panties and a thin pair of sleep shorts to his chest. When my vulva and clit reverberated down his pec, I fought back a savage cry.

"You're eager," I called out, struggling to keep my voice level.

Cal's wild bucking stilled, but he kept toying with my nipples while staring at me. The bare lightbulb deepened a feral gleam in his eyes. "What are you going to do about it?" he asked.

Oh, he was in *that* mood. I didn't fight the devious smile rising as I put together what he wanted, or how bad I wanted it too. Opening my legs, I released my grip on the ceiling beam and slipped down Cal's hard body. He took every advantage to caress me on the way down. My shirt caught between us. His thick cock strained against the boxer briefs and pressed to my bare belly.

I stood there, staring up at him, breathing deep so my breasts pooled against his chest. A low growl rumbled from below and I reached for the chain. In an instant, Cal snapped to attention, his eyes wide. I tugged the metal loops over and hefted the leather strap in my hands. "You need to be taught some manners," I declared, slipping the strap around Cal's neck.

He helpfully raised his chin, holding his breath as I tightened the collar and folded the loose end into a set of silver loops. When the leather fell flush to his neck, his cock hardened like a brass pole. I stepped back, staring at him nearly bursting out of his boxers, his body shivering in anticipation. He'd been shifting a lot lately, leaving his multitude of taut muscles bulgier than usual.

God, I wanted to rake my nails over his lats and bite into his biceps. But that wasn't the game.

Cal looked down at his cock and traced a hand around his hip toward it in a tease. His head snapped up and he surged forward. I took another step back. The chains rattled in the eyelet, each link catching until he reached the end of his rope.

"Ah-ah. Manners," I chided, waggling a finger.

He dropped the hand racing to catch me, but didn't lean back. If anything, he leaned farther out, tightening the collar. Fuck, the way his eyes darkened with hunger nearly sent me racing for his cock. To snare my attention, Cal dropped his hand under his waistband and jerked once around the bulge in his pants.

At my shiver, he grinned, showing a single long fang.

"What are you going to do with me?" he asked, toying with his cock while keeping it all hidden from me.

I could drop to my knees, turn around and bend over just nearly out of reach. Or...? I dragged the little end table over and stood before it. Placing my hand to my chest, I coyly crossed my legs while staring him straight in the eye. "You are going to stand there." As I spoke, I danced my fingers down, each tip dipping between my cleavage until I lifted my shirt off.

Cal's growl echoed through my core. I cupped and caressed the breasts he couldn't reach, every rattle of the chains wetting my panties. He fought hard against his restraint, but he couldn't break free. I risked taking a step closer to the panting beast, bending at the waist so I could feel his wild breath.

As he stared, one hand clenched to his cock, I whispered, "And watch."

Cal reached for me, but it was too late. I leaned away and tugged off my panties and shorts in one go. The sight of me completely naked and out of range caused him to whimper before he jerked his fist around his cock and his eyes rolled back. When they focused, I hopped back onto the table. It wasn't very tall, so I had to lean and arch my heels on the floor. But all of Cal's attention was on the sight of me nearly spread eagle before him.

Slowly, I traced my fingers between my thighs, trying to prolong his torture, when Cal tugged the edge of his underwear down so half of his cock popped free. *Fuck me!* My toes curled and I swept straight for my clit. My own heat threatened to consume me while Cal toyed with his cock's head. He danced his thumb and finger over the crown, swirling to match my own steady beat.

As he watched, I closed my legs tight, then opened them wider. He didn't strain against his bonds, but jerked himself off faster before stilling. Red stained his chest and cheeks, the exertion nearly breaking him, but Cal held back and watched. I swept across my wet vulva, taking in as much lubricant as possible, before plunging two fingers deep inside.

Cal howled and pumped himself hard. He used his whole fist to travel from the base of his cock to the near head. All the while, he kept trying to tug his boxer briefs lower with his other hand. It wasn't working so well, his reach limited and the other side caught on his hips, but he refused to release the hand bringing him to the edge.

"A little help?" he asked, darting his gaze down to his trapped underwear.

I eased to my feet, a cramp already rising in my arched heels. Carefully, I reached over while staring Cal in the eye. He lifted his hands on his own, abandoning his pleasure, and I tugged his shorts down. "It wouldn't do for you to come all over them."

"Not when I can come in you," he growled. Hands clasped around the small of my back. For a brief, glorious second his rock-hard cock brushed against my lower belly and down until I dodged out of his reach.

"That was...very naughty!" I tried to condemn him, but every fiber of his body looked ready to leap and fuck me hard. God, I wanted to run straight back and let him, but that wasn't the game.

Struggling to breathe, I slicked the dew off my forehead. Sex sweat glistened down his abs. Finding me in such a state, Cal smiled deviously and clenched tight around his cock. Even his big hands couldn't fully reach around, but he tugged the skin higher until a bead of pre-cum welled up on the tip.

"You..." I waggled my finger, fearing I was losing fast, when a wicked idea entered my head. "You must be punished."

"What are you going to do?" he asked, his head quirked.

I only needed a second to think of him. "I'm not going to do a thing," I said as a pair of naked warm hands swept over my breasts.

Hot breath caressed down the side of my cheek as Ink whispered, "You called?" He bit my neck and I squealed, clenching my thighs together. The chains rattled harder, Cal sputtering in rage even as he jerked himself off.

"I see someone's been bad." Ink surmised the situation in a second before he drew his hand between my thighs and pressed them apart.

"Enjoy your punishment, dog," he declared before thrusting his cock into me, "while my bond savors her reward." Ink drew his full palm over my breasts, one after the other. With his second hand, he kneaded into my thighs, then flicked his thumb against my clit. All the while, he nearly pulled his cock out before ramming it in as deep as possible.

Cal glared at the sight, one hand swiping through the air to reach us while the other pumped his veiny cock faster than ever. The once still chain rattled like a Vegas casino. Cal strained hard against his collar, his neck turning bright red at the force. Was he choking himself? Fear percolated in my mind, when Ink brushed back my hair with his chin.

"Do not fret so. He is safe under our watch, though we may yet drive him mad."

"Oh, fuck!" I cried as Ink pushed me forward, changing the angle of his cock. The rumbling rapids of pleasure became a geyser pumping through me. I knew I wasn't going to last long under his care. He nipped the edge of my ear, tightening his pinch with every gasp I made.

"Give in to the carnal delights," Ink whispered. "Cease fighting the inevitable and succumb to…"

The chains stopped clinking. Cal strained at the end, his body rigid and red. Ink cupped me under the chin, holding my gaze steady with Cal's feral eyes. With his other hand, Ink swept along my breast, lifting the bouncing flesh before he bellowed in a loud voice, "None can pleasure you better than I."

Metal shattered. I jerked just as Cal lunged forward. The iron chains snapped, the broken end ratcheting back through the eyelet while the rest dangled from Cal's neck. He didn't even pause to goggle at the feat he'd accomplished, but ran straight for me. Taking my hair by the nape of my neck, he pulled my head back and kissed me even with Ink still pumping away inside.

Roaring in my mouth, Cal grabbed my ass and pulled me off of Ink. I gasped in shock, rising into his arms. He ran his hands down my legs, putting them astride his waist, and he thrust hard.

His huge cock punctured so fast I couldn't speak. Stars shattered on the side of my vision, and my breath caught. Holding me against him, Cal drove us to the wall even as he thrust. My back struck the crumbling dirt of the crawlspace, mud slicking across my skin from the sweat, but I didn't care. The heat of my incubus had prepared me for the lava boil of my werewolf. I tried to widen my legs, when Cal grabbed my thigh and pressed it back.

Fuck! He clamped down around my leg, digging his claws in while thrusting as deep as possible. I grabbed him by the first thing I could reach and found my fingers tugging on his hair. Every thrust, I'd pull, tipping Cal's head back until he started to howl.

I wanted to join him but my breath was taken by the pressure mounting inside. As Cal rammed me deeper into the wall, I looked up and caught Ink, hand clenched around his dick, stroking himself. *Holy shit!* The orgasm walloped me so hard, I twisted back, arching my spine until I feared it would snap. Tremors sundered through me, clamping my vagina tighter to Cal who buried his head against my neck. His thrusting grew more shallow, but he bit down on my shoulder, setting off a fresh cascade before the first ended.

All I could do was whimper, praying my heart didn't explode from the freight train worth of orgasms slamming into me. Cal went still, his body tighter than the chains he'd snapped. I clung to the back of his neck, trying to pull him off for fear something went wrong.

"You..." His voice crackled like logs on a fire. Cal nibbled on my earlobe, and he breathed, "are mine." He thrust one last time, then pulled out.

All my strength vanished with him and I started to crash for the floor. In an instant, the pent-up animal I'd driven crazy vanished to leave only my concerned and slightly neurotic boyfriend. Cal caught me, though due to the sweat of our bodies, it was touch and go at first. As he pulled me to him, he ran his hands over my back, then frowned.

"Sorry, I got mud all over you."

I glanced back and laughed. "A little mud is worth it," I said. "That was amazing." He blushed at the compliment.

"Well, you gave me a good reason..." Cal jerked his head as the chain jangled and pulled taut. We both turned to find Ink at the end of the broken link.

He raised his hand and smiled. "Your dog's off his chain." He pulled again and Cal fought back. It looked about to break into a game of tug of war, when I slapped the chain in the middle.

Shaking my head, I undid the collar, letting the leather strap plummet to the ground. "Here I thought you boys were behaving."

"I am the picture of civility. My concern is for your werewolf imprisonment contraption. You require thicker links and more eyelets lest you break them again."

Cal swiped back through his hair, flattening the wild strands to his head as he turned to Ink. "And you just love the sight of me chained up, don't you?"

Ink blinked a moment before looking to me. "I care far more for Layla's response." Both men stared at me burning up and trying to hide in my hair. I wanted to burst into flames at my kink being laid out like that, when Cal drew his fingers up my arm and he pulled me close.

He was about to whisper in my ear, when Ink spoke, "Though, the image of you bound and on your knees is entertaining by rights."

Whatever Cal was going to say vanished in his sigh and eye roll.

"Now, unless I am needed to further your games of dominance and bondage, I believe my muffins are nearing completion." Ink smirked at Cal's soft grumbling, but when he looked to me, an emotion I couldn't place passed over his features. As he vanished into the ether, I'd swear I saw care.

Cal wandered over to inspect the shattered links, nudging them with his foot.

"Something's different with him," I said to myself, staring where Ink had been.

"Seemed the same pain in the ass to me. Though he's not wrong about the eyelets. One always seemed too few."

Ink was a pain in everyone's ass, a fact he took pride in. There was no way to prove he didn't find a perverse joy in his newfound love of cooking by making us eat weird food. But one fact kept nibbling on my ear. In all the time we'd been together, I'd never seen him touch himself for his pleasure.

Chapter Seven

The flowers had to be fake. I'd learned that the hard way the first time I'd visited her grave. I'd found a twenty on the floor of a bus and put it towards a huge bouquet of pink and white roses — huge to a ten-year-old, at least. When I'd laid them on the grave, I'd mourned properly like a good daughter. But while sitting outside the cemetery, waiting for the bus to take me back to the trailer park, a groundskeeper had swept up the fresh roses and dumped them into the trash.

This was the first time it felt right for me to be holding plastic petals and stems. Fake flowers for a fake grave.

"I don't know why I bothered," I whispered to myself, glaring at the nondescript plaque partially hidden in weeds missed by the mower. Usually, the cemetery was a dour and solemn place, save the loud roar of landscaping equipment. This was the only day when it echoed with the exuberant cries of children who found open space to run around and their parents chasing after before they all trucked off to a Mother's Day brunch. I hated it.

A warm hand slipped across my shoulders and I fell against Cal's chest. "Do you want to go?" he asked. He'd spent the morning watching me silently straighten my hair, put on makeup, wash it off, stuff my hair under a head wrap then do it all again. I never knew how I should dress. All in black was easy when I'd thought my mother was under this slab of dirt. What did I do now that I knew she had faked it and run?

I turned my head, staring down the dirt road that circled the grounds. Why did I think she'd be here? She wouldn't even answer my texts and left my DMs unread. This was stupid.

"Maybe a few more minutes."

"Ah." Cal followed my gaze to nothing, then he placed a kiss to my forehead. "We can stay as long as you need."

This was stupid. The red wolf was still out there, maybe not in wolf form by daylight, but he didn't need the fangs to be a threat. I should have stayed home. My mother wasn't dead, only pretending. No one put flowers on the grave of a faker.

A ring shattered the spirited chirp of birdsong. Mourners glared our way, wrenched from their tales of lost grandmothers and mothers by the call. Cal tugged out his phone and winced. "It's my mom." He looked about to answer before catching my eye. "I can talk to her later."

"No. Go ahead. There's a brook down that way not many go near." I pointed to the water feature that had once had a fountain and swans. When the swans attacked the fountain, no one had bothered to fix either.

Cal lifted his phone and pressed the button. But before he spoke, he pulled me over and pressed his forehead to mine. "Hey." His attention switched on a dime. "Happy Mother's Day!" Exuberance stampeded out of his voice as he slipped away. I didn't pay attention to what he said to his mother all the way in New Mexico. Instead, I watched him. They spoke often, Cal never dodging a call as if his life depended on it. After what they escaped thanks to his mother, how many life-or-death calls had they had?

"I think I have an uncle buried here. Great-uncle?"

I was left at the grave of my not-mother with the one person who knew death best of all. In the bright spring sun, Daniel looked washed out, like an old photograph fading on the wall.

"Of course, my murderer's a handful of graves down that way. Shame he didn't have any unfinished business to keep him trapped here."

"Can ghosts hurt each other?" I asked, not caring for the answer, only the distraction.

He shrugged, the burst of rage passing in an instant. The longer he had the answer to who had killed him with no closure, the quicker he seemed to cease caring. If the anger of his death was all that kept him tethered to this realm, what would happen if he lost the ability entirely? Would he vanish before I could even say goodbye?

"I'm surprised you're not back at home...studying the spell."

He chuckled and flicked the four safety pins holding together a tear in his jacket. "Not much to study. The spell seems simple enough. It's the ingredients that are proving a challenge. Unicorns are prone to inhabiting forested regions in Scandinavia, Slavic Europe and

Mongolia. Demons can only be summoned on the days associated with their creation. A bit like saints in a way."

"So, what, there's a demon Saint Nicholas? Or a demonic Saint Valentine?"

Daniel's gaze flickered behind me and he groaned. "I believe we both know who the demonic Valentine would be."

My mind filled with an image of Ink not in white wings but black as night, holding a whip in place of the bow. Instead of the white toga, he'd wear a leather thong and nothing else. "Ink's not—"

"As for the angel," Daniel spoke over me, not as if he wanted to shift away from mentioning Ink, but like he didn't even notice. "I have no idea. There are no first-hand accounts of angels anywhere in the books I've read."

I saw one.

The sentence died on my tongue. There was no arguing with the librarian ghost or my know-it-all incubus. Maybe I'd imagined the whole thing anyway. There was no mention of a winged man flying into the sky on the internet. It was like it hadn't happened.

Frustration tainted the summer air. I reached over toward Daniel, never able to touch him. My hand passed through the cold spot of his hip and I shifted closer. "We'll find an answer. I swear."

He raised his arm and held it behind my back as if we were holding each other without touching. "You would shake the very foundations of heaven and hell if possible."

For him? Without question. He'd been a rock I didn't know I needed, calming me after a bad night, assuring me that he was eternally vigilant and I never need fear the hunters' return. "Daniel, I've been wanting to tell you for a while…"

I turned my head to find him staring at nothing. He didn't blink, his eyes glazed over, while his lips hung stagnant. "She's crying," he whispered in a voice so quiet it nearly vanished on the wind.

Leaning closer, I tried to follow his line of sight, but there was nothing. Only a tree decorated in pink ribbons shook in the wind. "Who?"

"She never cried, not in front of us. Why...?" Daniel winced sharply before darting his watery eyes to me. "You were saying something?"

"No, you were. About a woman crying."

He raked his fingers back through his hair and stepped to the side. "I was? That can't be right. I'm here. No one's crying. Okay, that guy is. I should...I'm going to see if I can find my uncle. Great-uncle. Bye."

"Dan—" All I could do was sigh as my ghost made a break for it. Not that I blamed him. I'm sure I looked about ready to start jumping up and down on the grave while bawling. I wanted to be angry at her. I was! She'd abandoned me, let me think she died because of me. But...what would I do if I saw her again?

"You remain exposed, while also being stubbornly clothed. It is a confounding conundrum."

And there came the last of the fucked-up trifecta. Ink sauntered to the grave like it was a catwalk. If the residents weren't six feet under, I'm sure they'd give him a standing ovation.

He paused before reaching me, his feet at the side of the grave, while cocking his hip. "If this is all to maintain the illusion of your mother's death, there are none here to play to."

"I'm not pretending," I insisted.

"You bring a floral sacrifice to the grave even knowing it's not she who lurks below. Why?"

"Because…" I thumbed the plastic daisy heads, the unfinished edges snagging on my skin. Cal didn't ask, just accepted I had to do it. Daniel didn't say a word, just tried to distract me. Only Ink walked right up to my face and asked why I was wasting my time mourning a woman who wasn't dead.

"I don't know," I declared to the world and jammed the fake flowers into the plastic vase before the stone. They hid away dates and 'Leeland,' only 'Isabel' poking through the petals. I started to wrap my hands around myself, when another pair beat me to it.

Ink cinched around me like a cardigan, his hands clasping at my midsection while he placed the full weight of his chin on my shoulder. I girded myself for his laughter or snide comment, which I rightly deserved. But he kept silent, staring down at the flowers that leaned off kilter.

"I don't want to see her again," I declared to the universe. She'd abandoned me. She had no right to be in my life after that.

"My bond." Ink skirted the tip of his claw against my cheek, delicately pushing my already curling hair behind my ear. "That is not what you desire."

What do you know?

Everything. He somehow knew everything about what I wanted even before I understood it. Yet he chose to stay with me. I turned in his grip, searching through his flickering eyes for sense. Why did he stay when she didn't?

"What about you?"

"My desires are for you to be chained to the headboard so I can keep my eyes, fingers and tongue on you."

"No, not..." I tried to fight off the blush, suddenly growing aware of how many families were running around. "Do you have a mother? Had a mother? Are Sins born? How does it all work?"

Ink dropped his gaze and tugged on his ear. "I was born in a sense, but not as humans are. There is but a single parent, my creator as it were."

"And if you could see her again, would you?"

"Him. Should I search him out, he would be nothing more than a pile of ash."

Did another demon have to die to make an incubus...or did Ink kill him? I had so many questions, and no idea where to begin. "What do you mean?"

"From where comes this concern of my origin? I assure you, my ignoble beginnings are of little entertainment in comparison to what I can accomplish now." He leaned closer, placing a kiss to my neck then lower.

I didn't need to have magic incubus powers to know what he desired, but my question wasn't so easily shaken. "I want to know."

"Why?" The impertinent tone became guarded.

"I met Cal's mother, and...you know, with his father."

"Yes, I aided in that man's rightful end."

"Daniel's were both human. Mine... I just want to know. I'm curious."

Ink blinked slowly. He didn't stomp away or cut the discussion off and vanish. But he stared me up and down before saying, "As you are not a feline, I suppose you do not fear your overindulgent curiosity. Very well, but I assure you, the tale is not an interesting one."

I rested my cheek against his chest, listening to the stillness below. Ink glanced down at me and wrapped a hand around my back. "Sins are born of humans, though without the blood and afterbirth mess. Even though most mortals cannot actively tap into the wells of magic around, present lovely company excluded, humans are a part of it. They can bend it to their wills if they force the issue hard enough."

"You're saying you came about from, what, a really big orgy?"

Ink laughed at the idea. "I wish. I would claim that to the heavens were it so. Alas, no. There was a man, a scholar as he liked to call himself—though few were rushing to hear his speeches in the agora. A man of so little import, his name does not remain even in ledgers long lost to the sea. Time evaporated all aspects of his existence save the one he tried to rip from his soul."

Silence fell after Ink's statement, as if he'd revealed a deep secret but I was left confused. I waited for him to begin and turned my head so my cheek pressed tighter to his chest. He combed through my hair and spoke. "Sins are not born of flesh but vice. Or when you humans declare a natural function of existence a vice."

"He was extremely religious? Screeched brimstone and hellfire on anyone who jerked off under the covers?"

Ink chuckled at the idea. "As if hell would concern itself about the state of human genitalia. Most demons barely understand it."

"You're dodging."

"Not well enough if you noticed," Ink admitted. "Is this truly what you wish to know? What if I tell you of the time I fell in with a group of highway bandits and they demanded my money or my life? I chose theirs instead."

"Ink."

He stared skyward, nervously tugging on my hair and catching on the necklace clasp at the back of my neck. "He was not a pious man. Sins cannot come from nothing. In fact, he was a notoriously libidinous man, known even in Alexandria for his parties that'd put Bacchus to shame."

"Then...how did he make you?"

"Human fortunes shift so easily on the winds. One day he fell blind. I suspect it was due to the rotten wines he ingested hourly, but he placed his blame all upon one source."

"You?"

Ink shuddered at the idea. "If I am to be a single man's libido, which...perhaps that is what I am at the core. I do not know."

"That's all it takes to make an incubus? For a sex-crazed idiot to suddenly stop?"

"Hardly. He took his vow seriously, praying to the gods to rid him of his carnal fever. For five days he drank not a drop, slept nary a wink, only sat upon his knees, sacrificing every good at his disposal to be rid of his curse. The gods delivered and now I stand before you, while he rotted away to celibate dust."

Holy hell. "Did you...kill him?"

"Slaughter my creator? Do you think I wished to incur the furies' wrath? No. I abandoned him as a newborn, uncertain what I was in this vast world."

"That had to be terrifying." I flashed back to the first time I'd held my spell book when those monstrous scroungers ripped through my door. I had no idea what was happening or what to do. If Ink hadn't been there, hadn't helped me, I doubted I'd be alive. "How did you survive?"

Ink licked his lips. "I am not without guile, and I excel at all matters of sexual congress." He stared right at me with an 'as you know' in his eyes. I couldn't argue, but still...

I wrapped my arms tighter, crushing him in a hug. "I'm sorry you had to go through that."

He went rigid, as if he lost control of his body. I'd never felt that in Ink and looked up, concerned a basilisk had bitten him again. Slowly, he raised his hand and patted my back. "Do not waste your tears on me. I came out all the better for it. Had I remained entwined with him, I'd have died in that tiny room, tossed to the floor like a rag, coughing up blood. I do not deign him with a thought. I don't understand why you waste so much on yours. She abandoned you, tossed you to the side without a care. Why do you not do the same?"

"I don't know. Maybe it's not real yet. It took me so long to accept she was dead. Never see her, never talk to her, never sit on the couch with her watching Turkish *Seinfeld*. Then, in a second, it all changed again." I wanted to hate her, I did hate her, but I also didn't know her. She'd kept so much from me, her own daughter. What if she had a reason for it that I didn't understand?

"Well, if you wish to burn her in effigy, I am quite talented at stick binding."

I laughed at his offer when Ink brushed through my hair. He plucked an errant cherry blossom free. Twirling it, he smiled slyly and leaned closer. I closed my eyes and puckered my lips.

"Just 'cause I'm a few minutes late, you start making out on your mother's grave?"

Oh, god. Ink's kiss smashed into my cheek and I turned to find a fuming Dana standing behind him. He took a moment to collect himself and looked to the friend I never thought would show. "Wonderful, let the daily flagellation begin."

Chapter Eight

"Ink!"

"Layla."

"Dana." Ink smiled wide as if he'd won a game no one was playing. "I'm sorry, is this the point when I throw toast? I can never remember the steps."

I did not have the mental energy to understand what Ink said, all my focus on my friend who looked ready to haul Ink up by the nape of his neck. "You came?" I asked Dana. When Ink snickered, I elbowed him in the stomach.

He leaned close to whisper, "Do it again."

"Of course I did. Not that you didn't bother to drag your sidepiece with."

So we were gonna have that fight here. Well, what better place than above my mother's fake grave? "Ink?"

"Yes, yes, vanish into the ether. Yet another of my many, many talents." He took a step and I feared he'd do just as he said, but he cut his fiery eyes to Dana, picked up my hand and kissed it again. As we both groaned, Ink sauntered down the hill toward the single active funeral. I didn't have time to wonder how often he'd have hunted for widows crying over their dead lovers' bodies.

I held my breath, fearing that Ink would pop back in, or Daniel would suddenly need my attention. But only the chirp of happy robins and the rustle of leaves filled the air. Dana maintained her glare in Ink's direction, her arms folded tight. She was wearing her work polo, which meant she'd either come off a long shift or was about to go on one.

"Thank you," I said, meaning it. "For being here."

"Yeah, well…if I'd known you were here with him."

"You wouldn't have bothered?" I tried to not sound defeated but there was no escaping the sword dangling above our head.

"I'd have brought a spray bottle. Man's worse than a cat in heat."

I chortled at how close she got to the truth. "You have no idea."

"Angelo!" Dana spun on a dime at the exuberant cry of a small boy in a blue jacket. He seemed unhappy with said jacket, one arm dangling free. "You keep that on or your mother will hear about it."

"But I don't want to, Auntie."

"We all gotta do what we don't wanna. And don't step on the graves, that's how you get cursed." She shivered at the thought, watching from the side of her eye as Angelo flailed his arm around until the jacket went on. He stomped away to pick up fallen sticks under a tree.

"How long do you have him?" I asked, trying to remember if she'd told us. With school and spells, my memory felt like a bucket fountain. When the top pail filled up, all the information dumped out.

Dana sighed, her voice softening in regret. "I've got a bad feeling this time's forever."

"Your sister..."

She pinched her nose. "I don't want to talk about it. Family. You're lucky you don't have any."

Her comment struck like an arrow to the heart. I stared down at the headstone, my throat constricting. All of my uncertainty snapped straight to a gulf of grief as if I'd lost her all over again.

"Ah, shit, I didn't mean that." Dana held her hands out as if she needed to hug me, but I held back.

"It's okay. I'm used to it by now." I wiped at my cheeks, chasing away any hint of moisture and finally faced her. "You didn't answer my texts."

"Should we talk about this here? Right over your mom's...ya know."

Magic was real, angels and demons moved among us, yet Dana was the superstitious one, while I didn't care. I tipped my head to her and was about to step on the grave, when she glared. Carefully, I skittered around. Side by side, we started to walk toward the old mausoleum. Its yellowing bricks rose from the flat-stoned graveyard like a broken bone.

"You gotta admit, you lobbed a bomb at me. I mean, shit, not just Cal but that smarmy tatted-up walking mistake too?"

"Right. I'm selfish. Greedy." Every word stung deeper because a part of my heart knew she was right. Three men and I could give them a third of my attention. It wasn't fair.

"Okay, so maybe I overreacted," Dana said. "A lot. But Tattoo back there is fucking infuriating."

I laughed at her clenching her hands in agony from suffering one of Ink's moments. It dissolved the tension and Dana joined in.

"That level of dickheadness, he better be good in bed."

My head nodded on its own before I tried to walk it back. "He's not without his talents." That was easily the biggest undersell of Ink's skill.

"So the two of them know about each other. Like, do they *know* know?"

"What?"

"You," Dana said, counting on her fingers for emphasis, "that all-American boy-next-door and the tall, dark and smirking together...at the same time?"

My entire face burned and I tried to keep from jerking my head an enthusiastic yes. Sometimes Daniel was in there too, but Dana really wouldn't understand the invisible ghost in the situation. "It, um...sometimes," I squeaked out.

Dana snorted and shook her head at my wanton ways. "You got any pics?"

Uh... I slapped a hand to my purse as if to hide my phone deeper.

She laughed knowingly at that. "I am sorry for blowing up like that. It's just, it's all so weird. Two men, who ain't got a problem both fu..." Dana glanced up at the mourners in their Sunday best shuffling past. " — fudging you. It was a lot to take in."

"I should have told you and Fariah. How'd she take it?"

Dana tried to turn away, but I caught the guilt as if I didn't know she'd run straight to our third friend. "The way Fariah does everything, with a shrug and noncommittal response. I swear nothing rocks her boat."

We passed under the weeping branches of the willow, fading from the world of death into a private verdant one of our own. Dana paused in her steps and turned to me. "Look, if you're happy, and he's happy, and no one gives a shit about Tattoo, I'm glad. I don't get it, seems like a ton of work for the occasional orgasm."

She was completely wrong about that.

"But where is this all headed, Layls? I mean, what kind of future do you see here? Will you eventually pick one like it's a test drive or do you intend to keep playing this game of Bachelorette for years?"

"I…" The plan had always been that I'd wind up with just Cal. Now, I had no idea what to expect, much less want.

"Listen, if you can get it and…you're young once, so might as well. But that one, Cal, I mean, he's good. And so stupid hot it hurts to look at him."

"Wait, do you have a crush on him?"

Dana snorted. "Anyone with eyeballs does. Ain't you worried that adding all this spice will scare his ham and cheese ass away?"

My werewolf fighting against a murderous cult was the one adding the spice to my life, but I couldn't say that to her. Instead, I tried to compose my thoughts while hefting up the willow branches. "We're taking it all one day at a time. As for Cal, don't let his face fool you. He can be a ghost pepper some days." At least once a month, for certain.

"Now you got to tell me. Oh for…Angelo!" Dana dashed for the tree where her nephew had been. Scattered on the ground was the blue jacket that looked brand new. "What did I tell you? Angelo?"

Only the fallen young leaves tumbled across the ground in response. Dana ran forward shouting for her nephew. "This isn't funny, you little… If you say something, I'll give you ice cream!" The panic sharpened in her voice as I walked to where the jacket lay abandoned and bent low.

With my back to her, I fished out my spell book and quickly paged through Daniel's helpful sticky notes. The pages shuddered as if they were not a fan, but I didn't have time for my book's opinion. *There!* Keeping one eye on the ground, I whispered the incantation. Tiny footprints lit up blue, one after the other trailing the owner in the direction of the mausoleum.

"What the shit am I going to tell my sister? How am I going to explain that I lost him in less than a day?"

"Dana." I popped up and caught her rapidly waving arm. "He went this way."

"How can you tell?" she cried as her panic fought against natural skepticism.

I gestured to the ground where the feet kept lighting up to my eyes like a neon sign trailing away. "There's um, broken twigs here. And a bit of misplaced dirt." To back up my bullshit, I picked up a small clod and ran it between my fingers. "He's headed toward the mausoleum."

Dana stared at the nonexistent signs, then took off in the direction. "How the hell did you do that? You're not some secret elf, right?"

"I, uh, watched a video online," I said as an excuse that didn't answer her.

We hustled without running in the direction, when a sound jarred straight through my spine. Dana blinked and shook her head. "Who's breaking celery?"

"We have to run!" I shouted, dashing down the hill for the old mausoleum. I knew that sound deep in the pits of my nightmares — the crunch of bones snapping in half. Usually, a great lock rested on the door carved like the entrance to hell, but the metal padlock was shattered and the chain lay tossed to the side. No way a young boy had done that. What was in there?

What am I taking Dana straight into?

"Wait." I paused, trying to hold her back. "Why don't I go in first?"

"Are you crazy? If he's in there, I'm gonna drag him out by his ear for scaring the shit out of me." She clenched her hands as if about to wring his neck, when the air shattered with the splat of a body striking the wall. "Angelo!"

Dana took off before I could stop her. *Damn it!* Why did I have to be so much shorter? I trampled on the chain, the metal cracking to dust under my foot. Whatever had done that wasn't human.

When I burst into the cold marble of death, my vision went dark. I tried to blink to see through the black, when a shadow darted in front of me. *Shit.* I flung my hand out, spells on my tongue, and sparks struck on the marble.

Three sets of red eyes framed by fur black as pitch glared down a long nose against the ceiling. Its mouth hung low, fabric caught between the rows of fangs as the creature slicked its long claws down the wall once more and laughed. "Dana!" I shouted, pushing myself in front of her. She clung to me, her face ash at the terror stumbling on the coffins it had ripped from the walls, the chewed bodies at its feet.

What the hell was this thing? I didn't have time to consult my bestiary. I snapped my fingers, the flame catching then fading in the dead air. The monster turned, its tall ears swiveling at the sound. *Oh, that isn't good.*

Maybe it only ate dead people.

It dropped a hand to the ground, hunched over on three legs, and snarled, blood dripping from its fangs.

Nope, it ate live people too. *Shit, shit, shit!*

I called up the spell for lightning, hoping that'd at least distract it, when the monster leaped. *No time!* I shoved Dana to the side, prepared to take the hit and blast it at point-blank range. A hand pierced the darkness and latched onto the monster's back leg. It spun around, sinking fangs into whatever had it, but the owner didn't give in. The hand kept pulling it deeper into the bowels of the mausoleum.

The plink of broken marble falling from the ceiling and striking desiccated corpses filled the air before a great howl ripped through the entire crypt.

"Angelo?" Dana gasped.

The blood in its mouth! No, no, no! I flung my hands wide, prepared to leap on that creature and stab its belly Red Riding Hood-style.

Then, from behind a tall urn, a tiny voice called, "Auntie?"

"Thank fucking god!" Dana cried as a dusty but unharmed Angelo slipped around the vase. She wrapped him up in her arms. "What the hell were you thinking? Jesus Christ, you're okay? You're okay. I told you to keep your damn coat on. Why are you in here?"

A feral roar echoed so loud that my ears ached. I took a step back, ready to take them both away, when a lower, more guttural grunt broke from inside. There was that sound again of a body hitting the wall.

Whoever had saved us was fighting for their life down there.

"Get out of here," I said, pushing Dana and Angelo for the exit. "Run and don't stop. Get in your car and go."

"Don't have to tell me..." Dana began, already shoving Angelo out while putting his coat on. "Wait. Layla, you're coming too. You're not staying behind."

"Someone's in trouble," I said.

"Girl, are you out of your goddamn mind?"

Yes.

"We need to call the cops, or the National Guard or animal control. I don't fucking know."

I shivered at the mention of animal control. Was that who was down there? It made the most sense. Could it even be Stone trapped in a pit of bones and skulls fighting for his life? Walking right into that and revealing myself after all this time would be the dumbest thing I could —

"Ah!" a man screamed in agony.

"Get out of here!" I called my magic to push Dana the last of the way out and fling the door closed. Flicking my fingers faster, I conjured enough light that I could see a hole in the wall of the mausoleum. The floor had collapsed behind, a trail of finger bones and grandmas' jewelry leading me onward.

I struggled to slide, then caught my foot on the broken bricks. When I struck a collapsed section, my ankle rolled and I tumbled face first toward the ground. Arms caught me and swept me up like I was doing a dive. As I landed on solid ground, I knew who did it.

"Ink," I breathed, glad he had found me.

"Back to desecrating corpses, my bond? You do keep things lively."

I opened my mouth to explain, when a hand the size of my head smashed against the wall. Ink shifted to the left just before it decapitated him. The dust of the dead corpses erupted into the air, clogging my lungs and hiding the creature in shadow. It reared up, ready to strike again, when I did first.

Lightning erupted from my fingertips with enough volts to power a Prius. The air sizzled and stank of rotting fat from the dust of the dead, but the creature merely dropped to one knee. It needed more. Tapping deeper into the spell, I willed the magic to increase. Fire caught on the monster, its smoking fur burning my eyes. I turned my head as Ink caught my arm and broke contact.

"Why did you...?" I shouted, when he pointed to my feet.

Holy shit. The leather and rubber of my shoes had melted into a searing hot pile around my socks. I leaped out of them the second the heat touched me. Ink caught and spun me around when the creature rebounded for an attack. He slammed the flat of his hand into its chin, cracking a row of teeth.

As it whimpered away, Ink focused only on me. "I fear you are too powerful for your own good. Shall we adjourn and leave them to their meal?"

"Someone's in danger," I said and he rolled his eyes.

"When aren't they? I swear the entire human race hangs upon a razor's edge whenever we require donuts. Well, lead on. I shall provide backup."

I really thought he'd whisk me away, but Ink held his arm out like we were going on a walk. Rather than take it, I pulled out my spell book, prepared to cast or — should the worst come of it — bash something with it. We didn't have far to go. The cries of battle grew louder down the twists of an old cistern. At least it wasn't metal. My heart raced at the stench of sewage and I clenched tighter to the locket around my neck. *I've got my magic, it's not the sewers and Ink is here. It's okay.*

Fire surged in the middle of the room and my jaw plummeted. It wasn't one or even two of those things, but at least a half dozen slashing and screaming around a man. The light barely penetrated the deep ebony skin, though it flickered off his bald head like a beacon. He clung to one of the monsters, his arms bigger than my thighs as he wrenched its head clean off. Instead of being scared off, the others surged for him.

"Ah, you've found a nest of pishachas. Strange to find them here. Stranger to find them eating Christians."

"A what?"

"Devourers of the dead. Ghouls of a sort. Everyone has them," Ink said before he caught a leaping pishacha by the throat and hurled it back.

The fire vanished in the throng of pishachas. I flung my hand out and cast the first spell to come to me. As one, they collapsed to their knees, their weight quickly growing exponentially. When they fell, I caught the sparkling black eye of the man. His face came from another time, like a bust from Ancient Egypt one would stare at in a museum, or a forgotten statue hauled up out of the sea. Thousands of years circled his frame, making him timeless and immutable. Then he smiled, and it all vanished.

"Ah, my bond. They appear to be rising." Ink poked my bare arm and I watched the pishachas shake off the magic like a wet dog.

"Allow me," the stranger declared in a voice deeper than a canyon. Reaching from behind, he hauled out a sword longer than him. As the first pishacha stood, he swung it wide, bifurcating the head. It bounced off the wall like a basketball and the body tumbled to the ground.

"So that is the trick. Excellent." Ink leaped into the fray, his wings giving him lift. He plunged onto the shoulders of one pishacha and ripped its head off.

I touched my neck and grimaced at the sight of red tubes dangling from the severed head, which was when one pishacha noticed me. *Shit!* I raised my hand, ready to throw lightning. No, I was barefoot now. Bad idea. What about...?

"Ah!" It lunged and I thrust up my only shield, my spell book. Its steak-knife claws caught on the spine, digging into the leather. *If it's destroyed, I go mad!*

I fought to put all my strength into my arms and tossed the pishacha back. While the force twisted me, the creature barely moved. It stared at me panting and alone, and smiled.

A blade punctured its throat, then sliced clean through. The pishacha barely had time to look surprised before its head tumbled off its body like a hollow coconut. Gasping, I looked up from the dead monster into the face of my hero.

He swung his bloodied blade over his shoulders and held out his hand. "Hi." Massive white wings burst from behind him. "I'm Garavel."

Chapter Nine

"You're a…" I stared past the man with giant white wings to Ink staggering to his feet. I jabbed two fingers at them while waiting for him to look to prove I was right when the angel caught my hand.

Oh my god, he's so soft and warm. It was like his ebony skin glowed with a heavenly golden sparkle when I touched it, which shut my brain down.

Flecks of amber sparkled in his eyes — such a deep brown as to be black — as he shook my hand up and down. "You must be a witch."

Here it comes. I girded myself for the typical reaction of either fear or disgust. Didn't matter who it was — if they knew about witches they hated us at first glance.

"Wonderful!"

"Come again?"

Garavel smiled wide with teeth brighter than his shockingly thin robe. He wore two pieces of white cloth that clung to his wide chest and solid stomach before tapering at the hips and dangling near his sandaled feet. The cloths were attached via gold loops at the shoulders and a strip of gold fabric at the waist. The outfit left the entire sides of his chest exposed, which he didn't seem bothered by at all. Instead, he stared at me as if I were the answer to all of his problems.

My heart leaped at the idea I could mean anything to a creature of such divinity. Garavel sheathed his giant sword on his back and tucked his wings in. They vanished along with any sign of the blade. "I cannot believe my luck to find a child of creation here!" he bellowed like a kid at their birthday party.

"Well, I'm…that's me, witch lady. I mean lady who does witchcraft. Um, spells and stuff." I tried to smile through the pain in my chest at how stupid I sounded and twirled my hair around my finger.

A slow chuckle drew not only my attention, but the angel's as well. Ink tipped his head at my embarrassing fumbling, then he extended his shadow wings wide. *Oh no, he's a demon, Ink's a demon.* Demon and angel — they were going to rip each other to shreds in this underground pit of bones and I…

"Are you a demonic sin?" Garavel asked.

Ink fluttered his wings, blanketing the rest of the mausoleum in shadow. "Good eye. Lust," he said, pointing to himself.

Why can't he lie just once? I tensed up, trying to figure out how I could stun someone who'd taken out a room of corpse eaters.

"Delightful!" Garavel shouted, reaching over and taking the demon's hand. His massive palm nearly dwarfed Ink's, but the two shook with a disconcerting bonhomie, like two coworkers spotting each other outside of the office.

"You…you're okay with him?" I asked. Why wasn't the angel attacking? Weren't they always at war with the denizens of hell?

It was Ink who responded with a slow chuckle while Garavel stared down at his attire. "I am afraid I seem to have spilled a little soot on my robes."

"No, I mean you're a—"

"Layla!" Daniel's cry burst into the room right before he appeared, his face stricken in panic. "Are you…?" He reached over for me, the cold of his form barely competing with the chill of the tomb. Slowly, Daniel turned to take in the piles of decapitated pishachas on top of the mutilated corpses.

"As punctual as you are useful," Ink said, giving Daniel two thumbs up.

"Who's that?"

Ink slapped an arm across Garavel's fridge-sized frame. "Our newest addition to the coven." He gave me a knowing look and my mouth dried. I needed an angel to save Daniel, not to…gah.

"Hello." Garavel held out his hand and Daniel bridled beside me. He stared at the strange man like a wary cat.

"He's a ghost," I butted in, trying to explain why Daniel didn't share in the angelic handshake.

"I know." The angel reached over and clasped Daniel on the back. His eyes went wide at the touch and my jaw dropped. Instead of going through, Garavel was able to pull Daniel close in a hug. "Doesn't mean we can't be friends."

"You…you're touching. How are you able to…? Huh?" I'd read through everything I could on ghosts, Daniel'd done even more and neither of us had seen any mention that an angel could do that. Could other celestials touch him?

I had a million questions to put to him, but everyone was silenced by the sound of stone ripping away and a howl echoing from above. Were there more corpse eaters prowling the graveyard? I turned, prepared to fricassee whatever came through the wall.

Heavy footsteps lopped against the bones, not even pausing at the crunch. I wound my hand back, when a head of blond hair poked through. "Babe?" Cal asked, and I laughed out of joy at his appearance.

"It's all good," I said to him and reached to take his hand.

"A werewolf!" Garavel snarled, his once harmonic voice crackling. He rushed forward and clasped a hand to my stomach.

"Who the shit is this?" Cal demanded. He plummeted the last few feet and stared at the angel tugging me back.

"It's…"

"You shall not harm her, moon cursed!" the angel shrieked.

"Let go of her." Cal's words warped into a growl. He snapped out, "Now!" and his teeth sharpened to fangs.

"Okay, everyone's on edge, but…"

Garavel's wings snapped wide, blanketing the entire area in feathers. They didn't bend, but dug into the walls like unbreakable chisels. I tried to leap out of the way to defend Cal, when Garavel shouted, "I will shield you, my lady."

"You will not take her," Cal snarled. He planted one wolf foot on the ground and I felt mine raise off it.

What the…?

Tightness caught around my midsection and, before I could think, Garavel lifted us into the air. His wings beat an inescapable wind, shoving hard on Cal and not touching Daniel. Where was Ink in all of this? "Ink!" I shouted to my demon to break up the party.

"Ah!" Cal slammed his claws into the stone and slashed. In the blink of an eye, Garavel folded his wings around us and we shot straight up into the mausoleum and out the door.

"Holy shit!" I shouted. The cemetery ground was growing smaller and smaller below my feet as he flew into the skies. When it looked like a train model, I slammed my eyes shut. My stomach floated in my throat and I did my best to not think what would happen if he dropped me.

"What are you doing?" I cried against the crippling winds freezing my fingers and toes. *Please don't let him drop me.*

"Protecting you, my lady." He didn't explain at all.

"From what?"

Garavel stopped climbing and leveled out, his wings steady as we glided among the clouds circling above the city. I couldn't make out much below, but when the white puffs would break there'd be a highway as thick as a piece of spaghetti and the panic returned.

"Can we get down?" I fought to close my eyes, but the winds tugged on them, tearing me up until I had to blink to shake the salt away. There was a flock of geese flying under us.

"You are safe in my care," he said. Even though I was dangling from his arms four hundred feet in the air after he kidnapped me, my heart believed him. My brain was screaming at how I had to get away now, but the only way out was a very long down followed by a very painful stop.

"P-p-please!" I shouted, clinging to his arms out of fear he might open them.

"As you wish." Garavel sighed. He banked, the late morning sun shifting from our left to the right. The entire horizon tipped forty degrees and I tried to not upend my breakfast all over the runners in the park below. I cinched my eyes tight once again, refusing to open them until I felt ground on my bare feet. But when gravity grew stronger, I risked a peek.

Garavel glided for the roof of the bank building in downtown. I didn't realize that was what he aimed for until his legs dropped along with mine. I slipped an inch, but that sent me panicking. My nails dug into his skin and I held him as tight as possible.

"I have you," he assured me as we landed together on the freezing cold tower of Lakeland Bank. Garavel stood perched on the edge, the winds tugging back his wings while I fell to my knees and crawled for the center. A single tall pole stood in the middle, its tip glowing red to warn passing planes to not hit it. The light could also protect against potential angel takeoffs. Wrapping my arms around it, I slowly eased my way back up to my feet just as a gust of wind whipped against my body. The cute summer dress I'd put on this morning did nothing against the freezing cold this far off the ground.

"Wh-why are we here?" I pleaded, wishing I was anywhere else.

Garavel stared straight down at the ground, then he toyed with one of the tiny pennant flags tattering in the breeze. "You asked to land. This was the closest."

Okay, think carefully, Layla. I'd dealt with an incubus who couldn't lie and never told the whole truth. An angel that glowed like Christmas lights and seemed to have the attention span of a golden retriever couldn't be that hard.

Working my way around the pole without breaking my hold, I stared directly at Garavel. "Why did you fly me away?"

"For your protection, of course. That beast was no doubt sent to devour you by your enemies."

"Cal's not..." I wanted to insist he wasn't a beast, though that was more in the metaphorical sense. In the literal one, yeah, he was. The way Garavel stared, his wings straining then tucking back, and the hilt of his sword gleaming like molten gold in the sunlight told me to shut up and play along. "Thanks. What, um, what were you doing in that crypt?"

"I heard the sound of bones crunching and thought that seemed strange. I imagine you were there for the same reason."

"Uh, yep. More or less."

Garavel smiled bright as if he solved a math problem. "It's nice to know some things haven't changed after my long slumber. I hadn't seen a witch in weeks and feared the worst for this world."

"You, uh..." I finally risked lowering my eyes away from the clouds to take in his body. It reminded me of those old body builders in black and white photos. Instead of the skinny waist and twelve thousand abs like Cal, he had a sturdy belly that slightly curved out his white robe. Though, his chest looked gigantic in comparison to his belly. His pecs tugged so tight on the thin fabric, I could see the curve of everything below.

Angels had nipples. I would win that question at magical trivia night.

The arms could at best be compared to a bear, huge but not delineated like a man nearing death by dehydration. They looked big and snuggly, perfect for wrapping around someone in the warmest hug. What struck me hardest was the face. Every feature seemed like it was designed to intimidate, his brow heavy, the eyes sunken and small like a cobra's, his cheekbones low and lips pillowy but unshapely. Except, when he smiled, his entire being glowed with a light that sang of hearth and joy. And Garavel couldn't stop smiling.

"You like witches?" I asked coyly.

"Of course. I am devoted to them."

Holy moly. The way he said 'devoted' made my knees buckle. It wasn't just a word to him but an entire way of life.

"It is good fortune for me to find you. You may be the only person who can help."

"I...I want to help you." My tongue knotted at his ever-rising smile. He wanted me and I wanted...

"Not even five minutes. I believe that's a record for you."

At the voice, I spun, forgetting my death hold on the pole. The wind smashed against my chest, knocking the air from my lungs. My bare feet slid across the ground. I didn't even have a chance to squeak in terror at the long fall ahead, when a flash of wings parted above my head and those big bear arms wrapped around me.

On instinct, I rested my head on his pec, his chest soft but also strong like a memory-foam pillow. "It's windy up here," he said and all I could do was nod in agreement.

"Astute," Ink said. He stood in the middle of the blast, his hair whipping free, shirt tails undulating wildly. But he folded his arms like his bus was late. I looked down and spotted he'd sprouted his demon claws straight through his shoes and punctured them into the cement below.

There's a demon on the roof with the angel. He'd already panicked at the werewolf and flown me away. What if he tried again? "Ink…"

"Delighted to see you too, my bond. And still in one piece that isn't splattered across the ground. Daniel owes me a drink."

"Are you here to, uh…um?" The question of rescue died on my tongue as I realized I'd wrapped my arms around Garavel until I held him tighter than he did me. I tried to unwind myself, but the wind kept tossing me back against him, only for the angel to hug me once again.

Ink laughed at the pathetic display. I was trying to get away, and he sure as hell wasn't helping. "Do you wish me to leave you to finish with your awkward debauchery? I believe there is a bowl of minute rice I could attend to."

"Ha." I glared at Ink for his insinuation, both of them. Surely Garavel… Yeah, I wasn't contemplating how long an angel could last in bed.

"We were discussing negotiations," I said.

"Good to lay out ground rules first—orientation, number of men required, tools available, safe words."

I shook my head, ignoring Ink's needling, and focused on Garavel. "I need your help too. Maybe we could work something out."

"Be wary, she's a biter."

Ignore him for Daniel's sake.

Garavel let Ink's innuendo fall off him like water. *Oh god, him in the rain in that thin white robe…there'd be nothing left to the imagination. Focus, Layla.* "Whatever could a witch require of me?" he asked.

"I need an angel feather to help my friend."

He frowned and I flinched, fearing he was about to ask if he was a friend or boyfriend. It was Ink who chuckled. "Oh, my bond." He spoke to Garavel after patronizing me. "It's been many a century since I saw one like you. What are you, obsidian?"

"Ebony," Garavel declared, slapping a hand to his chest.

"Nice. Nearly unbreakable." Ink punctured his feet into the ground like a mountain climber's pitons to reach me. He caressed a hand to my back as he pointed to Garavel. "He's not a celestial."

"Dear creators!" Garavel's face lit up in a blush. "I couldn't imagine."

"But the wings…the — he can fly. What is he then?"

"He's a demi-angel."

"That's —"

"Nowhere near the same thing." Ink turned smug at that and I folded inward, wanting to run away. "I know you are heaven-sent on solving this ridiculous phantom problem, but he is as much an angel as I am a demon."

"Technically but not really?" I recited what Ink would insist to anyone who shrieked and called him a hell beast.

He caught my hand and draped my arm over his shoulder. I leaned with him, my hip knocking against his as Ink steadied me by my stomach. "I am sorry," he whispered before focusing on our not-angel. "Forgive my manners. I am an incubus of Alexandria. Ink, by preference. And you are?"

"I am Garavel, first and protector to my blessed creator, Ramiel. Nice to meet you. And you are?"

"Uh, Layla. Leeland. Future RN and witch of the fire nation?" I kept talking, trying to match their fancy titles. Ink had never mentioned he was from Alexandria before. Had he been around during the big fire, or had he caused it?

Garavel caught my hand and shook it. He seemed to love handshakes, giving yet another to Ink, who returned his palm to my stomach once it was over.

"Well, Garavel, creation of Ramiel, what brings you here?" Ink asked like they were running into each other at a bar.

"Can you not feel it?" He focused on me. In that moment all I could feel was queasiness from the wind trying to toss my ass to the pavement fifty stories below, and a burning embarrassment for looking stupid in front of the strange man that I kept wanting to hold. It wasn't a good day.

"Feel what exactly? It's chilly up here. I'm getting a tinge of smog from all the cars."

"My creator sent me on a mission of great importance. Said I was not to return to his side until I learned the truth."

"The truth of what?"

Garavel's tone plummeted, the lightness in his face sharpening to an existential dread I couldn't name. He stood taller and his wings popped out. "The end of the world."

Chapter Ten

The end of the world...

Ink laughed and shook his head. "When isn't this foolish rock trying to speed its way to doom? I swear it was designed to self-implode by mistake."

"This isn't funny."

The second Garavel said it, my heart sank and a heaviness grew in my stomach. It was like when the witch hunters took my magic, but in reverse. I could feel a knot that I hadn't noticed before.

"My bond. I could not count the number of doomsday cults were I a hydra sticking its heads in a fan blade."

"What do you mean the world's ending?" I put to Garavel, who leaned back and shrugged.

"I dunno."

"You don't, how do you not know?"

"My creator said, 'Go out into the world and determine who is disturbing the balance.' So I did."

None of this made any sense, but I couldn't stop getting hung up on how Garavel said creator. Not like he was mentioning a benevolent but absent god. No, he spoke of him like he was a favorite uncle or grandfather.

"Wait! Of course, you're a witch. And you're a...I'm uncertain how much help you can provide."

"Depends on his mood," I said, expecting Ink to laugh or nod in agreement, but he went silent.

"Wonderful. Then I'll take you to him."

Take me to him? "Wait..." I began, but Garavel had already pulled me flush to his body, his arm wrapped around the whole of my back.

"Hold a moment." Ink dashed forward just as Garavel unfurled his wings and walked us back. I caught worry in my incubus' face before I plunged straight off the tower.

"Close your eyes!" Ink shouted. "If you don't..." His warning whipped away on the wind. I crushed my hands over eyes, terrified to stare death in the eye sockets. The bulging forearm taut against my stomach pressed tight and my body, along with Garavel, did a full loop-de-loop. As we came out of it, he leveled us parallel with the ground. I could still stare down at the city now at the distance where if I fell I'd shatter every bone but probably live.

"Where are we going?" I shouted above the traffic. Garavel tipped, dodging us between buildings. I watched the reflection in black glass of a terrified woman trapped in the arms of an angel. It wasn't until he spun around to avoid a shorter building that I realized my jaw was open in a scream but no sound came out. How did superheroes make this look so easy?

"To Ramiel's side," he said.

"Oh, shit." The way Ink had talked about angels — the real ones, not Garavel — they seemed less like benevolent supermodels with wings and more short-fuse atom bombs. I was not prepared to face one. And what did he say about closing my eyes?

Garavel laughed, his chest rumbling against my back. "Don't beat yourself up. I forget things sometimes too. It's why I tie a piece of rope around my wrist."

I looked down at said wrist wrapped to my hip, and spotted ten different pieces of frayed rope tied up his forearm. The farthest one looked desiccated and about to shatter, while the one on his wrist was a piece of neon pink yarn. That couldn't be a good sign.

We flew even faster than when escaping from Cal. I kept trying to peer behind, hoping to find Ink, but also not. The last thing I needed was some demon and angel aerial battle with me caught in the middle. What about Cal and Daniel? As far as they knew I was kidnapped, again. What if they tried to attack the full angel to save me?

Wait. Garavel had never said where this guy was. "How far away is he?"

A cool wind rose from below and the clouds parted as we burst over the lake that sat to the east of the city. To the right, I spotted the dock where I had nearly been drowned by a kelpie. Good times.

"Not very, now. Beyond this water."

I tipped my head back to stare across the lake. Sunlight glinted off the small waves, whitecaps rising and falling below us as we flew. "At least if I fall here, it'll just be into water," I said, trying to make conversation.

"That would be bad. At this height, the water surface is stronger than a brick. But don't worry."

"You have me?" I asked.

"I can dive very quickly, and catch most things that fall."

Well, that was less than reassuring. I strained back with my arms, digging into Garavel's sides without touching the precious wings keeping us from dive bombing into the brick water. My fingers found their way under his robe, and—as I pressed my palms against his skin—a golden glow caressed my arm. A strange giddiness tickled in my throat, a laugh circling around my brain, but when it struck, it felt like a reverse ice cream headache. Fire hotter than the gates of hell erupted in my sinuses and spread across the front of my cerebellum. My eyes watered and the lake below me vanished into a charred pit of charcoal and...bodies.

The pit flashed with bursts of fire, and people with white wings marched forward. They weren't dressed in the simple white robes, but armor that glowed like magma, flames belching off their shoulders. Each carried a great sword, the hilt and flat of the blade pulsing with runes. What in the hell was all of this?

I tried to will myself closer, to see what they were marching to. Silhouettes of the enemy's army stood on the horizon, but I needed to drop lower to see who was... "Shit!" My sweaty palms slipped straight off of Garavel. They plummeted and, in my shock at breaking away from his memory, I twisted in his arms and fell.

It took a second for my brain to piece together that I was careening to my death. The pit of bodies was replaced by the threatening rocks of the lake's edge. "Ahhh!" I screamed, clawing at the air. My brain kept unhelpfully tossing up images of slow-motion water balloons bursting against the ground. That was going to be me, but with organs squirting out instead of colored latex. I needed a spell, a demon, a goddamn broom. Anything to...

"Oop." Hands slipped under my tumbling ass followed by the unshakable forearms and I rose away from my bone-breaking end. Garavel held me in his arms like a fireman plucking a girl off a burning ledge. Shaking, I snared my arms around the back of his neck and pressed my face against his cheek.

"No need to worry, my lady. I'm good at catching."

"Yes." I nodded, bonking against his cheekbones. "You are."

I didn't look up from his cheek that smelled like dawn's dew until he came to a hover. Slowly, I risked peering out to find an empty field of weeds below us, when Garavel dropped my legs. They slipped down, my body falling, but only for a millisecond, as he enveloped me in a hug. My shivering, water-splattered thighs trembled against his stoic ones. He pressed me tighter, our hips and bellies gliding across one another. I tried to calm down, but the way I floated against him set off a new panic in my heart.

What if I give an angel a boner?

What if I don't?

Garavel glanced down, his steady eyes dipping. "Hang on," he said, his first warning since this strange double-kidnapping had begun. I clenched around the back of his neck, lifting myself to hang off of him. As I went, a hard bulge pressed between my thighs.

In shock, I opened my eyes to find a blush across his cheeks. He smiled so innocently that I began to grin back. His wings folded inward and we dropped. "Garavel? Garavel!" He wasn't pulling up. We kept falling, the flat ground rushing to smash us into tiny pieces.

I held tighter, my entire body clenching for the inevitable when the ground opened. My toes caught on the edge of the grass, which was pulling apart to reveal a hole in the middle of nowhere. Dangling off the angel, I slipped into total darkness. The shaft of blue sky and sunlight above began to shrink before disappearing entirely.

There was no way to guess how long we were falling. It was probably thirty seconds but felt like thirty minutes. Garavel only had time to say, "You're safe," before the tube opened up and his wings spread wide. We rocketed back like a filled parachute and I gazed around at a cult's sacrificial chambers. Okay, that might not have been its exact purpose, but it would have made a great one.

The floor was of white marble stones. Pillars of the same material held up the ceiling, which was carved with various constellations made of poured gold and silver. Small altars sat around the area, though the middle was carved out for a purpose I couldn't guess. As we came to a gentle touchdown, I tapped my foot on the floor, expecting the whole thing to flash to someone's root cellar from the memory fading. Cold stone answered me back.

"How does this exist?" I asked carefully. I stood in an ancient lost city under the middle of America. That made no sense.

"It was built," Garavel explained.

"But by who?" As I turned around, I spotted a relief carved into the wall of a giant bust of a face but inverted. When I shifted, its sunken eyes followed me. Ugh.

"By the people who built it." He reached behind and hefted the now visible sword off his back.

I leaped away, ramming the back of my calf into a foot-high stone. The pain of a scrape jarred up my nerves, but my brain focused on the guy with the huge sword who had brought me to sacrifice city.

"Here." Garavel held out his hand, but I refused to move. "What's wrong?"

"You have a big sword that can cut me to many tiny pieces."

"This?" He stared at his giant knife as if he didn't even remember grabbing it. "You may hold it if you'd like." And he passed it over.

I managed to get one hand around the coffee-mug-sized grip before the entire thing tumbled to the ground. Shit! Don't drop the angel's sword. I raced to fall with it, as if that might protect it, when the strangest sound in the world echoed through this forgotten dead city — torn fabric. *Did he rip all of his clothes off?*

Oh…that, um. Damn.

I couldn't let go of the celestial sword, so I hobbled my legs around for a better grip and stared up.

He was still dressed. Which was a good thing. Alone in a lost Minoan palace underground halfway across the world with a naked angel sounded like a fun…bad time. Very dangerous. Who knew what could happen? Though I would have bet Ink could come up with some ideas.

Instead of tossing his clothes to the side and shouting he had to have me now, Garavel extended a strip of white cloth. I stared at it, then to the tattered hem of his robe. "You will need this," he said, "before meeting Ramiel." As I stared, Garavel slipped behind me and dropped the cloth over my eyes.

I jumped when it touched me but didn't rip it away. Garavel knotted it behind my head.

"Why are you blindfolding me?" I asked just as Ink's parting warning hit me.

"Humans, even powerful witches, cannot gaze upon an angel without..."

"Yeah, eye melting, brain popping. Got it." I didn't want to hear all of that again, not when I'd be walking into the possibility of my gray matter parboiling in my skull. I waved my hand in front of my eyes, terrified that if I turned the wrong way, the cloth would weaken and I'd see it.

A hand pressed over the top of mine and my first instinct was to rip it away. It didn't clamp onto my wrist or choke me, but took the sword out of my fingers. Without that ungodly weight, I tried to stand while blind, which for some reason was hard. I kept overcompensating, my body bowing to the left and right even though nothing was in my way.

The hand that I really hoped was Garavel's pressed to the top of mine again. I felt like a fancy lady about to be led around a ballroom...before I remembered I was being taken before a being so powerful Ink was terrified of it. Jane Austen didn't cover how to behave in that situation. Would there be cucumber sandwiches?

Garavel stepped forward, but I didn't come with. I was literally walking blind into something I barely understood. He returned to my side and in a gentle voice asked, "Do you need some time? I think there's a spot back there where one can relieve themselves."

"No." I uncrossed my wobbly legs to prove I didn't have to pee, then found myself teetering. Overcompensating again, I tumbled against the strong, immovable frame of a not-angel. Why was he so warm?

Not approaching scorching the way Ink and sometimes even Cal could. Certainly not the frosty bite of Daniel. Garavel felt like sticky buns fresh out of the oven and I wanted to melt in his hand.

World to save. Ghost to bring back. Melt later.

"I'm ready," I declared, steeling my spine for whatever was about to come. The sound of stone being dragged across cement shattered the air and a light brighter than the sun burst in front of me. I tried to close my eyes, but it was too late. In the darkness, all I could see was the light.

Chapter Eleven

Were my brains melting? I didn't see any flaming wheels or lion heads. I didn't see anything. *My name is Layla, I'm dating a werewolf, my mother faked her death.* God, that all sounded insane, but it was true. Unless my melting brain thought it was true.

This was a bad time to have a philosophical debate with myself.

"You've returned." The voice didn't boom like earthquake and thunder. It danced across the ground and burrowed into my head. Colors of pink and purple trailed the words even though I couldn't see anything.

"My blessed creator." Garavel didn't cause any colors, but I felt him release me and his form plummet to the ground. Hopefully on his knees in a bow and not because his boss was upset.

"What have you discovered?" The pinks sharpened to a mauve-red and heat struck my face. Ramiel had spotted me. "A human?"

"She is a witch, my creator," Garavel explained. He slipped away, abandoning my hand which I grasped at nothing. "Who would serve our cause better than a servant of magic?"

Pride sounded through Garavel's words and I rose higher, my shoulders back.

The angel laughed, each quick ha cracking the air like a gunshot. I dug my nails into my thighs to keep from falling to the ground. If I plummeted, I might lose where the door was should I have to escape. "Of course you would bring a witch to my domain. Tell me, conduit, what know you of the problems of the world?"

"Well, for starters, someone who calls people conduit and witch without asking for their names," I snapped back. *Eyeball-melting, world-destroying power, Layla. Shut up!*

The summer air froze in an instant. I slammed my jaw shut to keep my teeth from clacking as all of Ramiel's words became a jagged blue and black. "There is far more at stake than the nomenclature you've attached to yourself...?" He let his sentence dangle and I waited, too.

"She is called Layla," Garavel intervened.

"Layla." My name changed colors from a depressing green to a dirty gray. I tried blinking quick, then closing my eyes, but the colors hung there, telling me exactly how little Ramiel thought of me. "After so many passes of the sun, it seems the mortals have forgotten how to fear their creators."

"The hubris of man," I interrupted, trying to stave off a fight before it began. "Aren't there lots of Bible verses about that stuff?"

"I never much cared for your screeds against the darkness," Ramiel said. Over the thump of his voice and the strike of colors in the night was a soft swish. Was he dragging a long cloak over the floor? What would an angel wear?

A suicidal urge to take a peek ran through me, so I clasped my hands together in a knot.

"Why am I here? I mean, what's the problem you have?"

"My problems are yours, human, in a way you could not possibly comprehend."

I sneered at his arrogance. Damn thing was the size of a mountain. A snap broke through the air and the blinding light vanished. In an instant, I was thrown into total darkness, which was a lot more disconcerting than the eyeball-melting light. I tried to not shake as the air changed around me.

From the edges of the room seeped in tendrils of smoke...no, not the room. They came from between the room. *What the hell does that mean?*

"Even a simple solution to a universal problem must be capable of sensing what's happening." Ramiel declared it, but I took it as a question.

"You're drawing magic here. Why?" I could feel it now. The power radiating in the room came not from the angel I could barely understand, but a source I tapped every second I lived. I raised my hand, tugging the tendrils to me. They obeyed like a trained falcon, swooping through the air and pulling themselves inside my skin.

"Me? I do nothing of the sort."

"Then what...?"

"It's the realms themselves, conduit."

The realms? That unknowable line that separated earth from demonic creatures who'd pop a couple dozen humans in their mouths for a snack? "What about them?"

"They're breaking down."

An explosion with no sound or force burst in the air and, for a moment, I could sense the outline of Ramiel's body. It was gigantic. At that height, it could be ten feet or twenty. The head itself looked misshapen and strange while the body strained back like two metal wings conjoined by a flat strip. I tried to tilt my head down for the feet, but the sensation vanished and I was back in darkness.

"What do you mean they're breaking down? How can they be breaking? Does this happen a lot?" Was I required to find some mystical artifact built specifically to save the world?

"This is bad and new," Garavel said solemnly.

"What can do this?" Maybe I didn't fully understand the enormity of the situation but they were treating this like a pothole in the universe.

"I woke my defender to determine such a cause. No doubt you've noticed an increase in visitors from the twelve realms."

"Uh…" I'd been busy a lot. But Ink had never said anything about it seeming like there were too many monsters around. I thought it was normal to fight off imps and leaping dog creatures and corpse eaters. Had the world been falling down around without me noticing?

"This is who you put your faith in, defender?" Ramiel snorted, his words striking the air with a derisive brown.

A hand dropped to my shoulder and Garavel bellowed from behind me. "She's really brave."

My cheeks burned at his straightforward compliment.

"And who can find magic tears better than witches?"

The what now?

"I cannot fault you for that. Though, the world is not as it once was. The rules changed as you slept."

Garavel stuck his chest out until it bumped against my back. I shifted in place, then reached behind to keep myself steady. By accident, my palm landed on his biceps and I couldn't even reach halfway around.

"She can help us. She already said as much."

Ah, damn it, I did. Sort of. "I said that I'd try to help."

"Here comes the lie baked in the middle of a truth," Ramiel thundered before I heard more of that long cloak being dragged.

"Look, I don't know a lot about this realm tear stuff. I'm still learning how to be a witch. But, I have a crack team working with me."

"Yes, your coven."

I shrugged one shoulder. They were...kind of. Better than any other witches I'd met so far. Shame I couldn't call on Valerie, unless she too was working on this problem. A single word rattled in the back of my mind, traveling through my synapsis until it leaped off my tongue. "White."

"What?" Garavel asked.

"I fear she risked a peek and her brain is melting. Please remove her before her skull pops open."

"There's this...I don't know what he is. Calls himself Mr. White. Could he be causing all of this?"

"I've never heard of such a being, so I highly doubt it. The only creature of great enough strength to unravel what the creators formed is a high demon."

I swallowed hard. "Do you mean Lucifer?"

Ramiel laughed. "Don't be foolish. He far prefers hell to this dour existence. We exchange messages on the regular."

"You talk to the devil? About what?"

"Mostly literature. Hell's library is vast in comparison to the books you mortals have managed to lose over the centuries."

So it's not Mr. White. Probably. And not the devil, maybe. Unless he was deceiving an angel, but father of all lies so…

"You have no concept of what can be doing this," Ramiel summed up in an instant.

"But she can figure it out, with my help!" Garavel chimed in. He held tighter to me, as if afraid his boss might lunge forward and devour me. I did not want the last thing I saw to be an angel's mouth.

"Well, conduit?"

I nodded, then said, "Yes…but I require something in exchange."

"Ah, here we reach the selfishness of your species. Do go on."

I wanted to ask how was it not even more selfish for him to assume I'd do his job without pay, but years in retail taught me how to keep my mouth shut. Ramiel was another fuming middle manager. The thought calmed me and I raised my head. "I need one of your feathers."

Only the plink of water filled the air. The silence cascaded into a threatening chain reaction. "For what purpose?"

I leaped in place. Ramiel's words puffed against my face, the colors bleeding like an oil slick. He stood so close, I could reach out and yank a feather off. Though I was blindfolded, had no idea where his wings were and would probably be cut down before making it two steps out.

"What do you care? It's just a feather."

"Spoken like a child asking the king for a sword. What could it hurt? It's just a knife."

I could feel him lingering right in front of my face. The heat was like shoving my head against a hand dryer. It yanked my cheeks back and wetted my eyes. He didn't speak again, waiting for me to tell him what the feather was for. Or maybe he just wanted to berate me some more and required further ammunition. Either way, I kept my mouth slammed shut.

"So, conduit. Tell me — and without subterfuge — the world is in crisis, yet would you let it crumble if I refused to give you my feather?"

Yes. I needed it to help Daniel. Without it, he'd be trapped as a ghost until the endless nothing drove him mad. My teeth ground together, fighting to insist that I required his feather in exchange for my work and would not help otherwise.

"No," slipped from my lips and my head fell. He had no reason to help me, to give me anything other than a 'good witch' sticker and send me on my way. *Damn it!* As I mentally beat myself to a pulp, Garavel rubbed his palm over my shoulder.

"I see... You may leave my presence, my defender."

"Thank you, creator." Garavel must have bent over in another bow, the arm he had on me bending and sliding. But he sprang back up fast to take hold of my arm. With that, I was turned away from the angel, nothing to show for my dance with death other than another impossible task that could get us all killed. Exhaustion twisted my legs, my knees trembling as I tried to inch forward, one hand out. Tears built up on the blindfold, the salt digging into my eyes. I had to get free of Ramiel fast before I did something stupid.

"Witch?"

I whipped around to the voice, Garavel's hand falling off me.

"When you have found the source of the disruption, you will be given two of my feathers as compensation."

"How generous!" Garavel crowed, while a darker thought tumbled in my stomach. The angel liked torturing me, and he could do it without lifting a finger. Garavel pulled me away from his boss, but I kept staring in the direction, waiting for another pulse to reveal the outline of a snake in wings.

A warm hand landed on the small of my back as Garavel whispered, "You're so lucky. Not one feather but two. It's a...a gift to kings of kings. Wait here."

His lavish boss-praising switched to a spine-straightening command so fast, my shoulders launched back on their own. I lost my only guide in this, leaving me standing alone in the underground ruins realizing how thin my sundress was. When I heard the same stone dragging over concrete sound of before, I waited until it stopped, then reached for my blindfold. Another hand got there first.

"Allow me."

"Ink?" I spun for the voice, but my demon chuckled as he undid the knot behind my head. The meager candlelight burned in my eyes, and I had to shut them as soon as I caught the wind-swept black hair and cheeky smile.

"You gave me quite the chase, then unending tongue-lashing after you vanished from this earth."

"I met an angel, a real one. He's..." I wrung the blindfold between my hands like a garrote, my shoulders trembling as the entire situation hit me. Exhaustion struck and I fell into his arms.

"My creator agreed to her request," Garavel declared and extended a hand to me. I took it even though I was uncertain why. "We are to work together. Isn't that exciting?"

Ink stared him up and down. "I'm quaking in my hooves." He placed his chin on top of my head and asked me, "Another body to the pile? We're going to run out of beds at this rate, my bond."

"That isn't..." I tried to pull my fingers out of Garavel's grip, but they were stuck. Not as if he held them, but as if I couldn't let go. "Can we get out of here?" I asked, waiting for my demon to swoop me away.

It was the angel who scooped me into his arms. His wings burst free and he stared skyward, before casting a look to the lost incubus. "Would you like to climb on as well?"

"Interesting offer, but I'll carry myself."

Garavel smiled in response and he burst from the ground with a force that sent us rocketing up. His wings gave two flaps before folding in. I tipped my head back, watching the sun and blue sky appear above. It took longer to grow than it had to vanish. I tried to not calculate how much force he needed for us to reach the top, and what would happen if Garavel didn't use enough.

We didn't so much shoot out of the hole as lightly stumble across the crushed weeds in the fallow field.

Ellen Mint

Garavel released me and he extended his wings, sending him shooting high into the sky. I got one foot under me, only for the other to fold up and roll my ankle. Naked arms wrapped around me, turning me in place on my single foot until I stared into the terrified eyes of my boyfriend.

"Layla! Moon's sake," Cal cried. He pulled me into his arms, then tugged me back. "What did they do to you?"

"Nothing. It was... I met an angel. Why?" As I turned to stare around the field, finding Daniel and Ink, the sweet summer air struck my cheeks and they burned. "Gah!" I crumpled inward, trying to shield my face, but touching it only made it worse.

"Let me see." Ink tugged on my shoulder, but I refused to come away from the safety of Cal's nude chest. "My bond." When Ink placed a comforting hand on the top of my back, I gave in and turned. "Angel glow. Dangerous. It can combust flesh if exposed for too long."

"What do you know of medicine?" Daniel insisted, rushing to my side. He stared at my face. The angel's heat burned across the whole of it save where the blindfold had been. It grew stronger when the wind struck, bringing a tear to my eye. Daniel placed both his palms over my cheeks. The soothing cool of his touch knocked back the pain enough I was able to keep from crying out.

"I'm sorry." Ink sneered. "I forgot that the master of all knowledge in the twelve realms has attended to us. Please, share your thoughts on the cause."

"It could be radiation. What if that thing was like a nuclear reactor?" Daniel glared at Ink's heavy sigh, before focusing on Cal behind me. My werewolf's protective arm didn't drop away. Instead, he clung tight to my stomach even as I stared into Daniel's deep eyes.

"Ah yes, of course, it must be a common creation of this world and not the incomprehensible essence of life from a celestial. Truly, you are a sage among basil."

I shook my head, momentarily breaking contact from Daniel's cooling touch. "It doesn't matter. I can heal it away. The important thing is I met an angel. A real one." I placed my hands behind Daniel's and pretended to hold them while saying, "And he promised me a feather."

"Really?"

"And what did the celestial ask for in return?" Ink prompted.

I began to explain, when the sun fell into darkness above my head. Just as I glanced up, Garavel plummeted to the ground. He swung his wings back, a smile wide on his face. "My lady witch…" The grin fell, and he jabbed a finger at Cal. "I shall save you from the werewolf!"

"Like hell you will," Cal growled from behind me.

"Stop!" I commanded, in no mood for another round. "Put the sword down, and lose the claws, honey."

Both men grumbled, but at least had enough sense to do as I asked. Their heads drooped, yet they kept shooting warning glares from below their brows. Helpful. "Garavel, he isn't some werewolf."

"I'm her boyfriend," Cal declared.

"Urinate on her leg to show dominance!" Ink cheered from the side.

"Ink!"

The incubus shrugged and looked baffled, as if I didn't know he was enjoying this fight.

"You...you are *intimately* involved with a were-creature?" Garavel sputtered.

"Do you wish to see documentation? I have erotic still images." Ink extended up a notebook in his hand and I spun on him.

"What?" Yanking the notebook from his hands, I cracked it open. A random page had a hand-drawn image of Cal completely naked and on his knees. Before I could find more, I slapped it shut. "Why do you have this?"

"You regularly prune the images on your small phone," he said, as if this were normal.

"My lady witch, I refuse to cooperate with a werewolf."

"Well, I'm not exactly happy with how this angel keeps kidnapping you. Get rid of him, Layla, for all our sakes."

"Agreed," Daniel chimed in.

"Look," I began, when the wind struck again, reigniting my cheeks. I folded my fingers fast and cast my healing spell on myself. "We all have to work together in order to—"

Garavel snapped his wings wide. "You require time to rest. I shall find you after...away from the monster." He glared at Cal, who growled back, then the not-angel flew into the air away from us all.

"This is going well," I muttered to myself, when the burn stung again. Why wasn't the healing spell working? I tried casting again.

"What's he on about?" Cal asked.

"You're going to love this, mutt," Ink said while draping an arm over Cal's shoulder.

"We have to...gah!" The burn only grew stronger. "Why does it still hurt?" I cast the damn spell for the third time, but leaned my cheek against Daniel's. He caught on and pressed his hands back, wiping some of the agony away. "Don't tell me I lost my magic down there."

"I'm afraid no witch's magic, not even one as skilled as you, is capable of challenging a celestial." Ink scooped me up into his arms.

"Meaning?" I held on to him, exhausted.

Cal caught me by the chin and barely pecked my cracked lips. "We'll patch you up the old-fashioned way."

Chapter Twelve

"How's that?" With a gentle touch, Cal swept a large glob of aloe over my cheek.

As the goo worked into my crispy skin, I couldn't hold back an orgasmic sigh. He gave a small laugh at my response, then had to stand up to shift his pants. Somehow I'd wound up in the shared upstairs bathroom perched on an old counter while Cal stood before me in full protective panic mode. He dipped into the aloe pot and smeared his entire palm with the blue gel.

"Where are you going to put that?" I asked. My face was so covered I looked like a Smurf in a wig. With a sigh, Cal got down on his knees and placed his palm to the top of my chest. "Here's red too. Seems like the damn thing got you wherever skin was exposed."

"So don't visit the angel naked. Got it."

He stared up at me a moment before returning to his work. The rampaging wolf ready to throw down with an angel had vanished, leaving behind a man tenderly sweeping his cool palm over the top of my breasts. I'd be leaping on top of him until we fell into the empty tub if my whole body didn't ache.

"Ugh, I hate that I can't heal this away."

"I hate that it happened." He dropped the lid on the pot hard, and screwed it on while staring me in the eye. "First you get kidnapped, again, then burned. I don't like this, Layla."

"Or is it a certain winged, armed man of the celestials whom you don't enjoy?" Ink stood by the vanity, occasionally glancing at his face in the mirror. If I turned too quickly, I could see the outline of his horns and the demonic skin he kept hidden.

Cal grumbled and Ink leaned for him. "Sounds like someone needs his belly rubbed."

"Try it and I'll rip your arm off."

"Forgive me for lightening the mood, Beo-wolf."

I had to press my lips together to keep from laughing at Ink's god-awful pun. "I don't get it, why does Garavel—?"

Cal full on growled at the name. This was going well. "What does *he* have against werewolves?"

"Aside from their incessant howling, bringing fleas into the house and pissing in all your potted plants?" Ink asked. "Haven't a clue. Angels are not my purview."

"What is, exactly?"

Ink smiled wide. "Shall I list them alphabetically? Anal, anilingus, an—"

"Okay," I cut in, not needing those two to come flying apart. At least Cal had stopped lifting his lip to show off a fang. "We need to plan a way forward, then. I'll tell Garavel in no uncertain terms he cannot hurt you, and I expect the same."

"Oh." It was Ink who whined and not Cal. "But if you let them fight, it might lead to violent rutting. And my collection of erotic drawings could use a new chapter."

"Yet you he doesn't have a problem with?"

"Everyone likes me," Ink declared with a smile.

"I don't," Daniel called. He leaned back from the desk in the bedroom to stick his head clean through the wall.

"Everyone who matters likes me." Ink took my hand and pressed my knuckles to his lips. It was so silly, a blush rose under my burn. Then Ink drew his tongue around my pointer finger and lasciviously licked to the joint.

Cal caught my hand and pulled it away. "No, none of that. Not until she's had a good night's rest."

"Is that concern or jealousy for her newest toy not wanting you to share the bed?"

I tipped my head back until the crown touched the stuccoed wall and let them go at it. Not like...not like that. Though, the idea of those two... Ink paused in his arguing match to wink at me. "We need to focus on a plan of attack."

"Or, we ignore him, put out some angel traps and go about our lives," Cal bit back. For the first time I heard more than anger. Fear lurked in his words.

Forgetting Ink or Daniel partially in the room, I reached for Cal. He bent low as I took both of his hands. When he pressed his forehead to mine, I asked softly, "What's wrong?"

"You were kidnapped. Again! And I couldn't do anything but watch."

"Though you do look striking staring forlornly in the distance while the wind tousles your everything."

We both ignored the incubus wanting attention. "It wasn't like before. Garavel...the angel didn't plan it. And I was safe the whole time. Ink could get to me."

"More or less. Once you entered the angel's lair, I could no longer reach you. Demonic barriers. Angels can be such pricks."

"Tell me about it." I couldn't shake the feeling Ramiel had given me just enough rope to hang myself, but I couldn't figure out how. "Do angels even have...uh, you know?"

"Concerned about the state of your newest infatuation's holy trinity?" Ink asked with an elbow jab. "Truth be told, I don't know. Don't all glare at me like that. Yes, ghost, I can see your sour puss even with my back turned. Angels are rare, were rare when I first walked this earth. Barely any beings can stand to look upon them without bursting into flames, even powerful creatures such as myself."

"I'd like to see some hard stats on how powerful you are. We talking goldfish or baby hamster?" Daniel asked.

"Perhaps they do have a more human form. It would explain why they create their defenders to look so human. Or they are the spinning wheels of flame and feathers the humans saw, and happen to like having steely men and women of muscles standing around them. Who can say?"

"Are you saying that Ramiel created Garavel? Like, he's his father?"

"Nothing so exquisitely crude as him expelling the man mountain out of his whatever angels have. The demi-angels are carved."

"Ebony. He said he came from ebony. Like literally, he's made of ebony? But he's so soft."

Ink smirked at me for that and my stomach opened into a pit. I couldn't face Cal and tried to stare anywhere else.

"I only made an acquaintance with one demi-angel prior, a woman of quartz. To the eye they are human — skin, teeth, eyes, fingers…state of genitalia to be determined at a later date. But underneath they are stone, nearly unbreakable, requiring no rest, no food, nothing but to follow the orders of their creators. The first perfect soldier."

"That sounds…sad."

"So it's a rock that hates me. Great," Cal grumbled. I tried to soothe his arms, but he wouldn't look up. It took some time before he risked a glance over.

In a voice so soft I nearly missed it, he asked, "Why do this, risk so much for a feather? Is it…is he worth it?"

I jerked at his callow dismissal of Daniel, when Cal picked up my hands and raised them up. "One time with them and look at what he did to your beautiful skin. What if it gets worse?"

"Cal." I cupped his cheek, brushing my thumb nervously back and forth as he stared glumly at me.

"I know, you have to save the world, whatever that all means. I just…"

I caught his worrying lips in a kiss. All the aloe smeared between us, creating a slippery mess as I held him tight. I wanted to tell him it would be okay, that there was nothing to worry about. But he knew it'd be a lie and we'd promised not to do that. So all I could do was kiss him.

Cal parted his mouth and flicked his tongue across my bottom lip. I started to moan, tasting the aloe he had to be consuming too, but it didn't put him off. Instead, he slipped his tongue into my mouth. When it dove deeper, he slammed his palm against the wall and gently cupped my chin. I clutched my palms over his pecs, my fingertips pressing into the taut flesh as he breathed harder from my touch.

The force of his hunger pushed me along the counter. I reached for the towel rack to keep myself in place and caught the wily hand of an incubus instead. Ink placed his other hand to Cal's shoulder and pulled him off me. "Despite how near the full moon may be, do you consider it in her best interests to proceed?"

You have to be shitting me. Ink was calling this off? Even if he didn't participate, he'd always be standing by offering a helping hand, towel or play-by-play recap. Cal nodded, looking as stunned as I felt, while I stared at Ink. What had happened to him in that pit of vipers? Cal and Daniel lost him for some time in the sewers. What if the witch hunters had changed him?

"Your face is splattered in the healing unguent," he said, handing a washcloth to Cal. "Now, shall we return to the discussion at hand?"

"What was it?" Cal sounded punch-drunk, his eyes glazed over as he swiped the aloe off.

"The worthlessness of the ghost and how we would be wiser to put the angel feather to better use. As a quill, for example."

"You're such a dick," Daniel grumbled. He swept his head back into the bedroom office before I could see his face.

"I would not advise placing an angel feather there. Unless you know what you're doing."

This bickering wasn't getting us any closer to anything. "We need a plan."

"Seems like you have to figure out what's causing this realm breakage," Cal said.

"Assuming this Ramiel is correct and not simply misinterpreting a bit of swamp gas or solar flare for the complete annihilation of the realms. It can happen."

"Step two," I said, slipping off the counter to my tender feet. "Get the angel feather, then figure out how to find demon blood." I waited for Daniel to reemerge, but he didn't float through the wall at that.

"Step three," Ink interrupted. "I massage the finest oils of the Greek world across every succulent inch of your body until you orgasm from a foot rub." Ink caught my hand and pulled me to him. I fought off the wince of pain as he slipped his arm across the small of my back. "But first, you require rest."

"I'm fine. There's so much shit to…"

"No," Cal spoke up. "He's right. Layla, you…" His breath shuddered and he slicked the blue gel back through his hair by mistake. "You deserve a nap after all of that. We'll keep you safe. Those two have a few ideas on how we can protect against Eric."

"No anti-werewolf spells!" I ordered.

"Don't worry." Even with me in Ink's arms, Cal sidled up beside and brushed back my hair. "We're all working together. Can you…?"

"How dare you even ask such a question?"

Whoa! Ink swung me up into his arms, and spun both of us around to face Cal. "I'll carry her to your bedchambers. And if she tries to leave, I may be forced to tie her to the headboard."

"Ink…" I groaned, feeling like a worthless lump at all their attention. It was little more than a bad sunburn and they were acting like I had run headlong into a fire.

Cal stared at me a long moment before he stepped back. Fur sprouted off his chest. I tried to look away, but I was lost in the gray hair rippling across his abs. "You may need the handcuffs too."

Hey! I leaned up higher in Ink's arms, but Cal was already on all fours. When his tail sprouted, he turned and loped out of the bathroom, but not before giving me one last mournful look. Fine, I'd take a nap. But to assuage their silly concerns and not because I was...I wasn't sleepy. Though, against the heat of Ink's chest, it grew harder to fight to stay awake.

Ink stepped into the bedroom I shared with Cal. The incubus had been in the bed a few times, the chair and short dresser more, but he still moved as if this wasn't his space. With a dramatic flourish, he tugged back the covers Cal made every morning and lowered me onto the mattress.

"Please, for all that is debauched and dirty in this world, sleep," Ink damn-near prayed over me.

"I don't need it," I insisted even as my eyelids grew heavy. I'd forgotten how comfy this bed was.

Ink carefully pulled the thin blanket up, letting it fall right at the top of my breasts to avoid the goo. After tucking me in, he guided a fallen hair off my sticky forehead with his pinkie. "You may not, but we three need a break."

That caused my eyes to snap open, but my incubus was already bending over and placing his lips to my forehead. "Sleep, my..." A pause strained the air and I tried to reach for him, but Ink had already leaned back. He gave a cheery wave while practically shouting, "bond," then exiting the room.

That was weird. All of them were acting so damn... I couldn't fight the yawn. A few minutes with my eyes closed wouldn't hurt. Then I could get to work on fixing this angel problem. *Just as soon as I...*

Chapter Thirteen

A text notification pulled me from a bottomless sleep. With the curtains drawn so deep orange light broke through, the bedroom took on an air from another time. It was as if I'd woken in a storybook, waiting for three bears or seven small men to open the door. Though three men were enough, thanks.

Tipping up my phone, I had to twist it to make out the time below the numerous screen cracks. *It's only two? How long can this damn day last?*

A notification rose again with a text claiming to be from Don Juan. I made out the first few words, "Gazing upon you now, I would…"

I glanced back to the pillows that I'd managed to smear blue gel on. I couldn't have been down for longer than an hour, but I had to know what Daniel had said. Sitting up, I placed my back against the headboard and typed in my passcode. The screen jerked, as it always did now, but after glitching a second, it revealed the message.

Gazing upon you now, I would fight through a mile long thicket of thorns and climb a dozen towers just to kiss your sweet lips.

My cheeks warmed at the comparison and I curled my toes. I brushed back the soggy hair from my cheek and began to type.

What do you do after my eyes open?

Tell you my heart's every desire. How I ached from afar, unable to touch your delicate skin, to taste your flushed lips. Chained in the evil witch's clutches, I was only able to observe your beauty, not celebrate it, yet my love grew deeper with every moment.

My entire chest fluttered at his words. Daniel was equal parts romantic poet and punk rocker, both of which I couldn't touch.

Then what?

Then...

It took a moment, which was a little strange since he never had to physically type the keys. Maybe he got distracted, or he was in the middle of —

Then I shall caress your supple breasts while kissing you so deep, your thighs tremble in ecstasy.

My nips are so hard.

They poke through your dress, daring me to toy with them. I circle my palm under your breast, pressing my thumb and forefinger to your nipple, then pull.

I didn't realize my hand had risen to mimic Daniel's text until my thumb brushed over the nip in question and a jolt ran through me.

My panties wet and I gasp in joy. I reach for you, tugging away your...

What did those fancy princes wear in fairytales?

...Your doublet. The sight of you shirtless makes me squirm in anticipation.

I take your hand and place it to my heart. Your fingers scoop along the muscle and the heat of my blazing skin.

I bit my lip while picturing Daniel shrugging off his jacket and ripping away his black T-shirt. He was lithe and lean and his tan skin would glisten in the sunlight. There'd be no hair save a little black treasure trail leading straight to the tight pants.

I grab your belt and pull you to me.

Once again, the instant messages stopped. Had I pushed him too far? I wasn't very good at this. Half the time, autocorrect plus my dyslexia made my sexting sound like I was obsessed with plucking ducks. I dropped my hand off my breast, when Daniel responded.

The trousers come undone in your expert hands, the fly parting to reveal the crown of my cock.

Oh, fuck. I wanted to ask what it looked like, but would that be wrong? What if it reminded him that right now no one, not even him, could see it?

You gasp at the length straining free, the head a pinkish-brown while the dark tan shaft is thick with veins.

Yes! I could see Daniel straddled above me, one hand clasped to the base of his cock as he held it for me. I wanted to touch it, run my fingers over the smooth skin and jerk against the hard core. I wanted to taste it, to caress my tongue from the base up to the head and swirl it around the tip.

At the sight of you, I pull up my dress.

As I typed those words, I did exactly that. Digging my palm into my thigh, I rolled my fingers, slowly inching my dress up until it rested above my panties.

I take your cock in my hand and jerk the shaft.

At the thought, I circled a finger around my clit. Daniel would close his eyes and gasp silently as I touched him, his hips thrusting to match my rhythm.

Fuck, Layla. I…I rip off your corset, scissoring the ties with my teeth and bite down on your tit.

I cried out at the idea, my back arching as I plunged two fingers inside myself.

Then I catch your wrists, pinning them beside your head. All the while, I straddle your soft thighs, gliding my cock across your lower belly.

His breathing would grow heavier, his cock twitching against my skin. I'd whimper every time the crown would nearly press against my vagina before being pulled back.

I squirm in your grip, unable to take the torture.

But you love it. Your thighs part, sliding up my bare waist and I squeeze them hard.

I stopped fingering myself to grip onto my inner thighs. The thought of him doing the same sent my heart racing. *Damn it, where's the toy box?* Clutching my phone, I reached to the side of the bed for the red box. It had been Ink's idea to put all my toys in a red leather treasure chest, which made opening it tricky as hell.

I run my cheek up them, nibbling and biting as I press ever closer to your...

"Wait!" I shouted at my phone as if that would work. Turning away from Daniel's rapid-fire texting of exactly what his tongue would do to my clit, I found the damn vibrator. It was one of the cheaper options with a solitary setting, but I didn't care.

Falling onto my back, I held my phone up and typed with one thumb.

Duck me, my prince. Duck me so hard I black out.

I didn't have time to fix that. Aiming the vibrator, I pushed the bottom button and shoved it in.

I thrust my cock inside your wet, heaving pussy. It's so tight. I cling to your hips, pulling you onto me.

The tremors from the double-As were nothing compared to the rush from my imagination. Daniel, naked and grunting, with skin glistening from his run to save me, was back-arching, toe-curling. To have him thrusting inside of me and holding my hips so he burrowed deeper than ever chased me to the edge.

I raise your ankles and place them on my shoulders. God, I'd give anything to see you in that position.

The puncture of the real-world mess into the fantasy pulled me back. I left the vibrator rumbling away and focused on my phone.

I wrap my hands around your shoulders, pulling you down. A whimper at the pleasure of your cock pressing inside of me erupts. My prince, I cry, make me come.

As you wish.

I grabbed my hair and pulled, thrusting the toy in and out as the fantasy of Daniel kissing my neck while he fucked me hard rampaged through me. "Oh… Oh!" The orgasm came from deep within, rumbling forward until it set off a second at my clit. I writhed on the bed, pressing my legs tight together as I matched the slow rhythms of a man pumping me with his cum.

Layla?

God. I wiped at my eyes, finding tears, and focused on my screen. He'd typed out a long description of how hard he'd screw me, but my brain was a fog.

You made me come for real.

Time passed with no little dots bouncing. It was hard to know if Daniel had even seen my text. All I could do was wait for an answer and hope I hadn't…

"I know."

I sat up to find Daniel standing awkwardly by the end of the bed. He looked at me, then his gaze darted down. Ah, my boob had popped out of my dress from all the excitement. I began to try to stuff it back, when Daniel made a single cry in response.

"You're very naughty," I said playfully, adjusting my dress so the neckline swept across the middle of my areola. Daniel's unquenchable gaze burned at the hint of the deep brown flesh before he looked up.

"Am I not the knight in shining armor?"

As he drew a hand to his denim chest, my imagination flashed with the image of him naked. I'd give anything to see it for real...which was why I faced down an angel.

Gingerly, I touched my cheek, finding the burn had slightly cooled. "I'm supposed to be healing, which means no hanky-panky. Incubus orders."

Daniel scoffed. He stepped closer, the chill of his chest drawing my inflamed skin. "Do you do everything the demon tells you to?"

My eyes bugged at the very idea. I'd never be able to walk again. He chuckled as if reading my mind. I glanced to the cracked-open treasure chest. Cal was more of a rope and leather guy. Ink used anything he could find. Only Daniel would dive into the workhorses of my vibes and seeing what fun we could have.

I held out my hand. "Well, if you really want to stick it to him, no reason we can't go for seconds."

A mischievous smile flitted over his far too pretty features and Daniel reached to take control of my arm. The chill of his fingertips crested over my skin, then he shifted back. "Maybe the demon is right...for once. You need sleep."

"You know, out of all of them, I thought you'd be the one all but pushing me out the door to get this angel feather."

He winced at my summation, his head hanging lower. "I don't want you hurt on my account. I've since found tales of what happened to people who crossed paths with angels and demons. They're not for the faint of heart."

"You think that's me?" I'd survived two werewolf attacks, beat back witch hunters, outsmarted a genie then outsmarted the damn witch hunters again. "If anything, the angel should be scared of me."

Daniel chuckled in his low tenor. His gaze trailed from my eyes down to my barely contained breasts. He stopped at my neckline and furrowed his brow. "Where's your necklace?"

I slapped a hand to my throat and spun around to find it even as my mind pieced it together. "Ink..." I said while picking the locket off the nightstand. "He must have taken it off."

"After his threats, I'm amazed it hasn't wound up in the garbage disposal or flushed down the toilet."

It wasn't the gold heart Daniel cared about, but the piece of him inside. Without it, he couldn't find me. I drew my nail along the edge and gazed at it. One of the ruby chips was missing and the gold was tarnishing to a brass from how often I wore it. Instead of slipping the chain on, I stared at it.

"I doubt Ink knows what a toilet is. Or, at least, how to use it."

"Does he do that often? Remove the necklace?" Daniel practically growled at the easy threat the incubus proved.

I shook my head. "No. I don't think he did it with any ill intent. This time, anyway." Ink was quick to threaten to pulverize Daniel's bones and mulch them into potting soil or feed them to crows and let the wind take them. But he never did it. Nor did I think he would.

"It's not smart to sleep with a necklace on. You can choke." I repeated the same words of advice my mother would chastise me with when I'd tumbled into bed wearing a candy necklace. An ache pounded in my heart that wasn't anger. I swept my fingers around the locket that had been hers. She had never told me where it came from — only that I shouldn't play with it. Too late now, Mom.

"You're crying without tears," Daniel said, shaking me from my memory of that little house in provincial France where I'd chased chickens for hours.

"Oh?" I wiped the back of my hand over my cheekbones, even though they were dry.

"Would speaking of it help?"

"I have no idea. Just thinking about my mother and…the life we had before she went and abandoned me." I folded my knees up, sending myself sinking to the bed. I hunched over as small as possible and stared at the locket. "I don't want to think about her because it makes me so fucking angry. But how do I cut away all those memories? It's either erase my childhood or stay a rage monster. I hate this goddamn holiday."

Daniel sat next to me, the comforter not shifting at his non-weight. He brushed the tips of his cool fingers on my cheek and the tops of them stung like frosty water. I smeared off the tears, not knowing if they fell in anger or sorrow. Maybe it was both.

"I'm sorry. I don't mean to be such a bother…"

"I can't stop thinking about my mom," Daniel said over me. My apologies ground to a halt and I turned to him. He raised his fingers, staring at the pale skin. "If this works. If I get my body back, if I live again…"

"It will," I assured him.

He smiled sweetly. Even he was uncertain about this angel deal. "I'll be twenty-three again, and they'll all be thirty years older. My mom's in her eighties. My younger brother is fifty! What would I even say to explain that? Those bones you buried, well, they were mine but I got better?"

"Jesus, I hadn't even thought…" I'd been so hellbent on helping him, I hadn't thought about what came after. "Daniel? Should we not—"

"No. No, I want to live. To taste food, to touch your…perfectly succulent lips." He squeezed his eyes tight and started to turn away. As he did, his jacket fell back, and I spotted the bloodstain from his bleeding heart. "Every action has consequences, even the noblest of them."

"I just want you to be happy."

He drew his tongue over the lips I couldn't touch and quirked his head to the side. "And what would make you happy?"

I clenched my hand across my knee, staring at the skin that had almost blistered from the heat of an angel. What would make me happy was… That was an easy question. I wanted… Cal, Ink, Daniel all floated in my head. Yes, they could make me happy, but also infuriate me in equal steps. School. Proving I was capable of being so much more than my damn dyslexia and becoming a nurse? That'd make me happy, but it was also merely a job. *What do I want in life?*

A knock startled me and I fell through Daniel. He rose to his feet fast. Instead of the sound coming from the bedroom door, it was someone banging on the window.

"Careful," Daniel warned as I stood up and tugged back the curtain.

Like out of a horror movie, a face grinning ear to ear appeared between the gap. I squealed in shock before noticing the familiar obsidian eyes and the faint glow of heaven off the skin. Garavel waved his hand in front of the glass and shouted through it, "Lady Witch, are you ready to save the world?"

Chapter Fourteen

I barely had time to slip on a pair of tennis shoes and grab my purse before Garavel hefted me one-handed through the window. Good thing Cal's house came with big ones or I'd have stuck in the frame. This time I was better prepared and wrapped my arms around the back of his neck while keeping my gaze skyward instead of down.

He held me by a single arm, his forearm flexing against the small of my back as my feet helplessly dangled off of nothing. The rhythmic flap of his wings, raising us higher and higher with a slight jerk, became oddly assuring. I held my breath, waiting for each rush upward, then released it as we glided deeper into the city.

"How did you find me?" I asked, trying to not shout in his ear while still being heard.

"Divine intervention."

I laughed at his response and Garavel turned confused eyes on me. He was serious. *I should be used to this weird shit by now.* "You came rather quick," I said, then winced, expecting to hear a cutting remark from Ink, but nothing appeared. For the first time in a month, I was alone. Cal couldn't fly, Ink couldn't reach us and Daniel...

Oh no! I slapped at my throat, causing my body to jerk in his arms. I kept pawing, hoping it'd slipped to the side or down my back. But no, there was no chain around my neck.

"Is something wrong?" Garavel asked.

I'd left the locket behind. I'd been in such a rush that I'd nearly forgotten my spell book and fully forgot my only tie to Daniel. Which meant I really was alone with a winged man who carried a sword longer than my body. Said demi-angel cast his heavenly gaze upon me and I froze.

"Nope. Everything's good." It wasn't like he was a demon. If I wasn't safe with an angel's guardian, who would I be safe with? "Where are we going?"

"I have no idea," he said with such calm, I nearly skipped on past it.

"What? You're the one flying."

"Can you?" Garavel asked with so much sincerity, my cheeks burned.

"I, uh..." I clutched my book tighter to my side, growing more embarrassed with how many times I'd tried to find an enchantment for a flying broom. "No."

"Then I can do the flying for the both of us. Where shall we begin, Lady Witch?"

"Why do you keep calling me that?" It was better than 'Green Skin,' or any other pejorative the rest of the paranormal squad liked to toss my way. But he said the phrase how one would bellow 'First Lieutenant' or

'General.' It made my skin, which was not and never had been green, itch.

"I always have when working with magical bearers. They seemed to like it. Would you rather I call you something else?"

Layla, this cuddly and swole rock of a man wants to call you lady like some chivalrous knight. Let him! "No, it's…nice. Maybe in public you can call me by my name instead. So no one gets wise."

"Ah, yes, I've been trying to lay low."

I glanced at the man whose skin glowed gold, dressed in a bright white robe exposing the sides, spreading his massive wings across the blue sky. "You've done a great job," I muttered.

"Thank you. Now, where shall we begin our search together?"

I didn't have a clue. Usually Daniel would pry through my book to find an answer, or Ink would have a solution. Even Cal knew a few tricks of the trade in this world. But none of them could feel the magic the way I did. There had to be a way for a witch to trace where it was coming from. Maybe work back from that?

Garavel stared at me and I realized we were hovering in the air above a billboard for a McRib. There weren't many cars out, but someone had to see the black angel holding a woman in a sundress. I could try to comb through my book hoping for an answer while he stared at me with this expectant puppy look. *Or…?*

"I think I know someone that can help, but…"

Sybil. I hadn't gone anywhere near her shop since she had almost got Ink killed. There was also the whole trauma of me being kidnapped in the alley behind it. But I had no intention of forgiving or forgetting her attempted murder of my incubus. Too bad she was the only witch in the world I knew how to find.

"But?" Garavel prompted.

"You might have to use your big sword to get her to cooperate."

At his smile, I once again thanked heaven Ink wasn't around. He'd be having a field day. Meanwhile, I tried to not hyperventilate as Garavel flew us to confront Sybil. I had him land two blocks away beside the dumpsters for a Chinese buffet and a clothing outlet store. The summer air sang of rayon and sweet-and-sour pork.

Garavel kept his wings extended and reached back for his sword. I placed my hand on his chest to get him to stop, and my brain froze. He'd been holding me for fifteen minutes, but this touch felt far more intimate than all the wholesome kidnappings. I swallowed, fighting to focus through a warm fuzz rubbing across my brain.

"Keep it sheathed," I said. Another one Ink had missed. I needed a drinking game for all the fallen innuendo.

Garavel stopped reaching for the hilt. "But you said…"

"People are liable to lose their shit if they see you carrying a giant sword. Any chance you're bulletproof?"

"What's that?" he asked.

"It's…" How the hell did I explain what bullets were? Or guns for that matter? *It's like a big metal crossbow that can murder hundreds of people in a few minutes.* I shook my head, then stared down him. The sword was the least of his problems. "You need different clothes."

Garavel gazed upon his outfit that even up close looked like a catwalk experiment no one was supposed to wear outside. At a distance, all anyone would see was a big black man in a dress. "These are the robes my creator crafted specially for me."

"Did he not also order you to blend in? That ain't blending. That's a huge spotlight of angelic glory." Against all common sense ringing in my brain, I checked both sides of the alley, then popped open the dumpster. Black bags containing either clothing possibilities or rotten food awaited me. I took the risk and opened up the top one.

Piles of T-shirts advertising popular national parks tumbled out. That'd do. I sifted through the mess, trying to find one that'd fit. I had to settle for a large and passed it back to Garavel. "Let's hope the next one has pants," I said, only to find a rich vein of moldy fried rice. "Nope."

I kept digging, praying to hit jeans, but the best I could find was a pair of sweatpants. They'd been slashed on the hip to keep people like me from doing what I'd just done. At least it wasn't the crotch. I passed those back and abandoned any hope I had of finding shoes. He wore a pair of gold sandals laced up to his calves. Those would work.

Finished, I pushed out of the dumpster, and the stench of month-old takeout to follow me. Clasping my hand to my face, I waved my hand for Garavel to get changed quickly. He inspected the shirt, revealing the same deliberate slash done to the back. With a shrug, he dangled the clothing over his arm, reached for the shoulder straps of his robe, and the entire garment fell straight off him.

Holy hell! I slapped my hand over my eyes and tried to turn away, but it was too slow. Instead of the trim musculature of the Ancient Greeks like Ink, Garavel was built like an MMA fighter. All the power was in his wide shoulders, strapping pecs and oak barrel chest. I was a toothpick compared to the strength he carried. Which was stupid, as Ink could probably rip me in half if he had half a mind.

"How's it going?" I asked.

"I believe I am well disguised," Garavel declared. I risked taking a peek and had to fight a groan of exhaustion. He had gotten the shirt and pants on properly, but modern clothing was not designed for him. The shirt strained across his chest to the point the graphic for Yosemite looked like the bear had become a dachshund. I winced at the tight sleeves cutting into the skin of his biceps. At least sweatpants were meant to look awful on everyone.

Though…as Garavel turned in a circle, I had to bite back a yelp at how the cotton sculpted to his round booty. "I don't know what will happen if I use my wings," he said. "I fear this may tear."

Dear god, the tight navy shirt shredding off him when he popped his wings out… "We, uh." I composed myself and patted his arm. "We'll just have to risk it." I gathered up his abandoned robe, shocked at how light and airy it was without being see-through. I folded it up and put it in my purse. "Here." I extended my arm. "You can be my…"

I almost said boyfriend for some reason. No, I had enough of those, thanks. "Guide," I picked instead.

"I prefer to be your protection, La…Layla."

We started out of the alley to the old main street. Garavel stared, not at the vehicles idling and racing down the road, but at a top-heavy tree sprouting from a giant cement pot. As we passed the parking meters, he reached out and ran his palm over the top.

"Does this all seem strange to you?" I asked.

"There's so much more green than I'm used to," he said. If he'd been trapped in those underground ruins with Ramiel, it was no wonder the sight of a few maple leaves and a parking meter excited him.

A huge truck with its radio cranked to eleven blew past. "It's a lot louder than I could have expected!" Garavel shouted, causing me to laugh. He smiled too and cupped his hands to his ears. I mimicked him and we both giggled together.

"Ink was…elsewhere for a long time," I said, trying to find some commonality with the demi-angel. Except, the demon had seemed to adjust to this modern world so fast I didn't even realize he'd been in hell for four hundred years.

"How long have you been with Ramiel?" I asked.

"Always," Garavel said proudly.

"No, I mean, how long has he kept you underground with him?"

"Ah. I…have no idea. He said sleep, so I slept. He said wake up, so I'm here. That wolf is so tiny and fluffy!" Garavel's attention snapped to a small pomeranian trailing behind its owner. He held his hand out and waved to the 'tiny wolf' as if it would return the gesture.

"You do everything Ramiel tells you to without question?" I asked after the dog had passed. It was really cute.

"Of course. He's my creator. Don't humans?"

"Ha." I snorted at the idea, then we passed a hardware store with a banner telling people to get their mothers a bright pink toolbox. A pain churned in my stomach that I couldn't escape no matter how deep I stuffed it down. The anger came so quickly on the heels of grief now that it was like she had died all over again.

"You appear worried," Garavel declared, shaking me out of my funk. I was about to wave him off, when he slipped his arms around me and pulled me to his chest. "Does this help?"

I fell into his mega-bear hug, resting my cheek on the soft pec radiating a warmth of belonging. Instead of a steady heartbeat, a low rumble like the grinding of gravel echoed from inside. "It does, actually." I wanted to cling tighter to him, to listen to all the wonderful things he'd found, to shove aside every damn problem that kept catching fire and just let him fix me with hugs.

But that would make things worse.

With a gentle touch, I pushed myself away from him, needing that force to escape the gravimetric pull of his chest. I dabbed at my cheeks, fearing to find yet more tears, when Garavel brushed his thumbs over them. "You are in pain…"

More than he could ever understand.

"…from my creator."

"Ah." I stepped back and flushed. "Yes. It's… I can't magic it away, so only time can heal my burns."

"I forget how fragile mortals are. I won't make the same mistake again."

He said that like a man swearing on a grave. I stared, expecting Garavel to take a knee or raise his sword to the sky. Instead, he blinked and his infectious smile returned. I turned away, the heat on my cheeks too much for me to take. As I did, my heart plummeted.

Instead of the lopsided glass and wood shop, I stared at a blackened hole scooped out of the side of the street. Caution tape dangled from the door, dirty and tattered as if it had fallen after too many rainy days. The remaining sign was a tiny window cling that had fused into the rest of the door's glass, the witch's face melted into a scream of horror.

"What do they keep in here?" Garavel asked.

"Fire," I muttered.

"Oh. Interesting. I've never seen a shop for fire. Or is it a place where you home it?"

"No. I… This was Sybil's shop. She was a…a witch." I almost added "like me," but she'd tried to kill Ink. We weren't anything alike. "This place must have burned down."

Hunters. She was working with them, or at least they had her under surveillance. They must have torched her shop in retribution. I clutched my hand to my neck only to slap it to skin and nothing more.

If the hunters were here, we had to leave. Now. I wrapped my hands around Garavel's forearm and tried to tug him away, but he was fascinated by the smoke-damaged glass. He placed a fingertip to the gray surface and started to draw through it.

"We need to get out of here. It isn't safe."

"Don't worry, I'll protect you," he said.

"Not from these guys, you won't." They knew how to plan for a werewolf, a demon, a ghost and more. No doubt they could take down a demi-angel and probably use his body as a statue. That wasn't happening.

He finished his trace of a rune into the glass. I had no idea what it was, but Garavel smiled at it, then turned to me. "You are safe in my arms."

They are nice arms to be in.

Holy shit, Layla. Focus on anything other than the sword-wielding teddy bear.

I pulled harder, not budging Garavel an inch. How did I explain witch hunters to the only paranormal who liked witches? I opened my mouth, when a feral scream rattled between the gaps in the windows.

"Sybil?" I shouted and the scream stopped.

Holy shit, was she in there? I straddled the caution tape and gently pressed on the door. To my surprise, it opened without shattering and I walked into nothing. Where the small staircase used to be was now charred cinders. The few walls that remained were black and gray, the dust and ash long ripped away on the winds. Sunlight beamed down through the holes in the roof, one landing on the dark hair of the woman in the middle of the carnage.

"What happened here?" I asked, slipping my hand into my purse.

She spun on her heel, her eyes wild as they hunted for me. "They're here. Their march has begun. We're all doomed."

"Yeah, maybe you shouldn't have trusted the hunters after all. Seems they weren't big fans of your scarves and crystals and witch shit." I didn't let go of my spell book, but I relaxed a touch. It seemed highly unlikely she could do anything to me now that all of her relics were ash and melted iron.

A low chuckle rolled in Sybil's throat, lasting so long my stomach tied into a knot. She sounded like she was about to snap at any minute. "I was so consumed with out-maneuvering you all I didn't even notice. Every cycle like clockwork. It's all in here!" She raised her hands like she held a book, but nothing was in there.

Oh, no. Did they burn her spell book along with the shop? Sybil lunged closer and I fumbled back into Garavel's patient arms. I wrenched my hands out, prepared to fireball her ass, but she drifted to the side and began to moan.

"I was supposed to protect them. They were nothing, babes in the snow. And I left them to die." She clutched her wild hair and tugged her head back and forth.

"Who are you talking about?" I prompted. "Your coven?"

She made a soft yelp and I knew I had guessed right. Fuck, did that mean...? "Are the hunters killing witches?"

Her chest bounced, the laugh silent. She jerked twice more, then turned to face me. "The hunters are nothing. Your demon is nothing. What walks these roads heralds the end of all."

"Okay, I need you to start making a lot more sense. Did they...it, burn your book? Is that what happened? Did you lose your spell book?"

She barked once in a strangled laugh that became a sob. "Lose my book? Lose my book! What I lost...you can give back." Suddenly, she turned—hands outstretched—and ran straight for my throat. I flung my book up to deflect, but it and my arms went straight through her.

A familiar chill crawled up my spine as Sybil's hands impotently flailed inside my throat without touching me.

"You're...dead?" My knees began to shake and Garavel placed a steadying hand on my shoulder.

"Dead? Dead. I can't be dead. I'm the leader. The leader doesn't die. The leader dictates. The leader conquers. Ha ha haha!" The mad ghost tossed her head back and screamed. She hadn't made it out of the fire.

There, in the middle of her store was a single chalk outline. Sybil was doomed to haunt where her body had fallen.

"Who killed you?" I asked. "Who would do this?" Who could do that to a witch?

The mad ghost spun in a circle, giggling gleefully, before slamming a foot down and glaring at me. "You. You think you're so special because of your line. But it doesn't matter. None of it matters now."

An uneasy feeling surged up my spine, like a thousand eyes were watching. I hunched lower into my shoulders and walked backward into Garavel. "We need to leave. Now."

"But you haven't asked her about the realm tears?"

Rather than answer, I took him by the hand and pulled him away.

"You'll meet him soon enough, Layla!" Sybil shouted as I dashed through the charred ash of her store. I kept running, tearing away the last of the caution tape. Even in the light of day, her voice cut through the honk and rush of cars.

"The ride's already begun."

Chapter Fifteen

I was lost, my mind churning with chaos. Was what happened to Sybil what happened to all witches or just those killed before their time? Had she gone insane because her book was burned, or was she raving because of how she'd died?

Garavel skimmed higher, flying me across the city that I barely looked at. He made mention of various hot spots, but I couldn't sense anything. I didn't even know what I was looking for, because I had no idea how this witch stuff worked, because my mother had abandoned me.

My mother, Sybil, Valerie—every time I found someone to teach me what all this was, they abandoned me, or vanished or died. The only one to stick around was Ink, who seemed to be making it up as he went. If it wasn't for him, or Cal or Daniel…I'd either be dead, mad or brainwashed by the hunters. Even if they didn't give me any answers, at least they were there.

"What of this spot? It feels cursed, as if a thousand souls were wrenched free of their bodily constraints and smeared from this realm of existence."

"It's a dentist office," I said, trying to look down without fearing I'd fall. "People come here to get their teeth fixed."

"A dark lair, indeed," Garavel intoned, when my stomach growled loud enough to beat out the city sounds. "Are you okay?"

"Yeah, it's..." I blanked, trying to think when I had last eaten. Oh right, Ink's 'breakfast muffins' where he'd swapped baking soda with regular soda. He'd been pleased about that one, even if they were like bricks made of molasses. "I'm hungry. Any chance you can spot a restaurant around here?"

"Of course," Garavel said, lifting us higher. "What's a restaurant?"

"It's the place where people get food. You know, 'Here's some money, now hand over a fried sodium bomb. Thanks.'"

"Ah, what an ingenious invention. You humans, always scurrying about recreating the world." He sounded excited at the idea, until, when Garavel reached the end of his sentence, darkness fell over him.

I wanted to ask, but the only thing between me and broken bones was the man who turned insular on a dime. Instead, I stared down the street and spotted a familiar red roof. "You can land there behind that wall!" Once again, we found ourselves plummeting behind the dumpsters. At least no one could see the man fall from the sky then pull in his angel wings behind the privacy wall.

I took the lead, walking past the creepy statues of chicken nuggets with faces that lined the sidewalk.

They seemed to want to entice children into their play lair, no doubt to feast on their bones. I shook my head at the macabre thought and pulled open the door. Garavel stood in awe, his head craned back as he stared at the sign. It wasn't anything special. There were at least ten of these franchises around the city, but he gawped like it was the pearly gates.

"Okay." I slipped in behind and gave a gentle push. "We go inside."

"How exciting. This is my first time entering a human...tower?"

"Close enough." I left him standing beside a kiosk advertising the kids' toys for the month and gazed at the menu. My stomach leered at the cheesy, meaty offerings rotating on the screens. It hungered for the biggest burger and a bucket of fries. As I approached the counter, I reached into my purse and found nothing.

Shit. Where'd I put my wallet? I shuffled around inside, trying to peer around my spell book, but it and my ID were gone. Well, good thing I had my phone and...

I woke it up just for the screen to display a thousand backlogged notifications for Sheep Wars, shriek low battery and die.

"Welcome to Fry Shack, what can I fry for you today?" The fifty-something cashier sounded exhausted with life.

My mouth dried as I pawed around my purse, hoping to find anything. There, caught on the inside lining—I tugged out a single five-dollar bill. That'd get me a burger, with tax.

I looked back to Garavel, who was still gazing around in awe. All day he'd carted me around without a single complaint. I stared at the board anew, trying to find the cheapest thing, and one answer jumped out at me.

After placing my order, I handed the cashier the single bill I had to my name. He snickered at the cold hard cash, then returned a handful of change and told me to wait to the side. I was about to dump the coins into my purse, when Garavel drew his hand under mine and gasped.

"How did you acquire such pure metals?"

"That...it's my change?"

"Ah, transmutation. Of course."

"No, it's...this is how things work. It's the economy." At his bewildered stare, I realized I had as much chance of explaining economics as a goat would. "People exchange their hard work for coins and dollars. Then we use that to purchase food and clothing."

Garavel scratched his chin in thought. "Would it not be simpler for the necessary supplies of life to be given freely?"

"I guess?"

"Then the metal could be put to better use crafting spears and swords of the Almighty."

"Okay, that's probably not the best use for pennies. You seem to think about war a lot."

Garavel smiled patiently at me. "Of course. What else would I think about?"

"Life, love, friendship...cute kittens?" I kept babbling, trying to wrap my mind around this walking marshmallow of a man who was obsessed with fighting and battle.

He laughed, making me feel like I had missed something important. Before I could ask, the cashier called my name and handed over two cones of soft-serve ice cream. Mine was pure chocolate, which I had to lick fast before it dripped off the side of the cone. After getting it back in place, I handed the swirl to Garavel.

It took him a moment to take it in his hands. He cupped not one, but both of his giant palms around the tiny cake cone. I heard it crunch under his grip and winced. "What is this?"

"Ice cream. You lick it like this?" In the middle of the fast-food chain, I stuck my tongue out and swirled it with the dexterity of a porn star. It wasn't supposed to be dirty, but the focus in Garavel's eyes, then the way his face lit up with excitement, caused my stomach to roll.

Double-fisting it, Garavel raised his cone higher, and stuck half the cone in his mouth.

Holy shit! I tried to pull it back for fear of brain freeze or choking, but he bit and swallowed it all down and came up with only a smile. "This is amazing! I've never had anything like it. Creamy yet cold, like the prick of a ghost."

"Okay, we…" The judgmental eyes of a dozen people who just wanted some early dinner landed on me and the man shouting about ghost dick. I tried to wrap my hand around Garavel's bicep as he chowed down on the rest of his cone, but I couldn't reach far. "We should head outside. Nice day and all."

He followed as I guided him onto the little patio where a red and white umbrella provided momentary cover from the sun. I took my time slowly licking my ice cream while Garavel sucked his down without pause.

"You've got some…" I dabbed the side of my mouth where the vanilla ice cream clung to his, but Garavel reached over and touched me. Blushing, I drew the tip of my fingers across the top of his lip and down the side. It was smooth as glass, not even a single stubble hair prodding through.

As I leaned back, showing him the ice cream I'd cleaned off, Garavel caught my hand. He pressed his thumbs into my palm, no doubt feeling my rampaging heartbeat, and licked my finger clean. Good to know demi-angel tongues were as wet and hot as demon ones. As my hand fell away, a tingle ran across my skin that I couldn't explain.

"Who created such an amazing food? Was it Michael?"

"Uh…I'm not sure. I think the cone bit came about at some World's Fair." I studied mine, a sliver of chocolate remaining above the bland cone.

"This World's Fair must be a gathering of your greatest mages." He honest-to-god glowed at the thought of ice cream, his black skin sparkling with golden flakes. I held out my cone, offering him what I had left. Garavel's eyes lit up, before he looked to me.

"You should eat it. Unlike humans, I don't need food."

That was kind of him. I tried to finish my ice cream fast to not torture him. "Ink said something about how you were created by Ramiel."

"Yes." He beamed bright at the mention of the angel. "I am one of his defenders, the last after the great confrontation. I am entrusted to wield his power."

"What does that mean?"

Garavel smiled. "With my sword, I can channel the full grace of a celestial."

That sounded very useful. "Were you crafted in his image too?" A handful of random church services a foster family had dragged me to flared in my mind.

Garavel, however, frowned and shook his head. "Of course not, that would be blasphemous. None shall compare to the celestials, first and greatest of the creators."

"What do they, does he need you for exactly?" Couldn't an angel, a creator, a damn near god, just fix all of this with a wave of his hand?

"Me and my brethren were the solution to the schism problem. Angels can only create, and demons can only destroy. That is their destiny."

I'd never heard that from Ink. Was he only capable of destruction too?

"But oftentimes, a creation must be broken down, replaced, rebuilt. Thus we are created, the demi-angels, who serve as the third arm of the angels."

I fought through the minor brain freeze to focus on Garavel. His words sloshed about before folding together to make a stomach dropping statement. "You're saying your only job is to…"

"Destroy." He said it with such a happy-go-lucky smile, I was certain I had misunderstood. That would explain his tree-trunk arms and massive chest, not to mention that sword. But everything about Garavel was inviting, calm. I wanted to rest my head on his shoulder and listen to his breathing, not run away in a panic.

"What…" I gulped, trying to keep my voice steady and low, "what do you destroy?"

"It's not headboards, I'm afraid."

Ink! He slipped in beside me without warning, draping an arm over my shoulder as if he'd always been there. I was glad he found me.

"What are headboards?" Garavel asked, causing me to groan.

"A metaphor for se—"

"Okay, let's not have that discussion here near kids. How did you find me?"

Ink snickered and raised his hand to flash his wrist. "Though it proved tricky. You seemed to canvas the entire city before taking a break. And the wolf owes me a root beer."

"Why?" It didn't hit me until then how little Ink drank. Alcohol, at least. He drank anything else like a curious fish. The only liquor I'd seen him consume was a cupcake-flavored vodka, which he'd added a full bottle of chocolate syrup to.

Ink clung tighter to my shoulder and leaned closer until his hot breath brushed my ear. "Calvin believed you'd be in mortal danger the moment I could catch up."

"And you didn't?" That was surprisingly trusting of my incubus.

He shrugged, then trailed his tongue over my lobe, setting off exactly the reaction he wanted. "In truth, I assumed you'd be enjoying the original sin with our winged friend. He seems like a bottom."

"Ink..." I groaned. The heat of my incubus combined with the overwhelming glow of the angel melted my spine until I wanted to yank on his hair and shove him into the bathroom. He sensed the desire the minute it went into my head, Ink tipping his head down so I could grab his thick black locks.

"I'm good with orders," Garavel said so honestly it hurt.

"See. A loyal and trusting bedmate for the witch on the go. I assume you've found whatever source is destroying the realms and I can take you to the altar of a church for a proper desecration?" Ink beamed the full fire of his eyes at me, the flames dancing in hypnotic fashion until I stared deeper and realized they had formed the silhouette of a naked man thrusting.

That was a new trick. I had to physically pull my head away to focus on anything but the sex fire. "I went to see Sybil."

"What in the depths of hell's organ recital would convince you to do that? Did she hurt you? Did she try to scam you with a cursed relic?" He patted my hand like he was soothing a skittish dog.

"She's…dead."

"There is some justice in the world after all. That's a surprise."

"Did you do it? Don't scoff and look away, Ink. I have to know. After everything that happened with…you know, did you go back to her place and set it on fire?"

He drew his thumb down the side of his neck, growing the demonic claw out and scratching a long line against the human skin. "And if I did? What would you do, my bond?"

The last month of him play-acting at being the perfect helper snapped in an instant. I stared at a wild, untamable demon that'd do whatever he wanted without provocation…and it was fucking hot. "I'd hope you could explain what she was babbling about."

"You spoke to her? Oh delightful, yet another worthless ghost to add to the collection. I'm afraid I cannot help in your search. I did not end her life, nor do I have a streak of arson in me. I prefer a more visceral end to my enemies."

That was good. I hadn't realized I was sitting on pins and needles until he'd admitted it wasn't him. But, that raised an even bigger question. If it wasn't Ink, then who and why?

"What, pray tell—if you'll forgive the pun," he said quickly to Garavel who smiled uncertainly, "did that waste of human flesh prattle on about in her death throes?"

"Mostly nonsense," I had to admit. "What's weirder is she didn't look burned, not like Daniel and his bullet wound. As if whoever had torched her place did it to cover up her murder."

"Sounds like the work of our dear friends in Animal Control. I should really pay them a visit," he said, extending a full hand of claws.

I knew that was all bravado. So did Ink. If he got anywhere near their secret base, they'd use one of their bound witches to trap him. Our best bet was to avoid them at all costs, even if I too wanted to lightning a few asses after the hell they put me through.

"What about the ride?" Garavel spoke up, causing all of us to look his way. "The un-alive woman spoke of a ride beginning. Will there be mastodons?"

She did shriek about that. And what did a ride need but a rider, just like what Samuke had taunted us about. That wasn't a coincidence! I sat up to tell Ink, but he placed a finger to my lips.

"It is exactly a coincidence. You cannot believe the word of an insane, evil witch…who's also dead, nor the threats of a Marid."

"The Djinn have returned to this realm? That's not good."

I tried to focus on Ink, about to insist they too were related, it all made sense, but Garavel caught my attention. "There's all kinds of creatures on earth, this realm."

"By the rules of the accord, they were to remain in the realm of —"

A woman's panicked scream caused all three of us to leap to our feet. "Someone is in danger," Garavel declared and he plucked me up into his arms.

"Where are we going?" I asked as we took flight. I couldn't turn my back on whoever that was.

"To help," he said. I nodded in agreement. That was precisely what we needed to do.

Chapter Sixteen

Garavel dropped me to my feet in the middle of the parking lot of an abandoned retail store. Whatever was once here was long gone, the windows crusted in dirt and all the lights inside dark. He flew past, having to maneuver to land and pull in his wings, just as another scream burst from inside.

A shadow ran past the 'Out Of Business' sign. I raised a finger to point, when it burst through the glass. Holy shit! A woman rolled across the pavement, a smear of blood trailing her. I dashed for her as Ink appeared and held me back.

"Something's not right," he said.

Garavel leaped into the air, flapping twice to land beside the poor screaming woman bleeding out on the handicapped parking spot. He scooped her up in his arms, his wings falling around her.

"Be calm, my young one."

"Holy fucking shit, I'm dying! I don't want to die," she screamed in his face.

"What are you doing?" I tugged on Ink's hold. He let go, but kept glaring.

"Can't you feel it? The air is wrong."

I threw my shoulders back, prepared to shrug him off, when the dread landed in my gut. The little bit of ice cream in my stomach curdled and I pitched back to escape the death undulating in the air. A whimper snared me in place.

"Do not worry, you are in luck. A witch is here." Garavel raised his head from the dying woman and he held his hand out to me. Blood stained his pink palm and I took a step toward him.

"Layla..." Ink tried to warn me, but I shrugged him off.

"She's hurt," I said. Ink didn't fight me, but he sighed loudly. Running across the baking pavement, I slid down to her, scraping my knees through my thin dress.

"Hi, I'm Layla," I said as distraction. The whole of her skin was white as a sheet. Small bits of glass glittered inside her face from where she'd rammed through the door, but I knew better than to take them out.

"W-w-who are you?" she stuttered.

The only person that can keep you alive. I cupped my hand under her back and whispered my healing spell under my breath. "I'm a nurse," I said.

"Th-th-ank..." Whoever she was going to thank faded as her eyes rolled back and she sank into sleep.

I fumbled to check a pulse, the two years of nursing studies amounting to damn near nothing as I held a dying woman in my arms. Her heartbeat was still there and steady. She looked to be breathing too. "Ink, get my phone."

"This hardly seems the time for the great war of the ovine."

"I need you to call nine-one-one," I said through gritted teeth. She shouldn't have passed out like this. The wounds on her arms and face were slowly healing, but I was worried about internal bleeding. Not to mention whatever had sent her careening through a glass door.

"While I would love nothing more than to inform your barber squad where to locate us, your phone is without life."

Damn it, I forgot.

I wrenched it away from him before he did anything stupid, and stuffed my worthless phone in my purse. "You're going to have to take her to the hospital."

"No."

This wasn't the time for him to be obstinate. "What do you mean…?"

A bellow erupted from inside the store unlike anything I'd ever heard. It rattled like a moose giving birth to an elephant, then sharpened to a high-pitched shriek. The sound sent Garavel leaping to his feet.

"The mortal is tended to. Come, we must scout the premises immediately for an IAA." He held his hand out to me and I stared at it in confusion.

"You want me to what with an eye something?"

"Infiltrate, assess, attack," Garavel boomed. He plucked me off the ground just as Ink stepped in and scooped the dying woman up. Garavel reached behind to unsheathe his massive sword and extended it up, the entire blade glowing with haunting orange text.

"It's been many a year since I've fought by a witch's side."

"Uh…this is my first time doing that IAS thing."

"IAA. It's one of the many tactics employed in the war," Garavel said proudly. He looked ready to take on an entire army, the once cuddly arms flexing to rip apart a tank.

I gulped at the idea, but was willing to try. "What do you need me to do?"

"Let him go in and fight whatever that is while you remain safe out here," Ink said.

"You sound like Cal," I said, dismissing him.

Ink scoffed. "How dare you hit below the belt without asking if I'd like seconds."

"Get her to the hospital. You can do it in a snap. Then come back here to help me. Everyone wins."

The woman in his arms groaned, her head flopping back. I braced myself for a lewd response from Ink, but his face was etched in worry. "You leave me no choice. But..." He shoved the poor woman onto his shoulder in order to take my hand. "So help me, if you are injured, you will suffer a year of smug looks."

I reached over to assure him, but Ink vanished. Another noise, like a dozen metal shelves shoved across the tiled floor, burst from inside. I pulled out my spell book, prepared to run headlong into danger, when Garavel placed a steadying hand on my shoulder.

"I think it best if I inspect the perimeter. You infiltrate with a cloak of darkness, then signal me once the creature is found."

"Er, that cloak thing...I don't know how to do that."

He blinked slowly, then faced me. I braced myself for being talked down to, but Garavel nodded. "What do you have? Arcane magic? Resonance? Elemental?"

"I can do fire and lighting, and freeze stuff."

"Excellent!" The terrifying warrior cracked, letting the exuberant marshmallow out. But it was only for a moment before he hefted his sword up to the sky and his wings crashed down. He flew into the air, swooping around a broken streetlight as he ordered, "Utilize utmost caution in determining the creature's location, then contact me with an elemental."

"Which one?" I shouted, trying to chase after him as he began flying around the building.

"I trust you," was the last thing Garavel said before he too vanished into the sunlight.

Okay. I could do this. I'd walked into far worse, and this time I had an angel on my side.

"Boy," I whispered to myself as I crept toward the shattered door. "If this has all been a delusion for the past year, whoever's listening to me babble has to be entertained at least." I tried to scrunch down to make it through the broken glass, but my hair snagged on the splintered edges. Every slight touch of my foot caused the rest of the shattered plate glass to crack. I had bowed my head lower and shuffled one foot through the hole, when the creature bellowed in rage.

Without pause, I leaped into the darkening store. Everything had been ripped clean except for the fixtures. A promo table was toppled at the front, possibly from the bleeding woman. Metal wires that would have advertised the Going Out of Business Sale dangled from the ceiling. With the sun glinting off them, they looked like spiderwebs straining for a new victim.

I held my book closer to my chest and eased inside. I worked in a damn near replica of this store, same metal shelves we'd stock with impulse items over there, same fake wood displays for beauty items in that corner, except the energy was dead. I shivered at the thought that I was walking on my job's grave.

Or maybe it was the cold fog rolling across the floor. That couldn't be good. The summer heat collapsed into a winter's chill where no industrial A/C hummed. Deeper I delved, staring down the winding paths of clothing racks. What little light managed to catch them caused the bars to illuminate like the stripped bones of a gargantuan monster.

Another bellow echoed deeper in the store, somewhere near the hardware section if I had to guess. *Find it, tell Garavel. Don't do anything stupid.* The light dropped to nearly nothing once I reached the middle of the store. I had to glide my feet and keep my arms wide so I didn't ram into any forgotten rack and reveal myself. It made the going slower, until I turned a corner and a flash of otherworldly blue caught me.

Like a passing train, it radiated from under a door to the women's bathrooms. Holding my breath, I skittered to the wall beside them. *It's in there, time to call Garavel.* What spell should I use that wouldn't instantly attract it? Fire? Would he even see from in here?

I had to trust the man that used codes and acronyms for battle knew what he was doing. Folding my fingers into a fist, I whispered the spell for fire. A flicker caught on the tip.

"This is a disaster."

Shit!

"If you'd followed protocol…"

I threw my back to the wall, clenching my fists tight around my book. Panic clawed up my chest and cinched my throat, but I could do nothing.

"Don't get preachy with me, Stone."

Detective Stone was just behind that door. The man who'd orchestrated my kidnapping, who I'd let live, who I couldn't let see my face or my entire life was forfeit. I had to get out of here.

"These fucking rips are popping up everywhere now. Same time as White shows up in the city."

White? My body froze and the dread burst into a twirling fire. He had to mean Mr. White, a man who couldn't be a man who'd been plaguing my every step. What did he mean he was here? If the hunters were watching him then...did they know what he was? I leaned closer, but the voices lowered like they had moved deeper into the stalls.

Damn it. I had to know what they did about White and the tears. *Ink's going to kill me.* With the tip of my toe, I pushed open the ladies' door.

"You see coincidences where none are. A rise in activity is normal for one of them, but a full-on tear through the realms... There's something else going on," Stone explained, "and I don't like it."

"What do you like?"

Feet. I slapped my hand over my mouth to keep from saying that aloud. I had two men at home who'd be more than happy to rub my feet all day long and another that could write a sonnet about it. I did not need to remember Stone's fingers massaging me.

"A job done well," he said, followed by a grunt then the sound of shattering porcelain.

Memories of that same grunt flashed through my mind. *Stone's hands tugging my shirt off, his mouth over mine, his hips pressing me back against the wall.* Fuck. That hadn't been real. I tried to shake off the siren's illusion but it stuck to me like chewing gum. The harder I pulled at it, the longer it grew.

"Damn it, you hit the pipe," whoever was inside complained. A gush of water ran across the floor. It struck my toe, then kept going.

"How about you stop complaining and get a..." Stone's command died at the low, bone-quaking growl. No choice but to risk it. I turned to stare with a single eye into the bathroom. Stone stood in his white shirt, the jacket lost. He must have been exerting himself a lot as it was suckered to his back, revealing a handful of his magical scars. "It's coming, get onto the—!"

Before he could finish his order, a talon plunged through the ceiling. No, through thin air right below the ceiling. It smashed the stall, crumpling the cheap wood, as two long fawn legs followed after. The leg kicked, flinging the other hunter back, the edge of the talon slicing into his leg. He bounced off the wall, but didn't plummet.

Stone moved quickly, ordering his lackey to grab something on the floor. Both men bent down and reached into the water as the rest of the creature emerged from its realm. It fell onto turned-back hind legs, the ankles nearly three feet long with another set of talons on the joint. Its chest was the size of a small man, sunken in and covered with chestnut fur. But it was the face that'd scream in my nightmares for months. The jaws and nose were those of a wolf with the skin peeled away to reveal the bones of the gums and fangs. Giant, bat-like ears swung around off the head and horns towered off the head, every edge barbed with thorns. It was terrifying, eyes glowing red as blood, and it swung a massive human hand at Stone.

"Now!" They both yanked, lifting a net off the ground. As it touched the creature, the knots on the rope glowed. The monster bellowed in rage and lashed out. "The stun…" Stone shouted, when a fist the size of his chest smashed into him. He flew back into the mirrors. I winced at the crunch when his leg hit the faucets.

"Bad move, big guy," the other hunter joked and he shoved the stun gun deep into the monster's side. Instead of crying out, it began to…laugh between its skeletal teeth. "Oh shi —."

The creature dropped its head, trapping the hunter between its barbed antlers. He crumpled to a knee, kicking and punching, but impaling inch-long thorns into his flesh with each attack. Stone rolled off the sinks, landing in the ankle-high water. His blood washed over my feet, and a single gasp slipped out.

Oh, shit. The monster turned, impaling its antlers deeper into the hunter's back, and its crimson eye stared through the dark gap in the bathroom door. I fell back, flattening to the wall, clutching my hands tight together. Whatever this thing was, it had the witch hunters pinned and was going to kill them. So what? They had tried to kill me. They hunted me, and people like me. Why should I try to save them?

Let them learn what it meant to target the real things that went bump in the night.

Stone screamed and I kicked the door open. The monster had plunged a single talon into his leg, a maniacal grin lifting the last of the skin on its face. As it raised its head, impaling its antlers into the ceiling, I could only think of one spell to fix this.

Extending my palms, I dug into the power dumping into this room and cast sleep across the whole room. The monster was hit first, its massive nostrils pulling in boatloads of the enchantment. It bellowed, a shoulder slamming into the wall as it fought against my induced drowsiness. With one last low cry, it tumbled to the water. The rest of my spell billowed out, landing on the hunters. The one covered in antler thorns tried to fight it by shaking the monster's head, but he slumped to his ass, then fell backward against the wrecked stall.

Stone somehow was the last to go down even though he was nearest to me. He crawled an inch closer, his blood sloshing away in the water. Placing a hand to the floor, he raised his head up and stared at me. "La..." His face crashed into the water and he stopped moving. *Damn it, I didn't mean to drown him.*

I eased into the bathroom and less than gently wedged my foot under his chest. He groaned in pain as I pushed him over onto his back. The water washed up into his ears, but he was able to breathe. Strange. A green light glowed under his...

Arms wrapped around my stomach, pulling me out of the destroyed bathroom. I rammed my elbow back and dragged my nails over the skin, when a familiar voice breathed in my ear, "My bond. What did you do?"

"That was all them. I was just...trying to help."

"I had no idea you carried so much vandal in you. It's quite impressive..." Ink's pleased tone snapped away when he caught the man I'd nearly been touching. "That is one of the witch hunters. You risked yourself for them?"

"Well, I couldn't let them die."

"Why not?" he pressed, and I didn't have an answer. *Because it was the right thing to do* didn't hold much water given the havoc Stone alone could cause. I glanced down at the man who, unconscious—with his legs twisted and shirt torn open—looked as dangerous as a kitten. I didn't realize I was staring until Ink caught my chin and turned me to face him.

He waggled a finger at me and huffed, "You... Your wolf will have shit puppies if he finds out. Come, before they wake and we have to erase even more memories." Ink locked a hand around my waist and pulled me across the water, when the entire floor shuddered. Waves lapped against my ankles and I trailed them to the source.

The creature folded its hand into a fist and ripped straight through the solid brick. Smoke curled from its nostrils. It raised its head and opened its bloody eyes.

"Run!"

Chapter Seventeen

Ink laughed and held his ground. "It's nothing more than an overgrown fawn. From which satyr's hunting grounds do you hail?"

The monster didn't answer, but as it stood, its antlers plunged into the ceiling tiles. Had it been that tall before? It bellowed in rage and, with one quick jerk, ripped the entire ceiling down. A blizzard of dust fell, blanketing the creature into nothing more than dark shadows lurking in the white.

"Perhaps you bear some logic after all," Ink said, darting back to my side. "A spell or two would be wise at this junction."

"What do I cast?" Sleep hadn't worked. "If I throw lighting, it'll hit everyone."

"So you're more concerned with the hunters at its feet than the deer taking revenge?" Ink pressed. That wasn't what I'd meant. I slammed my foot into the water to try to make my point, but a hand slashed through the air. Ink shoved me at just the right second, sending my ass bouncing off a display table. The pain rocked through me, but I didn't have time to feel it. When the monster found nothing in its palm, it spun its hand around and lashed out for me.

Fire came fast, spurting from my fingertips when I thought to use it. The heat blew back my hair, igniting my already burned cheeks, but I wasn't giving up. I aimed the flames higher, sending them dancing up the creature's arm. Orange and red flickered off the fur and I dampened my spell.

Ink called to me, "Excellent use of…"

One by one, the fires poofed out. No. They didn't vanish. They were sucked into the creature. It threw its arms back in a great stretch and they kept extending, the whole thing sprouting another foot then two more. *Oh, that isn't good.*

"New plan," Ink shouted. He flew across the ground and scooped me up into his arms. "I believe it's time for the retreat."

I closed my eyes, expecting to wind up back home, or on the other side of the world. But we stared up at the murder deer ramming its antlers into the walls to make a hole large enough for it to chase us.

"Ink?"

The deer snorted, dropped a hand to the ground and charged.

Ink took off like a shot, running at inhuman speeds while I struggled to stay in his grip. But the monster was right on our tails. Its smoky breath billowed behind as I tried to find any way to take this thing out. "Ahead!" I shouted, spotting a pillar. He did as I asked, running straight for it. I leaned forward, wrapped both my arms around the pillar and used a little momentum and a lot of magic to send us hurtling to the left.

Ellen Mint

Unfortunately, my incubus couldn't compensate, and his flying feet struck the ground, sending both of us rolling. The first bounce hurt, the second was jarring and the third didn't happen. Ink already had me and we huddled together under a large shelf while listening to the terrifying clomp of giant talons somewhere in the dark.

"What are you doing?" I asked in a whisper. "Why are we still here?"

"It was your idea to run."

"Yes, literally anywhere but here. You're the one with the demon powers that can zip-zap all over the world."

"Well…they appear to be refusing to cooperate at the moment."

"What?"

The whole half wall rattled. I leaned tighter against it, shutting my eyes and listening for the snuffling nose hunting for us. How good a sense of smell did giant murder deer have? Average? The nose sniffed deep right above our heads. I clung tight to Ink's hands, wishing the others were here too while also so damn grateful he was.

A squeak of panic built in my throat, my leg shaking in terror. I clasped both my hands and Ink's over my mouth when the deer's fangs swung away. Thank god. I was about to breathe just as the deer's claws smacked onto a shelf and sent it tumbling for our heads.

Ink's hand shot up, catching the shelf. He held it a mere centimeter from striking us. I stared skyward at the death shelf, waiting for it to fall even while knowing my incubus had it. Silently, we waited for the monster to move anywhere else.

With care, Ink placed the shelf on the floor, then helped me up into a hunched run. "It seems wise to move."

"It seems wiser for you to whisk us away. Is this some kind of punishment or a joke?" Ahead of us was an open aisle. Exposed. I had to run across it to reach the other side.

"I assure you, my bond, if it were a joke, I would be laughing. And if it were a punishment..." He suddenly grabbed my shoulders and yanked me back. The deer's foot slammed down right where I nearly was. I tumbled back into Ink, trying to not picture what those four-foot-long talons would do my skin and organs.

"You'd be enjoying this," Ink breathed in my ear.

How the hell did we get out of here? "My magic doesn't work. It only makes it bigger. And you're conveniently suffering from performance anxiety."

"I can perform with utmost perfection. It's reality that refuses to obey."

What do we do? Garavel! "The angel's flying around outside. If I can signal him..."

"You think he can take that down?" Ink asked, his voice rising to a sharp crescendo. The 'down' echoed off every abandoned fixture, ringing across the store until the massive deer head spun around and its fist-sized pupil contracted to a pinprick.

"Oh dear," Ink said. I wanted to scold him for the pun, but he scooped me up and we took off. The monster didn't care about carefully hunting us out. It ran full bore, ripping shelves off their bolts and flinging them into the air. They crunched like cans with every hit as I struggled to find a spell.

"What the hell do you use to signal people?"

"I'd say anything flashy and bright myself." Ink turned sharp just as the monster deer ran straight past, antlers down to skewer us alive. I barely looked up as its tips impaled the wall.

"Gah, I need Daniel."

"Yes, because a worthless speck will be of far greater use in this situation."

The deer screamed. A horrifying sound of breaking bones ripped through the store as it cracked off its antlers. "Well, that was my last idea. Have you found any in your book?"

No. It was impossible to read while being jostled in the dark. At least if Daniel had been here, he'd... "I need a hole in the ceiling."

"Why didn't you request that before? Our mutilated friend has been happy to provide. Turning around."

Ink somehow spun on a dime even with me in his arms, not missing a step as we ran straight at the deer. That seemed to catch it off guard. It tried to lash its hands out to catch us, but Ink deftly dodged both and sent us straight through its legs. I refused to look up while the sex demon openly gawked.

"Four. Interesting choice," he muttered as we raced back to the bathroom. The deer tried to turn to chase after, but its massive size couldn't handle that kind of three-point turn. As it shifted, its legs fumbled, sending the whole thing sliding across the floor.

I leaped out of Ink's arms, needing to brace myself for this. I'd only ever done it once, and it hadn't gone well. Holding my elbow tight, I raised my hand, just as a groan rose from the floor.

"So they haven't expired yet. If you can't trust eldritch horrors from beyond the realms to finish the job, who can you?"

I ignored him and focused on the spell. If I got one word wrong, I could blow my own hand off. And last time I'd had Daniel feeding me the incantation. *Okay, Layla, you can do this. Remember, it's almost like a song. All the good mothers...*

"Wait a moment...this is not any hunter. This is the one you protected prior!" Ink hauled Stone up by his hair and turned the man's sleeping face to me.

"So?"

He hurled him back into the water, face-side up and stomped over to me. "I know the depths of depravity your urges can reach, but protecting an enemy for the sake of rage copulation—"

"That isn't it. And will you shut up before... Shit!" The deer got a foot under itself and rose back up, though this time it kept low and bent the antlers down. All it had to do was impale them through the bathroom wall and we'd be skewered.

Forget the mnemonic. Raising my hand, I shouted, "Blow up now!" To my shock, a bright red fireball sprung from my fist straight through the hole in the roof. *Yes!* I didn't know how it had worked without the incantation, but it had.

"Now we simply have to trust he is a demi-angel of his word and that he hasn't become distracted by a pretty flower."

Ink stared up at the hole with me where my fireball reached its apex and dropped back to the roof, vanishing from sight. Did Garavel see it? Was he even watching? Oh, god! I didn't have time to worry about any of that. The deer finished stepping as far back as it could. It snorted, dropped both arms to the floor and took off.

"To the back wall!" I pulled on Ink, rushing over the shattered bathroom to get as far from the antlers as possible. When my spine struck the wall, I tried to guide him to my side, but Ink stood with his back turned to the monster.

"What are you doing?"

"It'll have to go through me first," he said simply and held my face in his hands.

"No!"

A massive crash broke, shaking the walls. I wrapped around Ink, pulling him to me and waiting for the antler to spear us both. When nothing came, we both turned to find the deer staring upward. The ceiling shattered and Garavel dove with sword extended for the monster. It tried to rear back, but he threw a hand out and caught it by the neck.

"Whoa, this is a big one!" he shouted as the monster bucked. Angel and murder deer tangled together. Garavel shrugged off its claws, his sword matching the attack and biting off pieces of the creature

"He has this well in hand. We should leave," Ink said. I was about to object, when he hefted me in his arms and took off for the door.

"We can't just leave him to fight this alone?"

"Don't you have enough toys at home already? How can you care for yet another?" Ink shouted.

"That isn't the point!"

We made it to the middle of the store, but the fight wasn't getting any quieter. If anything, it was growing in volume. I gripped onto Ink's hair, using it as a ballast to pull myself up and peer behind him. "Ink!" I slapped him hard on the shoulder until he turned.

"For fuck's sake," he cursed.

Even with the manic angel stabbing it every which way he could, the deer was chasing after us. Blood gushed from its eye, but its skeletal jaws hung open and the gray tongue dangled free. "What the hell does it want?" I shouted.

Ink froze in place, nearly sending me flying out of his arms. "Magic. Your magic fed it, that's what it hungers for. It's hunting you."

"Great. So how do we…?"

He dropped my feet to the ground, took my face in his hands and kissed me. This was hardly the time for… Oh, damn. Ink plunged his tongue into my mouth, flooding me with the taste of musk and charcoal, and my mind melted. It was a kiss that'd cause lightbulbs to explode. I clung to his hair as he pulled down the strap on my dress. Ink bit down on my collarbone, causing me to gasp.

Fuck. I need him right now.

The hungry, plying fingers became a gentle touch. Ink swept his thumbs over my cheeks and he pecked my lips. "Thank you," he said quietly, before spinning around and shouting, "Angel! Get her to safety!"

"Can do," Garavel shouted. He kicked the deer in the head and leaped off, diving for me as his wings opened up. It sent him gliding at breakneck speeds across the floor.

"What are you doing?" I asked when Garavel clamped his arms around me and hefted me into the air.

"I assume you have a plan," Garavel said.

Ink shook his head and laughed while bending over on one foot. "Not really. Hey, you, grass muncher!" He launched his shoe at the deer that stared wide eyed at him. "Let's have a little race, shall we?"

I glided away from my incubus running full speed for the door. "Ink. Ink!" All I could do was shout as he vanished into a speck, the deer too focused on the incubus to see the angel flying away.

Chapter Eighteen

The last of the roof tiles crashed around me as we flew not into the early evening, but a jet-black sky. I'd only been in there for a half hour at most, but it looked like it was nearing midnight outside. That question clanged through my nerves, but there was a far more pressing one.

"How do we get to Ink?"

Garavel flew, not after my fleeing incubus, but away, the building's shadow eclipsing both Ink and the deer demon. If it weren't for the loud screech of cars and horns reacting to something running across the street, I'd have feared he was already caught or worse. I craned back, trying to catch Garavel's eye, but he was stubbornly and stoically flying in the direction of the moon.

"Put me down. I have to get to Ink and help him…"

"Do what?"

The idea jerked me so hard, I nearly sent my spell book careening through the air. What could I do against some kind of demon that grew bigger with magic? I was nothing more than collateral damage in that fight, as useful as a napkin in a shark attack. But I couldn't let them risk their necks while I cowered. "Keep him safe?"

God, it sounded even more pathetic when I said it.

"You could give it your all, but I bet the ur-demon has it well in hoof," Garavel said.

I'd seen Ink shrug off werewolf attacks, bullets, burning tuna shrapnel. But I'd also held him as he nearly died in my arms. What if Cal or Daniel came in to help? What could they do against that thing?

What could I do against it?

"Here we are."

We hovered above a standard McMansion behind a locked chain-link fence. Weeds sprouted through cracks in the empty driveway while the dirty windows sported random graffiti tags. The house's wheezing structure seemed like it'd been abandoned for decades, but I doubted it'd been more than five years.

Garavel didn't drop us to the sidewalk, but flew toward the roof and a hole in the all-glass ceiling above an empty pool. He dove through the break, landed on the cement floor and let go of me. I stumbled back, struggling to clear my head. This was when I could run, chase after Ink to try to help him…

Exhaustion churned through my body and I couldn't keep my balance. The graffiti-stained floor rushed up to me. A single angelic hand clamped onto my forearm. I stared up his arm to the concerned eyes carefully watching me. Before I could say a word, Garavel plucked me off the ground into his arms.

"I don't know why I'm so tired," I whispered, struggling to focus on him.

"Your incubus drained you of your magic."

"No. Ink wouldn't..." I extended my hand, expecting fire, but a single twist of smoke rose from my palm.

"Quick thinking on his part. It disguised you while tricking the beast into believing he was the source of magic."

How did he...? The kiss. Just thinking about that one made my toes curl in anticipation of what would come next. I looked around, hopeful that my incubus would hear the message, but only the mournful hoot of a lost owl echoed in the cement room.

"You know what that thing, the killer deer, was?"

"Nope. Though at a guess, it comes from the darker realms where magic is at its most concentrated. Or the creators made a land of deer mortals. Who can say?"

Garavel didn't put me down again. Instead, he hefted me up like a swooning bride and carried me out of the pool to a hallway.

"But you figured out the magic thing. Like that." I snapped my fingers and he stared at them before holding out his hand and mimicking the movement.

"Oh, that's fun." He snapped against the small of my back as we shifted down an elaborate marble staircase with a cheap plywood banister. I could tell where the builders had skimped because half the railing lay in pieces at the bottom of the stairs.

"Do you humans do this often? I've never seen it before." He kept snapping his fingers, delighted with the sound. The imposing army captain of before vanished behind a veneer of simple joy.

"Uh, sometimes. Usually for attention or emphasis."

"Or to cast your fire spell? Which was excellent work, by the way. I could have spotted it from a half-mile away."

My cheeks burned at the compliment and I realized it was the first one I'd ever gotten for my spells. Most of the time people either freaked out about them or nodded and moved on. Granted, we were typically in the middle of the fight of our lives so there wasn't time to hand out gold stars. But as I stared up at Garavel's genuine smile, his eyes only on me, I wanted more.

I wrapped my hands around the back of his neck, pulling myself closer. His palm shifted from my move, cupping the top of my ass. All I had to do was lean up and I could kiss his compassionate lips.

"Do you approve of this for our base?"

"Wha...?" The hypnotic passion snapped away as I looked around the remnants of a galley kitchen. The oven was long gone. In its place between the granite countertops lay a single mattress. Candles ringed the floor along with maps not printed on paper but hand-carved into clay tablets.

"From this room we can keep an eye on all entrances to the building, while this wall is the thickest I've found." He dropped me onto the stripped-down mattress and slapped his palm against the backsplash. "Should the monster track us here, we can make a quick escape in any number of directions."

Right, the murder deer was still out there. Ink could be fighting for his life and here I was trying to make out with an angel. What was wrong with me? "It's...good," I muttered, sinking to the floor and pulling my knees to my chest. They were cold against my breasts so I hugged tighter and rested my cheek on them.

Garavel busied himself making barricades. He kept asking if I needed anything. Despite my stomach's rage at getting nothing more than ice cream, I couldn't answer him. I didn't deserve a thing.

A monster, one of the kind I was born to corral, prowled the streets. It threatened people, had nearly killed some poor woman. And I had made it worse.

"I'm useless," I moaned, crashing my face to my knees.

To my surprise, a soothing palm rubbed over my shoulders. I didn't look up, but didn't shy away from Garavel's comfort either. He didn't speak. Instead, he gently ran his hand across my back.

"He said we should leave, but I didn't want to. No. I thought I knew what I was doing. I always think I know what I'm doing even if I don't have a fucking clue. And the hunters…!"

The thought of Stone dropped another boulder of guilt in my stomach. He had seen me. Maybe, hopefully, he didn't remember kidnapping me, but he had seen me before passing out. What if he came after me or the others? What if I had put them all in danger? For what? To save my enemy's life?

"I don't want to have an enemy!" I shouted to the uncaring universe.

"An enemy? You mean the creature?" Garavel asked, the gleam of command back in his voice.

"No. The hunters. Witch hunters…" I raised my chin off my knees. Candlelight flickered off Garavel's ebony sheen. He must have lit them while I was moping.

He shrugged his shoulders so I explained. "There are these people, demented assholes mostly, who go around hunting witches. They used to burn us."

"What?" he thundered. A glint of rage I saw in Ink's eyes flashed across Garavel. "Why would anyone harm a witch?"

A half laugh, half hiccup of exhaustion rolled in my throat. It was a long list. *They're scared of us. They want to control us. They think they can do better with our magic.*

"I don't know," I whispered to myself, wanting to cave inward and never stop falling. "Wake up one day, I've got monsters trying to kill me on one side and these hunters on the other. I don't want to fight. I don't want to hurt people. I don't want to be the person deciding whether I can risk myself and the people I love or let someone die. I didn't ask for any of this shit."

"It's war," Garavel said softly. "When the trumpets are blown, you have no choice but to fight."

"No one wants war, no one goes looking for it," I muttered before thinking. The hunters could stop. They could walk away and leave us in peace. But they wouldn't, they couldn't. "Only fuckheads with superiority complexes look for war. The rest of us just want to live."

A chill radiated around my body, one so sharp it caused me to sit up. Garavel stared through space. "You believe all war is worthless? Every fight to be folly?"

"Yes!" I shouted, before fading back again. "I don't know. It seems like, like by the time you get to the point of random people having to decide who lives and who dies, someone has fucked up royally."

Ink believed fighting was inevitable, Daniel all but hummed with a vengeance he couldn't slake and Cal... Some nights when the bed was cold as he prowled through the forests, I feared a part of him believed taking over the pack would make all the abuse he'd suffered mean something. "I'm not built for this," I sputtered, staring at my hands. It was a lie. One I kept telling myself even as I'd run headlong into threats. The others would call me back and I'd push harder to fight. What was wrong with me?

Collapsing tighter to my knees, I whispered, "I don't want to be built for this."

Protective, unbreakable arms swept around me. I fell against the solid chest of the angel and deep into his embrace. Slowly, Garavel stroked back my hair as I blubbered against the strained bear on his shirt. This wasn't the time for me to be falling apart, my conscience screamed at me. People were in danger from that magic-sucking beast, including those that I loved. Instead of Ink, Cal and Daniel, all I kept thinking about was Stone paralyzed on his stomach and about to drown because of my spell. I had almost left him there.

I'd grown so used to fearing death that it didn't scare me anymore. What kept me up at night was an unending terror that one day I'd watch the lights go out in someone's eyes, and I wouldn't feel a thing. I'd finally become the monster everyone else feared. My tears dried up but I couldn't stop crying and shaking. There'd be another time, and another and another when I'd have to either slaughter the people that wanted me dead, or risk everyone I loved. How could I put my own soul above their lives? How could anyone want me?

"What would you rather be?" Garavel asked. He kept gently brushing his hand against my back until I leaned up enough to look at him. "If you could be anything other than a witch, what would you want?"

"I don't know…" I reached to worry my necklace before remembering it was gone. Human seemed an easy answer, but when the hunters had taken my magic, I'd only felt rage. I'd have done anything to get it back even before I knew I'd die without it. "What about you? If you weren't the right hand of an angel, what would you be?"

Garavel scratched his chin and he stared upward. A long moment passed as he held me safe in his lap, nothing but the candlelight flickering off his contemplative features.

"A butterfly," he said.

"Really?" I hadn't expected that. "Why?"

He smiled sweetly and exhaled. "They're very pretty and people are always excited to see them."

"Well, you're already pretty and I like seeing you." My mouth had run away with me. I had meant the words, but I panicked when they slipped out.

Garavel blushed and he cast his gaze down. Even while looking like a Renaissance painting of humility, he kept caressing his soothing palms down my back. "You're very quick, despite never fighting beside a demi-angel before."

"Have you fought with witches before?"

He smiled and raised his chin. "There's no other mortal I'd trust by my side."

Did that mean witches had once served angels too? That we weren't always these green-skinned, selfish monsters people feared?

"But..." Garavel glanced a finger to my temples. Slowly, he drew it back, tracing the edge of my cheek. "None of them were as pretty as you."

I cupped the back of his hand, pressing it tighter to my face as I lost myself in his eyes. His delight in life lingered at the top, but in the unfathomable depths I could see a wash of sadness that clutched at my heart.

With all my strength, I rose up and pressed my lips to his exuberant pair.

I've done it. I kissed an angel! The idea danced then rattled in my brain as I realized Garavel wasn't pressing back. I opened my eyes, terrified to find disgust in his face. Prepared to run for the hills, I started to lean away. He flattened his palm across my shoulder and pulled me back to him. This time he kissed me with a heat that ensnared my body and enveloped my soul. My skin sang like a choir on Christmas. A wave pounded through me that wasn't the insatiable lust I'd expected, but a heartwarming love.

Garavel drew his hand down my chin and he shifted, his bottom lip pressing below mine. I began to open my mouth, eager for a taste of him, when a black shadow leaped into the room. *Holy – !*

Panic shattered the moment. Garavel's golden glow descended into darkness as I stared up into a pair of bright green eyes. They floated in the void above Garavel's shoulder until he reached behind and brought forward a small kitten.

"Ah!" I squealed in delight at the little kitten barely bigger than his hand. Which, in comparison to mine, made the kitten as long as my forearm. "You have a kitty." As it happened to all humans in the face of an unexpected baby animal, I completely lost my shit.

The kitten bonked its wide head against Garavel's smooth cheek, then purred like a jet engine. He scratched a single finger the width of the animals' spine down its back, which it greeted with more purrs. "I do. I found her when I was trying to answer my creator's question. She likes my feathers."

He burst out his wings, causing the kitten to go wide eyed in delight. Tiny paws batted at the white feathers

Garavel kept sweeping just within reach. The little murder knives sliced through his wings, harming nothing and causing the angel to laugh.

"Can I...?" I asked, scooting closer. He nodded, though I suspected most of the decision was up to the kitten. For a second, the fun feather toy was forgotten, and her judgmental green eyes swung around to find me. As I held out my finger, the kitten booped its nose against me and rubbed her little cheek on the side. Another aww slipped from me at the rumbling from the baby.

"What's her name?" I'd never had a pet before. When I had been living with my mother, we'd never stayed anywhere for more than a year or two. My life had been in even more turmoil without her. Watching the tiny baby rub her thin, fragile body against my finger, I fell hard.

Garavel reached behind and plucked off one of his feathers. The wince told me it had to hurt, but he didn't say anything while dangling it before the kitten. "I don't know. She hasn't told me."

"Well, of course not. Cats don't..." Watching the winged man entertain the kitten, it hit me that there was a good chance back in his day he had known felines that talked.

The nameless kitten gave a feral squeak at her enemy, slicing parts of the feather away while Garavel laughed. He wasn't trying to hide it under a machismo blanket of pretending to not give a shit. No, he stared in wonder at the kitten, radiating an aura that he'd defend the helpless baby to the death, then play with it after.

I melted into a gooey puddle on the floor watching them both.

With a little grace, the kitten leaped off his shoulders to tussle with one of the clay tablets. "Do you like her?" Garavel asked. All I could do was stupidly nod. He smiled while watching his kitten. "Then you can take care of her."

"What?" Ignoring the fact I was living with a man who turned into a dog each night, there was no way I could separate Garavel from his kitten. "I couldn't. She's yours."

"She's hers," he said, summing up the cat parent experience. "But I fear what the world will do to her once I am finished with my task."

"What do you mean? After we found the source of the magical disruptions, I thought we'd maybe celebrate, then you could be my..."

He stared at me, the once unmistakable emotions clouding to inscrutability. I knew what was perched on my tongue, but I swallowed it fast. "Battle buddy."

"While it has been delightful to fight by your side, Lady Layla, I'm afraid that once I've finished, I will return to my creator's side."

He'd have to hide underground with the angel? For how long? "But you..." I'd never seen anyone so excited to live, and he only had a few more days left to do it? "You just got to try ice cream. You have a kitten. You haven't even gotten to try out a new pair of shoes. It's not fair."

Garavel plucked up the kitten and placed her in my lap, then he swept his arms around the both of us. "I am bound to the wishes of my angel, and happy to serve them until he has no need of me."

"What does that mean? Has no need of you?" I pressed.

He raised his head so his brilliant eyes fell into shadow. "He is my creator," Garavel said, as if that made any sense.

So what? Because the angel had brought him into this world, that angel got to decide his whole life? That wasn't fair. That wasn't how creation was supposed to work. "You should get to decide your fate. Not him."

Pain flinched across Garavel's face as if I'd shouted every curse word in a church. He shook his head slowly, lowering it until he placed his lips to the top of my head. I couldn't make out what he mouthed silently and reached for him. Suddenly, Garavel sat up and in a jolly tone, he said, "But until the answer is found, we can spend this time together."

I scratched the kitten's head while glaring glumly at my feet. With the angel's feather, I could save Daniel from death. But with it, I'd lose this happy, caring man. I didn't know what I wanted anymore.

With care, Garavel pressed me close to his chest. I didn't hear his heart, but I felt it pounding stronger than any I'd known. He drew back my scattered hair while I held the kitten, then placed a single kiss to the top of my head. When I moved to look up, he flapped his wings once to snuff out every candle. In the darkness of the crumbling mansion, the angel held me safe in his arms and I tried to hold him back.

Chapter Nineteen

A slamming vehicle door plucked me out of my shallow dreams. I tried to sit up for a heavy warmth to press on my chest. Before I could panic, the warmth purred and stretched. "Morning... I really need to get you a name," I said to the kitten.

Garavel was gone. The last thing I remembered was cuddling in his arms and now I'd woken up on the mattress. Where did he sleep? Did he even sleep?

"Yes, this is the place."

Voices wrenched me away from the baby kitten. I carried her in my arms, not that she was a fan, and moved for the window.

"It's only the fifth one we've checked."

"Forgive me for not having an intimate knowledge of every dwelling in this city."

"You wish you had one of every woman, however."

"How dare you wound me so. You forget men and everything in between."

I smiled at the far too familiar bickering. Placing the kitten on the ground, I ran barefoot across the cold tiles and wrenched open the unlocked front door just as the three men came to knock.

"You're alive!" I shouted, leaping for them all at once.

Cal caught me first, enveloping me in his arms. He buried his nose against my neck and breathed deep while holding me. "Layla," was all he said, swaying my body back and forth before he passed me over to Ink.

I was about to reach for him, when I paused and inspected him. He wore the same careless smile, as if the world were nothing but a joke. Yet the circles under his eyes and lines punctuating his grin told a far different tale. Ink held a hand out to me like a gentleman greeting a lady. I ran my palm across it, took a step closer then launched up into his arms.

"Why did you do that?" I cried.

"Good morning to you as well," Ink said, a laugh in his voice.

"Do you have any idea how worried I was?"

"Now you know how we feel," Cal muttered.

Ink opened his arms so he could look down at me. After the longest Mother's Day of my life, I was a complete disaster. My skin felt like the peel of a brown banana—soggy and bruised. My hair would get a tongue lashing from a scarecrow. It was not the state I wanted to have anyone, much less these three, stare at me in.

"Seeing you again makes the long night worth it." Ink said that. Not Daniel, not even Cal having one of his occasional romantic moments. My incubus.

"Really?"

He smiled and tipped his head. "More or less."

"What happened?" I held Ink's hand while turning to take Cal's as well. If I could have clung to Daniel, I would have.

"Well, that is an intriguing tale — "

"Give it to her," Daniel interrupted. He'd been quiet, his arms crossed as he glared at Cal.

Reaching into his pocket, Cal eased behind me. When the golden heart dropped to the top of my chest, I understood. Cal was careful to pull the chain up and Ink held my hair. "There," he said, placing his hand over top the locket. "Back where it belongs."

"At last." Daniel breathed a sigh of relief. "That was the worst night of my afterlife, not knowing how to reach you to make certain you were safe." He placed his palm just above my cheek. The cold of his touch zapped down my body, setting off goosebumps. Ink was the one to rub up and down my exposed arms, but he didn't shoo Daniel away.

"I'm sorry. Garavel arrived so quickly, I forgot to put it back on," I said to Daniel.

It was Cal who groaned. As we turned to him, he paused in tugging on his hair and asked, "Would it have killed you to call?"

"I'd have loved to, if my battery wasn't dead thanks to too much Sheep Wars." They glared at Ink, who only shrugged, then wrapped a protective hand around my midsection.

"I refuse to apologize for tending to my flock in their time of need. Especially when it was double diamond day."

God, I needed this, all three of my boys beside me — bickering and hurling judgmental comments, but safe. "How did you stop the murder deer?" I put it to Ink, but Cal—who kept staring toward the pink clouds of dawn—spoke up.

"Where's the angel? Why'd he take you to Saint Oak?"

That was where we were? I tried to peer around the neighborhood, but the fancy houses were shielded by overgrown shrubbery. It wasn't the richest block of houses in the city—that'd be La Villette—but this was the land where the new money built their huge houses fast and cheap. No wonder the place was falling in on itself.

"I don't know. He was gone when I woke. But that doesn't matter. Tell me about the deer. What happened when you ran away?"

"You ran away?" Daniel scoffed.

"I cleverly retreated, after making myself the bait. I daresay I deserve a medal for my noble sacrifice."

Daniel blinked slowly at him. "It's not a sacrifice if you're still alive."

"Then why would anyone do such a thing? You mortals. Oh dear, Layla's making that face."

"What? No, I'm not. I don't have a face."

Ink and Daniel both shot glances while Cal leaned in. "Sorry, babe, but you do."

"Like a frustrated governess who's about to bake her charges into a pie. Yes, before you pull out your rolling pin, I will tell you the tale. Not that there is much to say. I guided the creature away from as much of the city as I could. By the time we reached a forested area, all your magic had drained from me."

"What'd the murder deer do then?"

Ink shrugged. "Nothing much. It sipped from the lake, then munched on the dandelion greens."

Wings

"That was when I caught up with him, finally," Cal added.

"Along with me." Daniel stuck his chin out. "You wouldn't have found him without my assistance."

"Yes, your crystal worked. Congrats. Woo. Anyway, we didn't know what to do about the deer. I mean, the thing's huge, but it wasn't hurting anyone."

I flashed on the blood-red eye shuttering to a pinprick when it'd looked at me. Clutching tighter to my locket, I tried to fight back a shiver, but I failed miserably.

"Anyone that wasn't magically blessed, at least," Ink said. He'd been there with me and had no doubt felt its hunger breathing down his neck. We shared a look that I knew the others would never understand.

"So it's still out there. You need me to send it home or trap it. I'll go get my book..." I turned to run inside for my purse, when Cal caught my arm.

"Er, not exactly. The deer thing, well, it's..."

"Some friends of yours arrived to cart it away," Ink said over Cal's non-answers.

"Friends?" My smile dropped and I glared at him. "The hunters are not my friends."

Ink put on a pained smile. "While it is heartening to hear you state the claim aloud, that is not to whom I refer. Wolf?"

I looked to Cal, who wilted at the attention. "Okay, fine, it was the pack. But I had nothing to do with them."

"Do not worry, my bond. I made certain to pull him into the bushes when their garish carriage arrived. Despite my best efforts, there was no tête-à-tête among the prickers."

Cal shook his head at Ink, but didn't challenge him on any of that. He'd dropped his chin to his chest, which was a really bad sign. I tried to get him to look at me. "Cal? Sweetheart. What happened?"

"As is typical when a pack of wolves under the tutelage of a feral animal meet a solitary deer," Ink said.

"They killed it." Instead of the murderous claws and antlers, its panicked bellow echoed in my mind. The thing was confused and trapped in this unwanted realm. If we could have just gotten it back to where it came from...

"Worse," Cal said. "They captured it. I don't know why. I've never seen anything like that mutated deer before. It was like the pack knew where it was and how to weaken it. Not to mention the huge truck they brought to load it onto. What the fuck is Moon Blood playing at?"

My questions grew more numerous. In the bathroom of an abandoned store, a gap in the realms had appeared. The hunters were there to try to catch whatever came through, but they were unprepared, while a wolf pack cult that lived in the woods was ready for it. "I'd quite like the world to make sense now," I muttered.

"You and I both. I've been scouring the library to the best of my ability, but there's no record of that thing." Daniel twisted his hands up to mimic the deadly antlers. "I don't know how you escaped it. Especially with only Captain Fuckboy at your side."

I laughed at the summation and stared at said fuckboy. "I dunno, he has a few more uses outside of that."

"I would doff my hat, if they were in fashion. But there is another piece to this unending puzzle. Mutt, you may as well reveal it."

God, what now? I squared my shoulders for the worst as Cal reached behind his back and tugged something out of his waistband. A weapon, a deadly artifact, a cursed book of the dead? I was prepared for anything except the square envelope he placed in my hands. It wasn't addressed to anyone, but the back bore a wax seal embossed with a rearing horse.

After pulling an invitation out, I had started to read when Ink explained, "It seems Mr. White has come to town."

When I didn't react strongly to the news, I looked away from the curly script to my three boys staring at me expectantly. "The witch hunters said as much before the deer attack. What's on the rest of this?" My dyslexia was having a field day with the cursive calligraphy.

"He is doing what all the elite have done since time immemorial." Ink sounded a touch miffed that he didn't get to drop the boom. I raised my eyes to him as he said, "Throwing an elaborate party."

"It's a ball, a masquerade one," Cal interrupted, jabbing a finger to the text I couldn't make heads or tails out of. All I could understand was the huge name at the end. Mr. White didn't have much by the way of humility. Could he be a sin of pride? No, that seemed like too easy of an answer.

"How did you get this?" I tapped the heavy cardstock against my palm while trying to think. White certainly hadn't spared any expense. There was gold foiling and lace on the invitation.

My three boys suddenly went silent. Cal shuffled his toe in the dirt. It took a few more breaths before he raised his head and met me eye to eye. "It was…"

"Werewolf!"

"Oh for crying out…" We all turned just as Garavel divebombed out of the sky. He extended one hand, ready to scoop me away. Daniel stepped in between, but it was Ink who plucked me off my feet and teleported us a yard away. Which left the demi-angel facing off against the werewolf completely alone.

"Ah, nice to have that returned to me," Ink said. I didn't have time to process whatever was going on with him.

Garavel unsheathed the giant sword on his back and held it straight out at Cal's chest. To my relief, Cal folded his arms and tossed his head back.

"You've signed your death, abomination!" Garavel thundered.

"Uh-huh." Cal pulled in a big breath, raising his chest so the tip of the sword bounced against it. "Funny how I'm still standing here, being alive."

"That shall be quickly remedied." Garavel hauled his sword back and I ran for them. Without pause, I cast a spell that was supposed to pin the demi-angel in place. But the power running through me struck harder than I ever intended, hurling his sword out of his hands until it flew through the open door and struck the staircase inside.

"Wait!"

"Lady Witch, what are you doing? Has his mage enchanted you?"

Cal shook his head. "What? What mage? I haven't, nor has any imaginary mage, done anything to her."

"He's my boyfriend," I said, trying to get through to Garavel.

"But...he is a mortal whose soul was twisted into a moon-cursed creature."

"Tell the whole neighborhood, why don't you?" Cal muttered. He dug into his shoulders and began to rock his head.

"And you are a powerful witch. How can you even break bread with such a monster, much less —"

"Break beds?" Ink had to add in. At my glare, he pulled a face. "What? It's a wonder the floor doesn't give out."

This wasn't helping. I tried to get Garavel to stare at me and not the wolf. "Look, I don't know why you hate werewolves."

"I don't understand why you don't. After everything they did at the bidding of..."

"Yes, these mysterious 'mages' I've never heard of, or seen or met. I don't do a damn thing at anyone's behest," Cal fumed.

"Well, excusing the times your father used the blood of the pack to drive you and your brothers to enact some ancient werewolf ritual."

"Ink!"

Garavel jabbed a hand to the overly helpful demon and glared at Cal. "See! A lamassu doesn't change its feathers. You're not safe near him, Layla."

The attack I'd feared between them didn't come. Far worse happened. Cal's face pinched up in pain and his hands fell dead to his sides as he took Garavel's cruel words to heart. I swooped around him, rubbing his chest as I tenderly pulled aside his hair. "I love him. And I trust him with my life. I'm not saying you all need to be best friends, but he's not this monster you think he is. If we're gonna find your creator's answer, then we all have to work together. Okay?"

Garavel gulped deep, his wary eyes glaring at Cal. After a time, he nodded sharply. "What do we do about the hoofed creature?"

"Yeah, about that…" I turned to face Cal, who went from heartbroken to guilty in an instant. "Where did you get the invitation from?"

Cal closed his eyes and breathed deep. "Mark's mother gave it to me."

"You mean…"

"The werewolves are going to a masquerade."

Chapter Twenty

Standing between two pallets, I reached out to unearth a porcelain heart someone had shoved to the back of the shelf. It wasn't very large, the size of my palm, with 'Mom' written across the top. The rest of the lingering Mother's Day crap no one needed sat in the box for the discount bin. I'd been tasked with trading it out for the Memorial Day flowers and wreaths. From a celebration of life to one of death with barely a shrug.

I'd been straddling that line for so long, I barely noticed where the pinks of mothers ended and the reds of memorials began. The little box was so ugly it was almost cute, and the kind of thing I could see an edgy nine-year-old buying for their mother. Had they hidden it back here until they could scrape up enough allowance to buy it? The tab on the front was broken and, as I moved to put it away, the top flipped open. A tinny music box played an old song.

Halfway around the world, my mother had taken me by the hand and swung me around in our socks. The entire time she sang with that song on the radio — a hint of her past in America and my future. I'd laughed so hard I'd gotten hiccups and she'd pulled a lemon drop from her pocket just for me.

"Leeland!"

I jerked at the sound, causing the music box to slam shut. I risked a peek over my shoulder before diving deep into plastic flowers with miniature American flags. "Yes, sir?" I asked my manager while stuffing the graveyard wreaths into place.

"When you're done here, lend a hand to hardware."

But... The complaint died on my tongue. It'd put me into overtime, which he'd make certain I clocked out of before reaching. They were really good about keeping us to thirty-nine hours each week, officially. "Yes, sir," I muttered.

"What was that?"

Oh for fuck's... "Yes, sir!" I shouted, spun around, and snapped him a salute. He grunted, then marched away to harass someone else to account for his larger paycheck.

If I didn't need to eat, or didn't have a huge hospital bill looming over my head like a flying iceberg, I'd have given him a very different gesture. This wasn't fair. Shouldn't the woman who, upon discovering her magical abilities and that werewolves and vampires were real, also have some huge inheritance waiting for her? Maybe even a long-lost castle that her great-uncle Vlad had left in a will? Sure, it might be haunted, but it would be free rent and antique dresses that'd make a buttload on Poshmark.

Fancy dresses and elaborate parties were for other girls. I got to be the Cinderella who toiled in the ashes after her coronation.

"Layls!"

Uh-oh. The past twenty-four hours had been a blur. I was only on my feet thanks to Ink's energy bar, which contained enough caffeine to explode a moose. In all that time I had never once thought to call...

"What the shit?" Dana stomped over to me, then she paled and looked at her nephew. "Cover your ears." Angelo rolled his eyes and tugged up the hood on his jacket instead. "What in the...h-e-double-hockey sticks happened to you? I've been worried sick."

"Dana, sorry. I... How's Angelo?"

"He's fine," she said for him. The boy didn't look too traumatized as he played with an old phone. That was the funny thing about trauma — it didn't always strike like lightning. Sometimes it lurked under the still waters, waiting for its chance to pull someone under.

I dropped the last of the flowers into the box and took a knee in front of Angelo. "How are you feeling?" I asked him.

"Fine," he said, not raising his eyes from the screen.

"And your dreams?"

His button-mashing fingers froze and he straightened his tiny body. "Fine," he repeated. In his short life, he'd already learned that bad things existed and there was no use in complaining because no one would listen.

I stuffed my hand into my pocket and rolled across a single fun-size candy bar. "Would you like this?" I held it out to him and his eyes went wide.

"Yes!" he shouted, before looking to his aunt. "Please." Angelo devoured the treat in lightning time. I wished chocolate could chase away the bad memories.

"I thought when we'd run out, you'd be right behind us," Dana said, causing me to stand. "A sane person would have run away from that…whatever the fuck that was."

A corpse eater feasting upon the flesh and bones of the dead because magic and monsters are real. "I stayed to call animal control to help with the bear."

"That was no fu…" Dana winced. "Bear. It didn't have any fur."

"Mange," I said, thinking fast. "It suffered from a lot of mange and it'd been living in the mausoleum for a while. Made a big mess. Then the cops showed up and I had to explain what happened, a lot. By the time they let me go, it was late and I fell asleep."

"For twelve hours?"

"It'd been a long day," I said solemnly, glancing to the box of Mother's Day gifts.

Dana cringed at the scarlet O for orphan I wore, but she wasn't finished with me. "That's no excuse to not call."

I should have, to make certain they'd made it out. It was hard to believe the angel kidnapping, the burning, the murder deer and waking in a moldy mansion had happened in twenty-four hours. "You're right," I said, feeling even worse.

"Course I am," she declared before wrapping a comforting arm around my shoulders and pulling her to me for a side hug. "I'm always right about everything."

"Your test scores say otherwise."

"They're all against me," Dana grumbled, but the smile was back in her eyes.

"My bond, it seems your frantic phantom has…" Ink stood way too close for the others to have not noticed him walking up. Or at least they should have if he hadn't just dropped in magically. "Ah, you have company. Delightful." He folded his arms haphazardly, but let a trio of white envelopes prod from below.

"What the hell are you doing here?" Dana thundered, before she darted her eyes to me, then back to Ink. "Cal's working today."

"He does keep busy," Ink taunted. I didn't have time for this.

"You think he's fine with you wandering into his store to annoy the shit out of *his* girlfriend?" She nearly screamed the 'his' at Ink, who responded with a shrug.

"I prefer to not speak for others, but you can inquire it of him yourself. I believe he's hands deep into his meat at the moment." He flashed her his smirkiest smile and I braced for the worst.

Dana raised a finger at him, but she reached over, caught Angelo's hand and stomped down the aisle. "You bet I will!" she declared. "Layla...don't do anything stupid." With that she was gone.

Ink gave a cheery wave in her wake, before leaning closer to me. "She does not know you well."

"What you said about Cal, that's not a euphemism, is it?"

"Alas, no. He remains the model serf of the Bellpepper estate. Why are you not utilizing your spells to put away this freight?"

"Because I'm still feeling drained after you...you know."

He chuckled. "Shame there wasn't time for me to lift your dress above your hips and plunge you onto me. Monstrous deer do ruin the mood."

I could feel him poking around in my mind, trying to get me to leap onto him, but I shook it off. "Is that what you do every time? Drain my magic from me?"

"It's that or your life. I assume you'd prefer the former."

The box slipped from my hands and struck the floor. "Could you take it all?"

Ink's cocksure stance crumpled. He held his hands out even with the envelopes in them and walked toward me. When I didn't slip away, he hugged me. "My bond, even if I were capable of such a thing, I would never violate a witch so. Whether you believe me or not, you need not fear losing your magic from me."

"I believe you," I whispered, and I did. For a moment, he collapsed around me, sealing us together in his embrace.

"Layla?"

Ink's hold broke apart and he stepped back further than necessary. I caught his eyes, a haunted wariness in them, before he looked away and it all vanished in fire. "Speaking of the specter."

Daniel stood in the middle of the aisle looking more flustered than usual. "You're here! I was worried the necklace fell off." He rushed to my side and nearly slipped his hand in mine. I beat him to it and unearthed the locket from below my work polo.

"I've still got it."

"He's as easy to shake off as a venereal disease," Ink muttered.

"Did you tell her?" Daniel looked at him for a second before focusing on me. "I did it."

"Did what?"

"Oh, yes, I forgot. Your ghost has been wrenching his shoulder out patting himself on the back. Congrats."

"Jealousy does not become you."

Ink laughed. "You'd be surprised what comes because of me."

"I get it, you're jealous because I — the one you keep declaring useless — managed to save the day."

Save the day? What did I miss? "What happened? Was it the deer?"

"Nothing so entertaining. Your specter is merely bursting with hubris over his fingering of the electrical wires."

I blinked slowly, unable to figure out what the hell Ink was getting at. As I turned to Daniel, he blushed rather adorably, and shook his raised hands even as he struggled to talk. "That's not what happened. I got you onto the list. I hacked the guest list for White's ball and added three people to it."

"How? That's... You didn't use our real names, did you?"

"What do you take me for? You all have clever pseudonyms they won't be able to trace. I even gave you fake addresses."

"Wow." I reached over to take Daniel's hands and he slipped his inside of mine. While I'd been toiling in box world, these two had managed to break into Mr. White's high security. "That's amazing," I whispered. Daniel smiled brightly. He pressed my hands together, then began to raise a finger to my lips.

"Don't ladle him in bottomless praise. You are now known as Busty de la Crème," Ink tossed off while inspecting his claws.

"Really? Busty?"

Daniel shrugged, though he looked damn pleased with that cringey alias. I glanced to Ink. "What'd he call you?"

"I refuse to repeat it."

"Mr. P. Enis Limpit," Daniel said with vengeful pride.

Ink merely sighed in exhaustion. "If you intend to make an erectile dysfunction joke at my expense, must it be such a flaccid one? A dimwitted child could wound deeper."

"Guys!" I tried to snap both out of their death stares, but Daniel still controlled my hands. "Not here." It was the middle of the afternoon, and customers would flock to see what the one-sided argument was. I pulled my hands free of Daniel and resumed my job.

"While he was fondling the web, I took it upon myself to extradite three invitations from the White premises." Ink extended them out like a card shark and smiled wide. "None can deny entrance with a proper invitation in hand, unlike an easily mangled list."

"Thank you for the reminder that your logic is as outdated as your manners," Daniel said back. "Everything's on the World Wide Web now."

I grimaced at the nineties ghost take on modern tech, but he had the right of it. I doubted anyone at the door would look twice at an invitation.

"You wasted time and risked our discovery, while I blazed a trail forward."

"How you simper at Layla's heel for a bone... Perhaps because you haven't seen yours in decades."

"Okay!" I slammed a hand down between them. "Look, you both did excellent work. We've got a way in. We just need to figure out how we're going to do this."

"With or without your winged kidnapper swooping in to mess things up?" Daniel pressed at me, but he kept his war up with Ink.

"Fearing your meager place in the hierarchy is at risk from the demi-angel?" Ink taunted. "Assuming he has not abandoned us to his angel's will."

They both looked to me and all I could do was shake my head and shrug. I had last seen Garavel the same time they did. If he was joining us, he hadn't told me.

"There is another concern," Ink said. "If they are creatures of another realm, they will be able to sense we are not human."

"I think I might have a solution for that," I said, mentally tapping my spell book that had to stay in my locker.

"Then all is set for our infiltration this coming day of Saturn."

Only five days left until I'd finally come face to face with Mr. White. He'd been dogging our steps from the shadows for half a year. Thinking of him made my hands clench and heart tremble. Was I strong enough for this? We'd staked the world's future on the outcome of a black-tie ball.

"There's still one problem," I said. "What am I going to wear?"

"My bond." Ink swooped in and took my hand in his. "I always provide."

Chapter Twenty-One

"Fu—" My foot slipped off the bathroom sink, sending the razor straight into my unsuspecting flesh. I glared at the line that was welling up with dots of blood.

"You okay?" Cal asked. He'd crushed in beside me, both of us trying to make ourselves look presentable for the big ball. I'd have killed for a fairy godmother and two mice turned beauty consultants right about now.

"It's fine," I said, ignoring the damage and moving to the next hairy spot.

"But you're bleeding." He washed off the last of his shaving cream and flashed his big puppy eyes in the mirror.

I tore off a piece of toilet paper and stuck it to the wound. "Beauty is pain," I said, returning to the mines.

"I want to argue with you," he said, shrugging off the towel around his shoulders, "but it hurts how beautiful you are."

"Oh my god, that's so cheesy." I rolled my eyes and tried to focus on my task, even as my cheeks burned hotter than the sun.

"But you're smiling," he said, shooting finger guns for good measure. I wanted to laugh with him but there wasn't time. We had an hour to dress, organize and infiltrate what could be the belly of the beast.

The other side of the sink was where I'd left my spell book open. It radiated anger at the water drops seeping into its pages, but I was trying to cram as many spells as I could into my messy brain. Next to a complicated glyph on how to cloud a person's mind was a little note. Usually I ignored them — most amounted to little more than sixteenth-century gossip or shopping lists — but this was about angels.

An angel always honors their word, but do not be deceived by their heavenly graces. For they are creation and creation is — before all things — the greatest deceiver of them all.

What the hell does that — ?

"Son of a...!"

"Band-Aids are in the top drawer," Cal called from down the hall. I nodded my thanks without saying it and slapped one over my bleeding cut. It stood out even against my barely brown skin, but would probably blend into Cal's nearly translucent one.

"I don't know why you bother." A flash at my side caused me to look up from my leg and at the heart-stopping sight of Calvin Rollin in a tuxedo. Okay, the jacket was missing and his tie dangled off his shoulder, but it didn't matter. White button-up shirt plus tight black trousers equaled instant aphrodisiac. He cursed me more by flashing an inescapable smile. "I like hairy girls."

"That's reassuring coming from a werewolf," I said, forcing myself to focus. I abandoned shaving above my knees—no reason to risk further blood loss—and tackled makeup next. Big fancy party with lots of rich idiots who could also be secret mythological creatures—best to keep it simple. The smoky eye was easy, but I had no idea what to do for lipstick.

"Here."

I jerked as a hand reached from behind me to select the plum tube. When I turned, Ink already had it open and came at me with it. "Don't speak," he said, placing the tip to my lip and expertly swiping across. "Not until I'm finished with you."

All I could do was give him a look of 'Save it for later.' He was surprisingly tender and thorough and even added a lighter hue to create a subtle ombre effect.

"You're good at this."

"Your surprise wounds me, my bond."

"Let me guess, you've done the eyeliner of pharaohs and put on the lipstick of queens."

Ink chuckled while putting the tube back. "I'm afraid no one quite so lofty has requested my attention thus, but that isn't why. I could trace your lips blind and not draw a millimeter out of line." He raised the tip of his pinkie and held it just above the lipstick he'd applied, then began to swoop around while closing his eyes.

Forget the ball. Grab Ink, then Cal and drag them both into the bedroom. Play poor Hollywood starlet who can't pick between her handsome costars.

The edge of Ink's lips twitched up, as he no doubt had read my thought, but he dropped his hand and turned to the wolf lurking in the doorway. Poor Cal was pulling his tie back and forth over his neck, uncertain where to begin.

"Allow me," I said, taking the tie to knot it.

"How do you know how to do this?" Cal asked. I couldn't be distracted by his tempting blue eyes so I glared at the black silk instead.

"I had a roommate with a neurological disorder that worked for a bank. His hands couldn't make the loop. So I googled how to tie a tie and would help him every morning."

"A lucky man," Cal whispered as I cinched the knot up and laid it against his chest.

"And gay."

"Doesn't make him any less lucky." He caught the back of my hand and pressed it tighter to his chest. The thin shirt clung to him, revealing a hint of the pec below.

"I hate how hot you look in that," I whispered.

"Why?"

"Because I can't do a thing about it." As I faced reality, I looked down at my mess of unflattering shapewear. "Ink?"

"Yes?" He appeared in an instant dressed in flattering evening wear instead of his usual outfit he'd had on two seconds before. Ink's suit was plucked out of time. With only two buttons on the short coat, tails and a paisley crimson waistcoat, he looked like he'd fallen out of a nineteenth-century wormhole. There wasn't time to play the naïve governess who succumbed to the rakish Earl either.

"Where's my dress?" I pressed. All week he'd sworn he was working on it. I had no choice but to trust him as I sure as shit didn't have the funds to buy anything that wasn't from a Halloween costume shop.

"Allow me, my bond." Ink took my hand and guided me out of the bathroom to our bedroom. Stepping over the abandoned sock hills and piles of scrubs, I peered at the bed, hoping to find a garment bag or pile of satin.

"There's no dress," I said, fear clawing up my chest. Was this an elaborate plan on his part to force me to stay back? Had the others joined in?

"Patience," Ink ordered. He left me standing in front of the mirror. God, I did not need a full body view of the mess I looked. Beige spandex was yanked up to under my boobs, and a strapless bra was all but duct-taped to my skin to keep my wily pair under control. A silk bonnet with ducks on it hid away my hair.

"Close your eyes," Ink said, his protective grip slipping to a gentle touch down my arm.

I sighed at the idea, but did as told.

"Calvin?" A flurry of movement flapped around beside me. Cal took my hand and helped me to stand up as a presence slid up my body. Before I could ask a question, a cold piece of metal landed on my neck and my eyes opened in surprise.

Oh my god!

"You were to wait until I finished," Ink groaned dramatically.

A purple satin bodice with a sweetheart neckline clung to my chest. The off-the-shoulder straps hung precariously against my arms, each bearing a single silver link with a pearl at the end. The neckline was covered in silver beading, creating waves across my chest, and a huge opalescent pearl was tucked right at the top of my cleavage. It was beautiful and elegant, while the skirt was dramatic and daring. Silk panels of royal purple and eggplant hung from my waist, extended outward by a petticoat of tulle below. I hovered my hands above the dress in disbelief at what I wore.

"Please don't cry," Ink said, catching a tear on the corner of my eye. He finished laying a silver chandelier necklace with teardrop pearls on my chest, then added two matching earrings and finally removed my bonnet. As my fresh twists shimmied around my head like a halo, it all hit me at once.

"How did you do this?" I whispered to the princess in the mirror. She couldn't be me. That had to be some other far more beautiful noblewoman from a parallel world who was trapped behind a pane of glass.

"Do you ask the moon how it can raise the tides?"

"But it fits like a glove. You never once measured me." I looked up from the dress that didn't pinch a single roll of fat.

"My bond," Ink said, shaking his head.

My whole body burned red at just how well he knew it. I reached over for Ink, who softened as he caressed my hand. Then I wrapped my arm around Cal's. He brushed his forehead against my cheek, breathing in my perfume, and could only whisper about how beautiful I was.

We were nearly ready for this dance. Together, we walked to the kitchen where Daniel stood sentinel over a set of masks on the table. One looked like it was made of marble and covered all but the bottom jaw. Another was a cute lady's mask that didn't really hide the face below but had lots of pretty lace on it. The third was a wolf, a fact Ink couldn't stop laughing about.

"The spell should be ready to go…" Daniel looked up from the masks resting in the center of a ward and his jaw dropped. "Layla, you are…" He roughed over his chin and mouth while sweating ghost bullets. The entire time his eyes grew bigger and bigger. "I…can't think. I can't speak."

"You should wear couture more often," Ink chimed in.

Daniel didn't even glance at him. He floated his palms over my bare arms and up to my shoulders. Goosebumps rose in his wake, causing every sensation to increase tenfold. I'd have sworn I could almost feel his skin in that state. "Never have I seen a beauty such as thee. A field of lilies by spring's ascent compare not to your radiance."

He brushed his hands inside of my arms, bringing himself to stand right before me. My gaze kept darting away. I was overwhelmed by the awestruck love in Daniel's eyes. "Eyes, lips, bosom, face, a twirling star by night's grace."

"Are yet one more thing the ghost can never taste," Ink interrupted.

Daniel turned to growl at him but Ink held up his wrist...which I realized had a fancy watch on it. "Are we not running late?"

"The masks are ready. I just need to cast the spell." I unfurled the Post-It Daniel had helped me fill out earlier and raised it to my eyes. The masks had been boiled in a lavender syrup for six hours which somehow didn't peel all the cheap paint off. Reading the syllables, I chanted what sounded like drunk limericks to my ear over the three party-store masks.

They lit up a disquieting green before fading back to normal. Cal picked the marble one and held it up to his face. "How's this supposed to work?"

"An excellent question. I am not of a mind to don the mortal cloak once again."

"Don't worry." I patted Ink to assure him. After what happened with Sybil, I wouldn't have even offered it. "This doesn't change us inside, merely makes us appear human to every sense."

Cal snorted and started to tie his mask in place when a great crash broke from the backyard. All four of us ran out to see what happened. Rising from the burned grass of a small crater, Garavel appeared.

"I thought you said he wasn't coming," Cal whispered to me. He kept one hand protectively around my stomach while Garavel nodded in my direction.

"I didn't think he was." I hadn't seen him since the blow-up at his house. I'd only stopped by his house once but he wasn't there. If I'd tried again, there was a high probability the rich neighbors would call the cops on the strange woman snooping around an abandoned property.

The demi-angel took one step before he finally looked to Cal and his folded wings shot back out. I leaped out between them before any fists could fly. "Garavel, what are you doing here?"

"Are we not going to the dance? I wore my best robes."

Holy shit, he wasn't kidding. They gleamed brighter than any white on earth. Even in the shade, it hurt my eyes to look for too long. The golden rings keeping him decent had rubies embedded inside. I held up a hand to protect my eyes and tried to stare at him, but he wouldn't look away from Cal.

"We're going, but...I haven't seen you for a week. Where were you?"

"Reconnaissance. I believe I've found at least two weak points in the castle's defenses."

"We're going to walk in the front door," Ink said.

"But what if we can't go back out it?" Garavel explained and my heart dropped. That was a very good point none of us had thought of. "I've also been learning more about this Mr. White, Lady Witch." He took my hand and tried to pull me closer, but Cal still gripped me. It left me leaning over to the point I was about to fall in the mud.

Garavel glared over at Cal, then he dropped his voice to a whisper. "I have reason to believe that Mr. White is working with werewolves."

We all blinked slowly at him.

"That is hardly earth-quaking information, wings," Ink said, slapping Garavel on the shoulder.

"Do you not see? Layla, you of all people must understand the significance of... If he is willing to degrade himself to employ werewolves — "

My wolfy boyfriend let out a growl. I tried to reach over to calm him, but if I moved my hand, my body began to teeter.

Garavel caught Ink's eye, then he looked to Daniel before homing in on me. "I believe Mr. White is a mage."

He said it like a crash of lighting should have punctuated the sentence, but all we got was a robin chirping in the trees. "Okay. A mage. Ink, what's that?"

"Haven't the foggiest."

"But you know everything," Cal insisted.

"In terms of carnal flesh, yes. In the wide wonders of the world, alas, even my thousands of years have not afforded me omnipotence. Yet."

Mr. White might be a mage. That sounded like a bad thing from the way Garavel spoke of them. "So they can...what? Do magic? I thought only witches could harness the realm energy or however you put it."

"Only they can," Ink said before he too looked at Garavel who slowly backed up. But he wouldn't let go of my arm either, dragging me with him.

"Mages are vile monsters, my sworn enemy. Their blood has spilled hundreds of thousands of times by my sword alone."

Suddenly, the cuddly teddy bear grew fangs. I tried to pull my arm back but Garavel had it clamped tight. "The war. You must know of the war." In his exasperation, he yanked me not just out of Cal's hands but off my feet. I stumbled, my heels puncturing the soggy ground before he caught me by the shoulders.

"Which war?"

"The war. The first war!" He sounded near hysterics. I took a quick glance over my shoulder to Ink, who shrugged.

"You mortals break out into battles like a randy merchant does with pox. I can't remember a specific one."

Garavel closed his eyes and began to reach behind his head. *Oh shit, he's going for his sword.* I tried to tug away, when he unsheathed the massive thing and lowered it.

"When the world was created, all creatures were meant to live in harmony." Garavel held his sword out, the flat end turned up. As he spoke, he traced his fingers down the blade. Small carvings lit up, the first a hand. "The creators learned, forever crafting in new and exciting ways before letting their children loose on this world of theirs. One day they had an idea. Rather than make new versions of the same creatures when one died, why not give them a way to create new?"

"Are you saying angels invented sex?" I whispered.

"I should send them a fruit basket in gratitude," Ink quipped.

"It required a spark of magic, but that spark became a fire, and the fire consumed all the creatures of the world. Chaos was born not from the creators who'd blessed them, but the mages trying to seize the world for themselves." He waved over his sword, causing a clenched fist to rise from the blade. "They wanted control of people, of creatures, of the creators themselves, and many joined their side out of fear and lust. But the angels could do nothing to stop them. They can only create, not destroy. So they created us."

"You're..."

"I was carved from hardest stone, as were all my brethren, to protect the world from the greed of mages."

Garavel shuddered as he tapped a finger to the next carving, a fang. "The mages were cunning and created monstrous beasts from their own kinds. We called them abominations. They called them werewolves."

Shit. I looked over to Cal, whose hands dangled at his sides. I tried to read his face but he reflected back nothing.

"Mindless beasts formed from apocryphal magics and the babes of their own blood. My fellow soldiers, my brothers and sisters, were slaughtered by these beasts!" He cried out with a sorrow that wracked through my soul. My own heart squeezed in my chest with the same raw grief. I clasped a hand to his arm, hoping to keep him in place, but Garavel didn't attack Cal. He pressed another carving on his sword, this one a broom.

"The tide turned when witches joined our side." He smiled and placed his hand to my cheek. I heard three men shift behind, each one ready to launch forward, but Garavel smiled beatifically. "At last we were able to break every mage's foothold and the accords were born. They separated the realms, rebuilt this world and sundered the mages from power over creation. If this

Mr. White is what I fear, then it is my solemn duty to remove his head from his body until he is dead."

The last carving lit up, this one mimicking a palm sliced with a knife — his oath to his angel and reason to live. As I stared down the line of lit carvings revealing his past, I realized Garavel's hand was shaking. Gently, I cupped mine around his, waiting until he stopped trembling in grief, anger or both. "That's what we want, too."

He brushed his fingers back over my cheek and up into my hair, holding me so close I could feel the heat of his lips. *Please don't kiss me, not now.* Another growl broke the moment, and Garavel glared over my shoulder. "What of the beast?"

"He's not a beast," I insisted.

"Nor have I slain thousands and thousands of people with a big-ass sword on my back," Cal tacked on.

"Where do your loyalties lie, wolf, if not with a mage?"

It took him a half-second to answer. "Layla."

"That…" Garavel's gaze darted over to me. He pressed his lips tight and closed his eyes. After a moment, he breathed, "That could work. But if you turn on her for even a second…"

"Like you're the first to threaten me with that," Cal said, holding his hands up. For the first time, the tension wobbled a bit. It didn't snap, didn't recede either, but if what Garavel had said was true, it wasn't hard for me to understand his hatred.

With the terms laid out, he released me and slotted his sword back on his wings. "So." The loopy smile returned and he asked, "What's the plan?"

"We're gonna find this Mr. White, figure out what he's got to do with realms tearing apart then take it from there. But first." I glanced down Garavel's outfit and sighed. "Ink? Any chance you can find him a suit that will fit in?"

"A demon's work is never done."

Chapter Twenty-Two

Dressed in a heart-stopping dress with two besuited men at my side, I would have felt like the sexy spy about to break up a crime syndicate ring if I didn't have to slip out of the driver's seat of my sedan and help one of them fit through the door.

"Just duck your head. No, you have to…" White feathers smashed into my face, sending me reeling back into Cal's patient arms.

It was Ink who reached over and unlocked the seat belt around Garavel's waist. As it snapped back, the angel leaped out of the car like it was full of snakes. I feared he'd go airborne, but he stopped in front of me and retracted his wings. Though his stink eye didn't waver from Cal, at least he wasn't openly shouting, "Werewolf!"

We'd parked far enough from the fancy house there was no chance of anyone seeing us. Even still, I turned to Daniel and he vanished before I could ask. Ink joined the three of us and we waited, watching the five p.m. sun dangle above the skyscraper houses.

"No one's around. You're good," Daniel announced, zapping in beside me. I nodded my thanks, then popped open my purse. Three invitations for three guests and the three masks to hide them rested inside. I picked up the wolf one first.

Cal, Garavel and Ink stood before me and I felt like a very strange Bachelorette about to pick who'd risk their life for a date. "There's..."

"If you please, my bond," Ink interrupted. "I'd prefer to remain as my lustrous self for the eve."

I caught his eye, worried I'd find remnants of the trauma he swore wasn't there from the last time he'd pretended to be mortal. All he gave me was a sly smile as if he wanted to make the choice easy on me, but I grew uncomfortable. I'd gotten used to having Ink there when shit got real.

"Okay. Um..." I held the wolf mask out between Cal and Garavel. They both glared at each other from the sides of their eyes. An untimely wind ripped through the leering buildings, tugging on my skirt.

"Oh for..." Cal took the wolf mask and placed it against his face. "I'll take it." He began to tie it in place as I handed Garavel the marble one.

As Cal finished his knots, I expected for the same green glow to overtake him, or his body to shrink and grow less fearsome, but nothing changed. What if the spell didn't work?

"Am I human now?" he asked, swinging the longer muzzle of the mask around. He tipped his head back and sniffed deep. "I can still smell the demon... Did you eat my aftershave?"

Garavel knotted his on as well, his dark eyes cutting from behind the white and gold swirls of the mask. I trailed the ribbons on my pearl mask, watching them waft in the wind. If I'd fucked the casting up, we could all be walking to our deaths.

A warm hand brushed over my bare shoulder, drawing me to find Garavel's gaze soft even behind the unforgiving marble mask. "I have faith in you," he whispered, tugging me back to that single stolen kiss on the floor of the kitchen. I should have been stressed over that moment lost in the swirls of magic and chaos, a moment Garavel hadn't said word one about. But being near him wrapped me up in a blanket that tamped down my anxiety.

Nodding, I placed the mask to my brow and was about to tie it back when Ink beat me to it. As he did, double securing the knots, he whispered, "Be wary inside, Layla."

"When aren't I?"

Ink paused in his work to stare me dead in the eye. Fair enough. "Whatever this Mr. White is, maybe a mage, maybe worse. Watch what you say and where." He let the ribbon trail down, the end tickling the nape of my neck as Ink placed a hand to the small of my back. "I'd rather not face the bowels of hell so soon."

The edge of worry in his tone sent me reeling. I turned to Ink, when Cal suddenly jerked his head to the side. "Wait a second." He drew closer to me, causing Garavel to stiffen, and placed the nose of the mask against my cheek. It tickled a little as Cal breathed deep. "You don't smell right."

"Well, I had to take a quick shower..."

"No, I mean, the you that makes you who you are. It's gone. I don't like this."

He looked so unnerved, shaking his head like I'd vanished into a puff of smoke, that I had to take his hand and hold him close. "Don't worry, Cal. I'm still me," I promised. He held my cheek, brushing his thumb under the gap in the mask.

"While I'm not against letting the mutt get a deep whiff of all of us, I'd say you need to be reaching the front of this mansion before the clock strikes."

I nodded to Ink how that made too much sense. "Everyone knows what to do?" I asked while handing out the invitations.

"Wander around the party, try to look important," Cal said.

"Find Mr. White and cut his head off," Garavel summed up.

"After we determine if he's a mage," I tacked on. We'd had that argument the entire drive down. He seemed to think storming the castle was the only option, which I doubted Cal or I would survive.

"Yes, after he reveals himself," Garavel agreed.

"Let's just hope he's the cackling monologue type," Cal added while holding his arm out for me. I took it and patted his hand, praying for the same. If we were lucky, he'd believe no one would dare crash his party and have his guard down. If we weren't...at least my shoes were comfortable.

"One more matter, my bond." Ink held out a hand. "Your spell book."

I pried open my huge purse which I'd brought specifically to hold my book. "What about it?"

"There are few things that will give you away more than a large leather tome. If you wish your subterfuge to work, it will need to remain with me."

No, I couldn't give it to him. We were going to be at least three blocks away for hours. What if something happened to it? What if I went mad?

"I promise, I will protect it with my eternal life," Ink swore. Closing my eyes, I yanked my book out and passed it over. The pages radiated confusion like a toddler on their first day at daycare, but he was right. If they did a bag check, the first thing they'd notice would be my spell book. I tried to not give it a sad wave goodbye as I turned my back.

"And one other matter." Ink swept me up into his arms, bent me over and kissed me hard. I was in such shock, I didn't even have time to ruffle through his hair before he leaned away. A ring of purple coated his lips as he smiled and brushed his hand over my cheek. "So I can be a fly on the wall the entire night."

What was he...? As I scrunched up my face, cool metal touched my inner ear. I reached up to it, when Ink took my hand and placed it in Cal's. He held up a finger to his stained lips. "Our little secret." As he said that, his voice echoed from the listening device he'd slipped in there.

The walk was more of a hike up a hill to the largest house at the top. Even at a distance, I could make out the Grecian pillars and mountain-sharp roofs that gave the house an old Victorian feel. It was probably named something like Fanciful McButternut Estate. A handful of people milled about outside smoking, but it wasn't until I walked past that I realized none of them were holding a cigarette. Eyes that blinked two sets of lids watched us walk up to the front door.

This was it. I adjusted my skirt and raised my head, prepared to launch a thousand spells should the worst come to it. "You ready?" I asked the two men beside me.

It was Ink who piped up. "Always. Will you cease your prattling? What good would you even do in there? Unless you are attending a Dress As A Dockworker soirée."

I shook off Ink and Daniel bickering in my ear and pushed on the giant door with a rearing stallion for a knocker. No one rushed to pat us down for weapons or demand our names. There were no guards to see if we were really human or not. The only proof we were even in the right place was a simple sign written in a curly script—"Welcome to the White Ball."

The foyer wasn't much to look at. Aside from the sign, two lines of racks stretched across both walls and bulged with coats. Music pulsed from the room on the right, while the left was eerily still. Not silent like an abandoned house—still like a graveyard on Halloween. At any moment, it could come alive, then the real terror would begin.

"Let's start in there," I said, pointing to the right. I took a step, and my slippers snagged on the hem of my dress. *Damn it.* I gripped the sides of the dress and hiked it up to walk. "How the hell do princesses get anything done in this?"

Cal slipped his hand around mine while Garavel hung slightly behind. We weren't all going to fit through the door together, so I picked my wolf. Arm in arm, we walked into the party. The chandelier struck me first. Elaborate beyond measure, it boasted five levels of real candles, each sconce held aloft by a silver horse. Beyond the flickering flame, lights of every color darted between the candles and moved without purpose, almost as if they were alive.

Men in black suits and women in designer gowns half-filled what had to be a ballroom stolen from a gothic manor. The floor was a dark oak that I feared would whisper my death when I walked on it. The ceiling was even stranger, bearing a mosaic of various hooded riders traveling across every vista in the world, including the clouds. The walls themselves boasted a wallpaper of a vibrant green hue that struck a long-lost chord in my brain.

"Don't eat the wallpaper," I whispered. "It's made of arsenic."

"Why would we do that?" Cal asked. He raised his head and his pupils narrowed to pinpricks.

I turned to follow, and my heart nearly gave out. The big bad wolf strode down the gilded stairs. Eric stared out across the gathered throngs like they were a lost flock of sheep ripe for the eating. Unlike the miracles Ink had worked with Garavel, the werewolf was stuffed into a too tight suit. He either didn't want to or couldn't close the coat and had left the white shirt partially unbuttoned to reveal a tuft of red chest fur prodding from below. When he turned, I swore I could hear the sleeves straining from his heft even above the orchestra and murmurings of the crowd.

"What are you looking at?" Garavel asked excitedly before he too turned to find Eric in a domino mask. "That's a were—"

I clamped a hand over his mouth and pulled his gaze to me. He tried to fight it, narrowing in on the threat waltzing into the crowd along with a mass of more subdued pack members on his heels. "We're human, remember. Human."

"I'm beginning to think we might be the only ones," Cal said. One by one, the high society socialites, politicians and businessmen shed their skins—some metaphorical, others literal. Wings appeared, mostly of the shadow variety, though a few were gossamer. Crackling rock appeared below the soft flesh and others burst with magma. We were surrounded by horns, fangs, claws, scales and worse.

I tensed up, preparing myself for the attack, but nothing happened. The lizard tongues snaked down to lick pâté off crackers and fangs clanged against crystal champagne flutes. No one cackled manically or leaped for throats. The party continued as if nothing had changed.

"This may have been a bad idea," I said, starting to ease back. I gripped Cal's and Garavel's arms. Both were too entranced with the crowd to notice. I took two steps for the door before the stench of wet dog and rotting mud punched me in the stomach.

"Watch the door," he ordered. I closed my eyes tight and tried to breathe. *Don't pass out, don't draw attention.* Even without looking, I could feel Eric pacing behind me like a nervous wolf trapped in a tight cage.

"He doesn't want any surprises tonight. Watch for anything that don't..." Eric's order trailed away and I heard him breathe in deep to smell the air. "Something ain't—"

The lights crashed to near darkness, save the early evening sun peeking through the windows. The murmuring of the monsters faded to a drop as a single spotlight landed at the top of the balcony. Standing in the middle was a plain man in a bright white suit. His bald spot caught the glow, reflecting it back onto the ceiling. I squinted to make out his features, but the harsh light did him no favors, elongating his nose and causing his eyes to sink deeper than seemed possible. Otherwise, there were no wings, no horns, no massive shoulders or fins. He looked as human as everyone else had two minutes ago.

"Gentlemen, ladies, creatures and creations of a fervid mind. Welcome to my humble abode."

Hands and flippers slapped together to clap in glee while my stomach dropped. This was him, Mr. White, the man who'd been nibbling at the back of my mind for nearly a year. He was even more terrifying than I could have imagined.

"Please, partake of the vittles, brought to you from the deepest of realms courtesy of my friend Garkong." He extended a white cane to the crowd where the spotlight swung to reveal a massive yeti-like creature humbly raising a hand and blushing. "Dance, drink, divine deep into the realms for tonight..."

Mr. White bowed his head and he placed a white fedora on top. When he looked up, his eyes were blacker than death. "Tonight we take the first step to carving out what we deserve from this world. In the meantime, do try the pie. I understand it's baked with ambrosia." He raised his hand and waved just as the spotlight winked out.

The rest of the flickering candles caught and the party resumed. I stared at the balcony. Mr. White was completely gone. What he deserved? The phrase wouldn't stop rattling in my head, every bounce sparking in the darkness. What did he deserve? What did any of us?

"Are you cold?" Garavel asked. I jerked in surprise and found I'd been worrying my skirts.

"No. Why?"

"You've gone all bumpy." He reached over and rubbed up and down my arms. It didn't quell the strike of fear in my heart, but his nearness helped.

"Thanks," I said, patting his hand.

"We were always having to do that for witches in the mountains."

I bobbed my head in thanks, when I caught another head in the crowd. It too stared up to where Mr. White had been. The hair was covered in a silk scarf, though a single braid of white hung off the side. I could only see the profile of the mask, porcelain and perfect, hiding whoever was under there.

"Layla?" I jerked again, nearly knocking champagne back onto Cal's chest. Wincing, I took the drink he offered, before glaring at it.

"Should we be drinking this?"

"It is a party. You'd appear stranger for not," the bug in my ear piped up. I had nearly forgotten Ink was listening in on all of this.

"And if it's poisoned...?" I tried to whisper, uncertain how he was hearing me. Cal bunched his eyebrows at my comment and he glanced around while the bee in my ear laughed.

"We find a goat with intestinal distress."

"Ink is no help." I sighed, wishing I could pull the damn thing out, but people were watching me. I raised my glass at the narrowed eyes and put it to my lips. Taking the barest sip of the probably expensive champagne, I turned back to Cal who'd finished his whole flute.

At my look, he shrugged. "It's hard to poison werewolves. This whole thing feels like adult prom. Tight suits, long dresses, boring music. All it needs is a steer to tear through the place with the school banner on its horns."

"You went to prom?" It was hard to picture the three brothers in that tiny house on the outskirts of Santa Fe being social enough to brave a school dance.

"We all did," he said with a smile before it cracked. "Two girls asked Eli and he didn't have the heart to turn one down."

I rubbed a soothing hand over Cal's chest, the beat of his heart increasing erratically at the memory of his dead brother. "Did some wacky hijinks ensue?"

"Nah. He took both. They had a good time. We all did..." The forced smile he wore to avoid the pain slipped to a sly one. "Except for Mark. He broke into the teacher's lounge just to blow smoke into all the cupboards. It was a damn miracle Mar graduated."

Cal blew off the memories of his youth like a teenager trying to disrupt authority via a cigarette stub. Turning to me, he smiled and held my hand. "I bet you were prom queen."

I snorted hard at the thought. "I'd have to have gone first." Also been nominated or had anyone look twice at me.

"Well." Cal held his hand out to me. He tucked his other behind his back and stuck his ass out in a half bow. Carefully, I placed my palm in his. He clenched his fingers around mine and pulled me to him in a flash. "No reason we can't dance now."

Music for fancy jewelry commercials twirled across the ballroom along with a handful of couples making their way into the middle. I folded into Cal's embrace while he stood rod straight like a gymnast. At the edge of the dance floor, he paused, raised my hand and spun me on my toes. I stumbled to form a circle, Cal guiding me like a wayward top until he pressed me against his chest.

"I need to tell you how beautiful you are before the blood starts flying."

I blushed and glanced down at the pearls across my cleavage. "You really don't."

"Pretty sure I do. Think it's in the boyfriend code. Compliment your girl when she's so hot you don't know how you haven't screwed her against the wall." He raised his hand and this time I twirled in step with the music before laying my arm across his shoulders. I toyed with the handful of hairs left on the nape of his neck.

Leaning closer, I whispered, "Full moon?"

Cal shivered and closed his eyes. "It feels like one every day when I'm with you. That's a good thing, I mean. Maybe not for my sheets, but..."

"If you two do not rut in the bathroom, I will come in there and drag you myself!" Ink thundered in my ear.

Instead of giving in to the incubus, or the obvious bulge pressing against my silk skirts, I lay my cheek on Cal's chest. He bent his chin lower, tenderly cresting it over my hair as we swayed in time. It was a magical moment, the princess finally having her dance with the dashing and charming prince. So it all had to come crashing down.

Cal stiffened in more than just his trousers, shaking me from my dreams. I followed his line of sight to spot Eric shoving his way through the crowd with a massive turkey leg in his hand. At least I hoped it was turkey. A handful of people with bent heads trailed behind the werewolf's towering form.

I didn't realize how tight Cal's grip was until I tried to breathe and couldn't. "Cal." I tapped my palm against his back, pulling him from his fugue state.

"Sorry, I... That's every werewolf left in the pack behind him. At least the ones I knew. That can't be good." As we watched, Eric and his minions shouted and shoved through the crowd before stopping by a nondescript door on the side of the ballroom. The bombastic werewolf peered around and quietly cracked it open. One by one, each minion followed.

"Go," I said.

Cal spun around from watching them to stare at me.

"We're here to figure out what's up and…you should follow him."

"Are you sure?"

No. Cal was strong but he sure as shit wasn't invincible. When he was out of my sight, I couldn't protect him, and he couldn't protect me. But I couldn't keep forcing him to stay by my side either. "Yeah. I trust you."

"Babe…" He didn't run off. Instead, he pushed a wayward curl off my cheek. Pulling me close, Cal brought his forehead to mine and he whispered, "I know you do."

I kissed him, fear snapping through me that this would bite me in the ass. He kissed back tenderly with a promise for more. Cal gave one last swoop of my cheek with his thumb, then he turned and took off for the door.

"I love you," I whispered to myself alone out on the dance floor.

"How long until he will require rescuing?" Ink asked.

I could only close my eyes and hope, when a long shadow fell over me. Before fear could percolate, Garavel boomed from behind, "Have you tried the green stuff?"

At least he was less 'kill all werewolves' in the face of free food. I turned to find he had napkins full of little hors d'oeuvres running up both his forearms. "You've been busy." I picked up a cracker with a green blob on it and took a taste test.

Smoky guacamole with a wasabi bite washed across my tongue. It was good. I shared Garavel's smile. He stared down the line of food with the wonder of a child on Christmas Day.

"We could eat all of those in one sitting," I said, carefully pulling the napkins off his arms. He dipped the tip of his pinkie into a pink pâté that had to be salmon and scrunched his face up. Not a winner.

"Or...would you like to dance?" I held out my hand. Garavel watched the couples sweeping around the floor, then he nodded vehemently.

"That looks like fun!" he boomed. His massive hand covered mine as he pulled me onto the floor. I didn't even have time to put the food down. All those cute little treats tumbled to the ground.

We ended up right in the middle, Garavel towering above nearly everyone twirling around us. He watched them go past, then held his arms out the way the others did. I placed my left hand in his, and swept my other around his shoulders. He slipped his hand behind my waist, and his entire palm reached across it.

"You know what they say about men with big hands..." Ink whispered in my ear causing me to burn inside. "They can strike both buttocks with one swing."

"No one says that."

"Well, they should, as it's far more true than any other foolish aphorisms."

Garavel didn't sway like Cal. He raised a foot up, stomped it purposefully on the ground, then shuffled after it with the second. We moved like a marching elephant with a limp, but it kept anyone from getting too close. "This is different," he said after a time. "I don't know how to dance like this."

"Neither do I. Did you do a lot of dancing?"

"Yes. Nights around the fire, our battalion would leap to our feet and give in to the pounding rhythm of the drums turned from war. This is...nice, I guess. Peacetime dancing."

I watched the others all perfectly following the same set of rules, fingers barely touching, bodies separate enough for the holy ghost. I took a half step closer to Garavel, my feet slipping between his. "I think I prefer your dancing."

"It was more energetic." He raised his head and the blinding grin dimmed to a bittersweet smile. I could nearly see the beloved memory turning painful in his eyes.

"What else do you love?" I prompted, trying to break him from the barbed memories sweeping through his mind. "Other than dancing and ice cream and kittens."

With each suggestion, Garavel smiled wider. "I like you."

"Really?" We'd only spent a day together and he was already using the little l word?

"I like all witches."

Right, the witch thing. "You must have served beside a lot of them. Or did you have a special one assigned to you?"

"It was one to a squad. We all relied upon her to protect us, keep us safe. One time, Serapha found a brook of pure water and we all leaped into it, even..." He frowned deeply and looked away. "They're all long gone."

"I'm sorry."

"You shouldn't be. You're here. You're exactly what I need. You're...nice."

"I'm nice?" I repeated, a hot coal bubbling in my stomach at the thought. It was dumb. I didn't need the demi-angel to fall in love with me. But nice?

Garavel drew closer. His once awkward steps smoothed out, and I didn't realize we were gliding across the floor until he lifted me onto my tiptoes. "Nice to listen, nice to talk, nice to touch. And what you did with your lips on mine…that was nicer than ice cream."

"Young lady!" Ink scolded. "How dare you take advantage of an inexperienced demi-angel without telling me of it. What is the state of his genitals?"

That all hit me at once. "You mean when I kissed you? Are you saying you'd never kissed before?"

Garavel shook his head. "It's softer than I expected. Warmer, too."

He was a dawn of creation virgin and I'd given him his first kiss on the floor of an abandoned kitchen? Oh, I was going to hell. As I fought to ignore the crass incubus comments buzzing in my ear, I stared up at Garavel. He didn't just glisten — he full-on glowed like the angel at the top of the Christmas tree. Instead of light, he radiated joy, and instead of warmth, my skin tingled in acceptance. My heart skipped about in my chest as he swung me in a circle, fully matching with the beat.

"There's so much more than kissing."

Garavel's cheeks pinked. "I know," he whispered, his head dipped as he stared at me sheepishly.

Whew, at least he knew sex existed. But then, how in all of his long, *long* years of existence had he never tried it? "Have you not wanted to give it a go?" I asked, then full body winced.

"If you do not pull that poor demi-angel into a room and ride him like a wanton Valkyrie, I shall lose all faith in you," Ink thundered in my ear.

We were in a room surrounded by the enemy on all sides. This was hardly the time or place to even be thinking about Garavel in that way, even if he held me so tight I could smell the sunlight on his skin. "I'm sorry, I shouldn't have asked."

"You're pretty. I like you, Layla. But I can't stay long. Once this is over, I will return to my creator's side."

"But that doesn't mean we won't see each other again. We can work together to fix all these other creatures threatening humans. You could even take a break for ice cream with me."

"No. My orders were to find what was causing the cracks in the realm. After that, my mission is finished."

This didn't make any sense. We worked well together. He'd worked with witches before. "Think of all that we could do to help people. Witch and demi-angel, together again, saving the world."

Garavel's radiant face crumpled into an internalized agony I couldn't understand. "While I'd like that a lot, it can't happen. I'm sorry."

"You're talking like you're going to die."

"I will not expire the way mortals do, not even the way my cracked and crushed brethren have. But I will be returned to slumber, waiting in endless sleep for when my creator has need of me again."

"When will that be?" My voice rose to a sharp crescendo that ended in a cymbal crash of tears.

Garavel tightened his hold on me, pressing my cheek to his chest. "I don't know."

"But you...you just got out. Woke up. Got to try ice cream. You have a cat."

I had a cat now, because he knew the whole time he wasn't long for this world. "That's not right." There were thousands of experiences Garavel would never know—careening down a waterslide, shoving his fist into a chocolate fountain, making love before a crackling fire. And the next time Ramiel deigned to wake up his bodyguard, nearly all of this world could be long gone. I'd be nothing more than dust in his eye.

"He can't do this to you. Tell him you need more time."

"I cannot lie to my creator. He formed me from the bones of this realm. I owe him my existence."

"Just because someone makes us doesn't mean they own us," I shot back, starting to tremble. My mother had abandoned me, walked away and left me to a system that'd rather I'd have died with her. I didn't owe her a damn thing.

"You do not understand." Garavel pivoted from a heart-wrenching pain to patriarchal patronizing in a second. I expected him to call me "child" and pat my head. Instead, he placed his cheek to mine and whispered, "You do not know duty."

I slapped my hands to his chest and pushed back. "Oh, I know duty. A duty to the people I love, to my friends...to myself. None of that means a thing to an..." Slowly the gap in couples around us and the heads swiveling in our direction dawned on me. "A real parent wouldn't take away their kid's life for their ends."

Garavel's once open and round face sharpened to deep shadows and hard lines. He stood even taller and folded his arms across his chest. "I'm not here for you," he said, stabbing the knife in just a few inches before finishing it off by walking away.

Fuck. I picked harder at the skirts, worrying the edges as my heart dropped into my stomach, then kept going. The band played louder, covering for the woman ripped of all dignity in the middle of the floor. The couples turned their backs, dancing in a circle so I was left out of their company. Loneliness was an ache that froze from the toes up to the eyes. This was an ice pick to the heart, stabbing incessantly with every reminder that in the end, everyone left me.

I tried to shuffle away, when my damn shoe caught on my hem. In my state, I was ready to rip the skirts off and run, but a cold hand caught my bare arm. Before I could even plant my foot, someone spun me around and I came face to face with my savior.

My jaw dropped.

"Shall we?" Mr. White asked, pulling me into a dance I couldn't escape.

Chapter Twenty-Three

One hand clamped over mine like an iron shackle and the other jammed against my waist like a spike. I tried to fold inward to escape, but he turned on his heel and there was no option left but to follow. Unlike with Garavel, these steps were precise and inescapable. My body had to obey.

He didn't say a word. Only the rising tempo of strings and French horn accompanied us as the guests moved farther and farther from their host. From the edges of their eyes, the monsters at the ball stared at me with pity.

Think of an excuse. Anything. Tell him you're going to bleed through your dress. That had to gross out male demons. I flexed my jaw, prepared to fling the first sentence that came to mind, when I stared him in the eye. His face would blend in with a board of top swindlers at any finance company. It was the eyes that revealed the truth.

Swirling in the nondescript gray irises marched a blanket of smoke. Inescapable, this smoke covered the sky, blotting away the sun until all hope drained away. Subjugation chilled through my marrow, breaking my shoulders and bowing my head. If he didn't have me pinned up, I'd have fallen to my knees.

What was the use of fighting? There was no challenging a creature like this. Even if we won, he'd return stronger than before.

Blink, Layla. Close your damn eyes.

It wasn't Ink yelling at me but my subconscious. I fought to do as it told, shutting my lids tight and turning my head away. The constraining smoke broke, tearing away the cloying defeat, but not the pressure constricting my chest. My skin itched where he touched me, like a caustic chemical slowly peeling away my flesh. I tugged, managing to slide my palm a half-inch out of his, when he finally spoke.

"You surprise me." Mr. White's voice should have boomed through the entire room, shaking walls like the blast of a sonic weapon. Instead, it was constrained and tight, each syllable emphasized with clarity. "I've never had someone daring enough to crash one of my parties since…since I began."

A panicked laugh slipped from me. "You must have me confused with someone else. I'm on the list."

"So I noticed. Crafty of you to employ a spirit. Who knew such old magic could finagle modern technology?"

Crap crap crap. If he knows I'm not entirely human, then what about…?

"A witch forming inroads with a ghost, most interesting."

"A…a what? You think I'm a witch? Like with crystals and incense? I think they prefer to be called Wiccans."

Mr. White pulled our conjoined hands closer and placed his thumb on my mask. I jerked away, trying to keep him from pulling it off. He smiled at that and I trembled from the maniacal glee.

"A cute parlor trick, my dear. To some here it might have even worked, but you're playing in the big leagues now. I'd suggest you employ better guards beyond a single werewolf and a demi-angel."

Don't hurt them. I squeezed my eyes tight, willing the panic out of them and my voice. "Mr. White, I presume."

"Ah, we're standing on formality. It's been many a century since I've enjoyed the pomp and ceremony." He dipped his head like a man greeting a fellow officer in the army, then he stared through me. "Is that it? Are you not going to declare my utter destruction? What about a grandstand upon the balcony about ending my reign?"

I kept my mouth shut, knowing when I was being handed the rope.

Mr. White tipped his head in surprise. "No? How interesting. Why then have you willingly walked into my domain if not to challenge me?"

"To party." It was the first stupid thing that came to mind, but it made him chuckle.

As he laughed, he turned us, and I realized every other couple had fallen into lock-step with him. When he put down his right foot, they did the same a millisecond after. The feet hit the floor like a drum line marching to battle. I spun my head, trying to see what magic was causing this, but there was nothing. No tingle raced through the air other than the oppression radiating from his being.

"What are you?" Oh, no. I'd said that one aloud.

The jolly laughter of a spider taunting the fly fell off. Mr. White's nondescript face contorted into a rictus of surprise. "You don't know? The wee witch willingly walks into the den of a master without knowing whose it is." He tipped his head back to laugh derisively and everyone else did the same.

I froze in place, but I couldn't stop dancing. Instead of moving my feet, he did it for me, pulling me with him without pause. Anger bubbled inside the harder I tried to stop and the longer I couldn't. He wouldn't cease laughing along with the others. I shouted above them, "Are you a demon?"

"A demon? I am as much of this realm as you are, as everyone here is…and soon shall be. I am the first, the trumpeter, the carrier of the banner to bring about the end of all things and the begging of the new. You know me without putting a name to it, as do all mortals scurrying about during their little lot of years. I consume, I take, I own, I am."

"You're greed."

"Ha! A puny sin such as that is nothing more than one man's regret in this world. I am both fear and want formed and fed by billions of souls." As he thundered, the suit melted into metal armor atop a white leather jerkin. His fedora transformed into a crown of tall black spikes. Red liquid continuously dripped down them.

"I am…" he boomed, shaking the windows and whipping the chandelier into a frenzy. In a snap, the armored king vanished. The Southern white suit hung off his shoulders, the crown returned to a fedora and the rest of the couples danced at their own speed. "That I am."

But the pressure wouldn't break. It hung off him more than any cloak could, shattering people's resistance in the name of…

"How many years has it been?"

I jerked in his arms, surprised to find I could. At my look of confusion, Mr. White smiled wider. "Sixteen? No, it must be fifteen."

My mother, he was talking about my mom. How did he...?

"It is quite easy to recognize the resemblance. You have her gritted jaw. She too read through the scattered spells of her grimoire, believed herself to be the next anointed champion of the cause. Perhaps you should ask her what happened next."

I clenched my hand tighter, digging my nails into the back of his. "She's dead."

"Now, we both know that isn't true. Though she did give me the slip for quite some time. Put me in a bit of a pickle there. Here I was fearing I'd have to spend the energy to hunt down her newly realized daughter. Thank you for coming straight to me and so unarmed."

Oh, shit. "It was you. You killed Sybil."

"I can't abide any free-roaming witches now. You'd understand if you could comprehend my plans. They come out the better for your kind as well. No more hunters, no more hiding behind snake oil stands and pretty rocks."

He was going to try to kill me. I moved to take a step, prepared to launch a fireball, when Mr. White pulled me into following him. I couldn't resist. He didn't have to try. He was going to kill me.

"Where are you going to do it? Here, in front of all your guests?"

Mr. White chuckled. "You think any here would weep for another dead witch? The applause would be thunderous. Perhaps I should remove your mask and reveal you to them." He dropped his hold on my back and reached for my mask. I managed to wrench my arm behind my head and grip onto the ribbons.

His gloved hands pierced through the eye holes. I strained against the force for my life. It was as if I stood in the middle of the hurricane. If I let go, if the ribbons broke, I'd be surrounded by a hundred enemies with no book and no hope. I leaned back, my teeth gritted, and a ribbon ripped.

Suddenly, Mr. White let go. The mask bounced against my cheekbones and nose, but I cinched it up twice as tight behind my head. In the commotion, I had managed to slip free of his hold. We stood staring eye to eye like combatants in an arena. I raised my hands, uncertain if I could go for my marker or make a fist, when he crossed his arms.

"I've decided I shall wait to finish you off. The night is young, after all."

"What?"

He smiled and turned away. The dancers shifted, giving him a gap without even looking. As he went, he raised a hand to wave goodbye. "Please, enjoy the party, Ms. Leeland."

For it will be your last.

Chapter Twenty-Four

"...Layla?"

Air hit my lungs like a lead weight, my body sucking in oxygen as I emerged from the dire dance of the man threatening to kill me. My vision wobbled and I grew lightheaded, but I clamped a hand to a wall and kept myself from falling. The party continued on without a care, people and creatures gathered in small groups to gossip about worldly affairs. But everyone gave me a wide berth.

"Layla!"

I jerked up and turned around, expecting to find Ink behind me. A man with scales and huge black eyes stared at me, then licked the top of his own head with a giant tongue. *Don't shudder.* I nodded my head, keeping my expression locked.

"Nice party," I said to him, hoping Ink would respond.

He sighed in exasperation and I could nearly hear him slapping his chest. "Finally. I seemed to be incapable of reaching you for some time. Yes, ghost,

I've reestablished connection. Calm down before you agitate the azaleas."

I glared away from the dance floor where Mr. White had captured me and up to the balcony. He stood before it, surveying the party with an amused sneer. "Do you know anything about a man of white who wears a crown of jagged black spikes?"

"A crown...?" Ink's cheery voice plummeted off a cliff. "Get out of there."

"We have to find proof of — "

"Forget the damn angel or his infernal feathers. Layla, if that is who I believe, you do not stand a fly's chance in a hurricane against Con–"

The giant French doors behind the ballroom burst open and the deer of my nightmares ran through. I reared back, along with the rest of the panicked guests, when the deer jerked and its fawn knee crashed to the floor. It bellowed loud enough to collapse the candles on the chandelier. A rope swung from the left and lassoed its muzzle. Whoever it was pulled on the deer's head, twisting it to the side, where another person in a floor-length white cloak grabbed the antlers and shoved the creature's head to the floor.

When it struck, my heart cried out for the poor thing. Its tongue flailed between the ropes, trying to work them off while it was held immobile below the foot on its head. The magic it ate must have worn off as the deer was no bigger than a basketball player. Its strength was drained, the creature only able to flail against the assholes pinning it down.

"We've brought dinner." Smoke roiled from inside the mysterious room, a shadow stomping closer. He dragged something on the floor, but I knew that voice in an instant. Eric raised his smarmy face to the crowd and, at their attention, he smiled below his tiny mask. "And dessert!" With great effort, he heaved a bag from behind him and hurled it across the floor.

The black fabric rolled, sending people skittering away. I struggled to peer around them to see what it was...when a human arm tumbled outside of the bag and to the ground. *No!*

Everyone ran away from what I dashed for, my mind screaming in rage and my heart refusing to face what I saw. "Cal? Cal!" Was he moving? I couldn't tell. *Please, god, let him be breathing.*

"Get the damn green skin," Eric ordered without a care.

Two of the cloaked werewolves advanced, hands out to grab me, but I wasn't having it. I wrenched out my marker and popped the cap off with my nail. Holding my hands wide, I conjured up a ball of fire. The mask on my face dissolved, the fire and ash rising into the wind. I revealed what I was to the entire room.

"If you..." I gulped, unable to say the word. "Hurt him—" I spun my marker down like a knife, and prepared to drop to my knees. "I'll hurt you."

"Cute." Eric snickered. "The meat shouldn't have been poking where he wasn't wanted. Kill her."

I didn't wait for them to make the first move. I planted my knee and jammed the Sharpie's felt tip right onto the oak floor. With a fast swipe, I drew the circle, then four lines through it. That glyph gave me lots of options. The werewolves took off, shedding their human skin and cloaks as they leaped into the air after me. I swung my hand around, willing the flame as large as a bonfire.

"Stop."

The werewolves fell to the ground in an instant in subjugation. Though they kept glaring at me as I too lowered my hand and snuffed out the flame on the floor. I didn't want to, but I didn't have a choice. Mr. White took complete control.

"You've displaced my itinerary, Eric, son of Lucien."

"I'm sorry," he murmured, the wild beast cowed into a sniveling pet by one look from Mr. White.

With everyone staring at him, the host glided toward the staircase. "It was to be cocktails and appetizers, then a dinner of delights in the grand hall before we approached the main event. Creatures of the moon, always in such a hurry."

Below Mr. White's bluster, a soft moan cut me to the quick. I spun around. Cal struggled to lift his head from the black bag. "Holy shit, thank you. Don't move." I caught his head in my lap. Cal groaned again and he raised his hand for my arm. Bending over, I placed my lips to his blood-stained hair and whispered the healing spell.

"Lay…la." He struggled to speak.

Heal him, damn it. His skin was so pale, his lips were turning blue. How much blood had they taken from him? How badly had they beaten him?

My tears couldn't stop, each one gumming up my mascara. I fought to blink. Whatever was happening with the deer and wolves was beyond my ability to care. "Cal, sit still. I'm here. I've got you. You're being healed, I promise."

"Layla," he said again, his voice growing stronger. That was the first sign of hope in this mess. He raised his head on his own and stared me in the eye. "Run. You have to get out of here."

"Not without you," I swore, casting the spell again. It was like pushing an elevator button over and over but I couldn't do anything else.

"I know what he is...what he wants." Cal dug his fingers into my shoulder and he hauled himself up. "He's going to—"

"Friends, compatriots." Mr. White stopped beside the poor deer, which was struggling to sit up. Eric's foot covered the entire deer's head while the scariest monster here stood next to them both. He folded his hands together like a patient priest. "Since time began, we've existed under the tyranny of the accord. A decision made by absent celestials to unfairly punish those they created constrains and demeans us. Is this fair?"

A chorus of "No's" rang out around us.

"We did not choose the order of the cosmos—they did. We did not decide our place within the realms— they did. We did not pick our jailers—they decreed it."

My skin prickled and I caught angry and murderous eyes glaring from all corners of the room. Not at Eric, not at Mr. White, not even at the mutant deer. It was all aimed at me.

"For too long we've accepted their decree as law. But what use is an absent god? What fear can they instill in their creation once they've abandoned it? Do we not have the right to govern ourselves?"

"Yes!" the lizard man from before screamed, his fist raised to the air.

"I've danced to their tune, delighting in the destruction of the mortals they've coddled in their quest for equality. Destruction they so ordained. But it grows wearisome to renew the cycle, hoping for change while knowing that nothing in this realm truly changes.

Life begins, grows, dies then begins anew. So it is for each of us, trapped in this miserable realm of static."

"What are you going to do about it?" a brave voice called from the back of the room. "What can anyone do about it?"

For a flicker, the crown appeared on Mr. White's head, his mouth black as pitch and teeth gnarled as thorns. But when he smiled, it all vanished. The picture of civility returned. "That is why I invited you here. You see this creature before you? Beautiful, isn't it? Impossible, as well. It is a feaster of magic, a creation before the realms came to be, kept to the lands where the celestials dwell."

Mr. White stepped closer to the trapped deer. He brushed his palm down the velvety antlers while staring around at the crowd. "I brought it here."

"You're full of shit!" the same voice shouted. Mr. White didn't respond. He didn't even glance at the owner. It was Eric who jerked his chin to one of the kowtowing werewolves. In an instant, they transformed, bounding through the parting crowd.

I could only hear a soft shriek of panic, then the clamp of teeth puncturing and tearing flesh before the silence returned. Mr. White continued to pet the deer at his feet. The creature rolled its doe eyes up to him, as if it believed he was its salvation.

"All those realms, separated in the name of protection, equality, constraint, punishment. Realms of wonder and beauty, never before seen or long since lost to those trapped here." He stood and a long sword of steel appeared at his side. It shone so bright my eyes burned. Mr. White steadied the blade, then he looked to the deer. Raising his weapon high, he shouted, "All those realms are about to come crashing down."

"Conquest!"

White's blade froze mid-decapitation and he, along with the crowd, turned to the man perched on the balcony railing. Garavel too had his sword raised, his wings extended as he glared down at the man. "You shame your betters!" he shouted and aimed the blade at Mr. White.

"A celestial's lap dog has come to stop us." Mr. White swung his sword around just as Garavel leaped to him. The angel's blade was twice the width of White's light beam, but when the two clanged, it was White who pushed Garavel off.

Sliding across the floor, Garavel unfurled a wing and dipped it to the ground. His head shot up and he stared with radiant rage at White. "After everything they gave you, you would tear this realm to pieces." Garavel swung hard. When the blades met, a crumpling energy reverberated through the air. I folded down against Cal, pinning his head against my chest.

"Your war is over. Return to dust like the rest of your kind," White said.

Garavel's eyes opened wide and he screamed, "For the honor of Ramiel!" He ran, fueled by a blind rage, straight at White. Garavel had the strength, the reach, the blade. He slammed his sword down through White's, knocking it to the ground. But when he reared back, prepared to strike a killing blow, White clasped his hand to Garavel's forehead.

Oh, shit! The dark brown skin began to peel away, Garavel's eyes rolling back as he sank to his knees. "If you think I of all creations can be cowed by an angel's tin soldier!" White thundered, staggering to his feet. As he did, blood wept from his eyes, staining his cheeks.

His skin turned as pale as his name. He jammed his hand tighter, causing Garavel to cry out. "Know that you failed him. Grind to dust with the final thought that your creator is nothing but another casualty."

I had to do something. Garavel was flailing, trying to get a grip to White's arm, but every time he touched it, he slipped away. *What can I even do in the face of so much...?*

Power was magic and White was throwing around a shit ton of it like an all-a-deer-could-eat buffet. I bounced my hand, trying to get a small fireball going. The others weren't looking at me, not the werewolf cultists, not the guests. But when I threw it, White dodged. He pivoted his chin to stare at me.

"Your aim is as abysmal as your plan."

I formed another fireball, trying to concentrate as much magic as I could into it. This one I hurled even wider, causing White to laugh while he peeled away Garavel's life. A bellow shattered the windows and White's chuckling stooped.

The deer shook its head, snapping the ropes. It rose to seven feet, then ten and it kept going. The antlers strained across the whole of the ceiling of the ballroom. As it got a hoof under itself, it turned its blood red eye on the tastiest meal in the room. White released Garavel just as the deer's massive hand swiped for him. He unleashed his sword, slicing into the deer's palm. The creature screamed, the sound ripping apart the floor below us.

I rolled along with Cal, the entire ballroom shuddering. White swung his sword. The deer slammed its antlers down, deflecting the blow and sending a slice of light straight through the chandelier. "Fuck!" I shouted, pulling and scrambling with Cal as the massive light fixture pulled a *Phantom of the Opera*. It crashed through the rupturing floorboards, the silver horses on the chandelier whinnying in rage and fire dancing across the shattered oak.

"Layla, get out of here," Cal said, fighting to get to his feet.

"What about Garavel?" As I asked, the angel shook his head. Dust rained from the open gash in his forehead, but with each twist, his skin regrew, hiding away what White had done. He reached across the floor for the grip of his sword and began to stand. White turned from the deer, matching him blow for blow.

"Eric? Rid me of this troublesome angel."

"No problem." Eric strode forward and reached for Garavel. The angel slashed with his sword, but he was still drained from White. Eric dodged the first slice, causing Garavel to stumble. He scrambled to right himself and face Eric. The werewolf glared at him and swung his fist.

I only saw the blur, gray and white fur leaping past and latching onto Eric's arm. He screamed, proving the brute was capable of feeling anything, then Cal bit down even harder. Blood spilled across the floor, slicking up both shoes and paws. Eric couldn't shake Cal off, so he brought his other fist around to punch in his skull. Before he could strike, Garavel caught his arm.

"Mage-damned werewolves," he cursed and smashed in Eric's nose. The crunch churned my stomach, but all the werewolf did was laugh.

Cal got his feet to the ground, and he tried to tug Eric back. The thug lashed out with his foot and Cal had no choice but to let go. As he did, he dashed out of reach and planted his paws. Garavel shifted his sword to his other hand, then revealed a flail from his wing-arsenal.

Eric laughed, his arm and face both dripping in blood. "Two on one hardly seems fair," he said, taking a step back. Neither Cal nor Garavel would give him an inch, both prepared to go in for the kill, when the bleeding nose sprouted longer. Red fur erupted across Eric's back, shredding his tuxedo. He grew even bigger than before, muscles sprouting on top of muscles like a demented comic book character. The grinning smile filled with fangs. In a strangled voice, Eric said, "Now the fun begi—" He finished transforming before the setting sun and leaped for Garavel.

The angel swung the flail, aiming for Eric's jaw, but the massive wolf caught it and bit straight through the metal. Eric lunged for Cal, who had enough sense to keep his distance. I folded my hand into a cone and whispered the spell for ice. As each one formed in my palm, I hurled the makeshift spears at Eric. They bounced off his fur like headless arrows.

"Witch!"

Oh crap, I forgot about the bigger problem.

Garavel lunged, making a dent in Eric's armor, but I had to look away from my guys in the fight of their lives. My own was on the line.

With one arm, White held on to the antlers the size of a bus. The deer screamed in rage, kicking its hooves and pulverizing the wall. There wouldn't be much of the house left when this was over.

"I've had enough of your interference." He extended not his sword but a beam of light from his hand that sharpened to a razor edge. Without taking his eyes off me, he yanked the deer's head and plunged the blade straight into the poor animal's brain. It stopped fighting and crashed to the ground. The eyes faded to milky white and its tongue tumbled from the bony jaws.

The blood of the deer sparked off of White's blade. It crackled like lightning, splattering burning clots against the walls. But the blood on the blade charred to form a new weapon, a spike of such power I couldn't look at it nor could I look away. My jaw clenched so tight, I could hear my teeth bending.

"Enjoy oblivion," White said. He hurled the spike of blood and power straight at me.

"Layla!" Garavel shouted.

As the spike flew, time and air shifted. First it hardened to solid steel, then water, then to smoky oxygen. I struggled to follow the spike with my eye, its ends straining back then looping forward and around into a circle. There was no time for me to escape, no time to do anything but move my toe.

A shield flew up from my glyph, my foot connecting all four corners at once. With a massive clang, the spike burrowed straight into a wall of iron and I breathed a sigh of relief. It was my last hail Mary, but it worked. Whatever White could throw at me, I... The iron wall began to shake and the outer layer rusted up as if a thousand years had passed in a second. In a blink, the rusted section collapsed, only for another layer of orange rust to form around it. The blood spike was still moving.

I took a step back, trying to think of the incantation for the shield that stopped bullets. *There's a da, no, it started with a nell... Ah!* My brain flipped every syllable in the spell I'd memorized. I needed Daniel. He'd know it. I was worthless without him.

Fighting off the tears, I clenched my hand tight and willed my lips to remember what my mind couldn't.

"De nala te—"

The wall shattered. The spike broke free, flying at the same speed as before. I held my breath, hoping death wouldn't hurt, when a leg smashed into my knee from behind. I tumbled to the left, watching the blood spike come close to striking my chest...then just my arm, before it would sail right on past. My side bounced on the hard floor, causing me to breathe and twist up.

The edge of the spike sliced along my cheek and I fell into darkness.

Chapter Twenty-Five

The world was nothing and everything. I closed my eyelids but could still see a sky that pulsed with the beat of a heart and an unending valley not of grass and dirt, but flayed tissue and muscle. No wind tugged at my hair. The air was dead and thick as pudding. If I raised my hand, tendrils of other hands followed behind before ramming together to form mine.

"Hello?" I called. My words punctured through the sky like a rock tossed into a pond. I watched them travel up in a curve before falling back onto me. The one word pounded into my ears, slamming my brain deeper into my skull as I crumpled to my knees.

Cradling my head for protection, I bit my lip hard to keep from whimpering in pain. Any other sound would hit harder. Where the hell was I?

I raised my right arm and heard the heavy clink of a chain. A shackle was locked around my wrist, the chain trailing ahead down the narrow passage to darkness.

Oh god, was this actually hell? Had he killed me and I'd been dragged into the pits, same as Ink?

The chain tugged, rising higher and pulling me with it. I thought to try to pull back just as it slackened and drooped to the floor. It coiled like a serpent waiting to strike and I tried to step away, and my back slammed into a wall. I spun around and stared upward at the edge of nothing. The sky, the ground, the very air all vanished to a darkness that was colder than anything in nature. Shivering, I leaped away, only for my foot to catch on the chain.

At the sound, I ducked deeper into my shoulders. Slowly, the chain rattled back behind me, tightening the links until it extended taut off my wrist. If this was hell, then shouldn't Ink be here?

The chain flew up again, wrenching me around to stare down the path. Before I could fight back, it fell once again. Wait. *Ink?*

Sure enough, the chain pulled. This was our bond, the way he'd find me. The cold of nothing froze my back. I gripped onto the chain and started to walk, then run. Ink was at the other end. He'd know how to get me out of here. He'd shown me this place once before when revealing himself. Except the sky hadn't looked like an inside-out heart, and there'd been flames everywhere. *What has changed?*

Lightning twirled across the organ plains, spreading up into the clouds. It branched out, forming a nervous system clear above my head. I'd almost think it beautiful if everything wasn't trying to kill me.

"Ah!" Cold bit into my heel. It surged through my feet, causing them to ache worse than going barefoot in the snow. I feared I'd fall over, but I couldn't stop. Ink was at the other end. I kept grabbing the chain, yanking myself ahead while the nothingness pursued me from behind.

My foolish cry burst ahead like a runaway train. It punctured the darkness, swirling it apart like smoke to reveal an outline. It wasn't even a shadow, but a hint of a lighter gray among the black. A man's silhouette turned toward me. Ink?

The cold seized through my fingers and bit at my nose. I couldn't stop, even as I watched my loud cry of pain turn around and come rushing back. It tunneled the air apart, splitting off into chunks of razor blades. As they spun off, the sky cracked, edges of the red torn away to reveal an icy blue or turbid green. At the center of the spiraling vortex was a death-punch barreling straight for my chest.

Ink! I kept running and closed my eyes tight. Even so, I still saw my end coming for me from both ahead and behind. They'd smash me to pieces in this hell world. The shadow twitched, Ink's silhouette growing more opaque. Eyes of fire blazed from the face as it turned to look to me. I worked link by link over the chain, the cold metal burning my palms. The blast of my scream shuddered the air, shoving the last of my oxygen out of my lungs, while the frozen nothingness drenched my back in ice. I couldn't dodge. I couldn't run.

I was out of options. I'd die in this inside-out world without anyone even knowing. Fear pounded in my chest and I opened my mouth to shriek. My palm touched a warm hand in a shackle just like mine. I clung to Ink's forearm and the world inverted.

Light pounded into my eyes and I stumbled against hard, inescapable ground. Blind, I reached out for my incubus, but felt only air. *Ink? Where are you?*

"Layla?"

Even though they burned, I fought to open my eyes. It felt like a paper cut was searing across my eyeballs, but I kept going until I caught the tattered edge of a jean jacket. "Daniel?" I gasped, wanting to reach out to touch what I knew I couldn't. He dropped to a knee beside me. Why would he have to do that? He wasn't very tall.

"Layla." Daniel raised his hand to my cheek, his ghostly cold warm against my frozen flesh. "What the hell happened?"

"I don't…" I began when I raised my hand to him. Instead of my fingers, withered clumps of flesh dangled from the knuckles. I stared in shock at the gnarled tree roots where my hand should be and screamed.

"What happened to you? Layla?"

"Fuck!" My other hand was the same, and my feet… They'd curled in on themselves, rotting away to nothing until my shoes fell off and I'd crashed to the ground. I couldn't stop screaming and shaking, my gray and brittle corpse hands trembling before me.

"Layla. Listen to me. You have to heal yourself."

"I can't. I can't. I can't. Help me. Please?" I tried to reach for him, but Daniel recoiled at the horror on my arms. The stretch was too much and I crumbled to the ground, slamming my gnarled palms down. Pain seared up both my arms so hard my jaw fell open but no sound could come out.

"You can do it, Layla." Daniel dropped even lower until he could look me in the eye. But I wouldn't turn away from my mutilated hands. "Look at me. Listen to me. You have to heal yourself. It's the only hope before this gets… Layla, please!"

Daniel reached up. I tried to wrench my horrifying hands away, but he cupped his over mine, hiding them from me.

"What if it doesn't work?" I moaned, my future twisting in the wind. The pain bounded against my head, shoving my despair deeper into my skull with every swing. I couldn't escape this. I wasn't strong enough.

"It will. Layla, I believe in you. Say the spell. Please."

The spell. I'd whispered it to Cal, who... *No, don't think about him recoiling in horror at these*. I pictured the page in my book, trying to recall the words scrawled across them. I had left them, Cal and Garavel. They were fighting for their lives, but I wasn't there.

"Cal's in danger, someone has to... Ah!"

"For the love of god, Layla, heal yourself now," Daniel thundered in a voice that drilled straight through every fear in my head. The words came to me. I struggled to get them out through the gasps of pain and tears.

But as the last syllable slipped past my lips, the agony dampened. Daniel held my hands, keeping them invisible, so I kept repeating the spell on myself while he spoke. "Push through this. Please. You have to keep fighting, then we can save the rest. Right now, you're all that matters. Please."

Daniel bent his head over mine, the chill of his lips caressing my forehead as he whispered, "Don't give up."

I strained my hands, every joint aching, but they were whole again. Red and puffy fingers popped out from between Daniel's clasped hands and he slipped back. I patted my palms together, wincing at the pain, but so glad to feel them. With a grit in my jaw, I stood up. My feet felt even worse than my hands and my body teetered as I rose and met Daniel eye to eye.

"Thank you," I said, and my protector smiled.

"I can't find her anywhere..." Ink shouted, appearing out of nowhere just as I had.

"Oh, thank god." I crumbled into Ink's surprised arms.

He caught me and tenderly caressed the back of my head while asking, "Layla? How are you out here? I went to retrieve you from the ruckus."

"I don't know," I moaned, burying my face into his shoulder. The old-fashioned coat smelled of cedar and backstage, but I kept breathing until I found the brimstone below. "I think...I think I traveled between realms."

"That isn't possible," Ink said.

"I followed our chain back to you, but you weren't here," I explained.

"Oh, my bond. I heard you, I tried to find you, but it was as if..." He cupped my cheeks and stared at my tear-stained face. Slowly, Ink placed a kiss to my forehead and he guided me back to his warm shoulder. "As if you vanished from this realm."

"Whatever it was, it damn near killed her," Daniel said.

"Mortals are not designed to travel through the between. How? Why? How again?"

We could puzzle all of this out later. I tried to push back, but Ink held me longer as if he couldn't let go. "It doesn't matter. Garavel and Cal are fighting for their lives against..."

An explosion erupted into the air. Debris rose into the sky, splintered floorboards and roof tiles twisting in a miniature tornado directly over White's house. The entire structure was obliterated, the frame sucked into the vortex and sprayed across five city blocks.

"I don't think that's as much of a concern now," Ink said.

I shoved him aside and ran toward the twister of destruction. *I'm coming, Cal.*

"If you intend to risk ruin, you will require this." Ink appeared beside me, keeping pace without showing any strain. When I saw the red leather, I scooped my hands around my book and clutched it to my chest. As I did, my locket knocked into my arm and I cupped it in my hand.

"Thank you," I breathed. I hadn't realized how wrong I was without it.

"Now I know I made a grave error, but we are out of time to question it." Ink jabbed a finger toward the carnage on the street. Car alarms shrieked from walls smashed through their windows. The catering van had the entire chandelier on top of its crumpled roof. People lay in the streets, dazed or worse.

The decadent Victorian home was gone. It looked like a bomb had landed on it, ripping away every nail and beam down to the foundation. I skidded to a halt, trying to peer through the haze of sheetrock dust and whatever secrets White had blown up in his quest for power.

Darkness rose from the ashes. I hoped for the heads to look familiar, but they huddled close in formation and walked on all fours. At the lead was the red wolf, nearly as big as a compact car. Eric stepped into the moonlight, tipped his head back and howled. The rest of the pack joined in, werewolves quickly filling the sidewalk. As their cry faded, Eric turned his head and beamed death from his eyes. He pulled his wolf lips back, leaving a terrifying rictus rimming his bloody fangs.

I raised my book up, prepared to cast spells and smash his head in with it. "So help me, if you did anything to Cal!" I screamed, when a shadow dropped behind me. Before I could turn to fight it off, hands locked around my stomach and lifted me straight off the ground.

"Fuck you, you—"

"You're very wiggly. Good thing I can grip tight," Garavel said.

Despite his gentle chiding, I turned in his arms, not believing he was alive until I saw his face. "You're...you're okay? Where's Cal? What happened?"

"Whatever you did, or Conquest did, made the house get very angry very quickly. It expelled everyone inside, except for the cursed werewolves."

Cal...

I remembered the blood oozing from Eric's teeth and I shuddered. "Where are we going? I have to go back!"

"That's probably not a good idea. Conquest didn't seem very happy." Garavel flapped higher, taking us away from the destruction of the party to the silent shadows of the rooftops.

"I don't care if White's shitting hot tacks right now. I have to save him. Let me go!" I banged my fist on Garavel's chest, but the angel wouldn't let up. His powerful wings gave a downward burst, rocketing us up the sheer windows of a bank building. "Please. Please, let me go back to him."

Garavel didn't say anything, only held his head back as we both flew up over the edge of the building and he dropped a foot to the roof. Now his arms opened and I stumbled away, unable to reach Cal, to save him if he was...if they'd...

"Layla?"

Oh, god! I flung my arms around him, nearly sending both of us tumbling to the ground. But Cal held me up as I blubbered against his naked chest. "I thought you were dead!"

"I thought the same of you. You just... I don't even know what happened."

"Me either. It was..." I shivered against the heat of his nude body, my mind filling with the chill of nothing that had nearly consumed me. "Bad."

I waited for Cal to argue, or even give me an 'I told you so', but he gently pressed back my hair, peeling each twist from my sweaty forehead. "I can tell," he whispered.

"How are you here? On a roof?" Not eviscerated by his half-brother.

Cal raised his head and tipped it to Garavel. "He saved me. When the house exploded, he plucked me off the ground and flew the both of us out of reach."

I reached over to take Garavel's hand. He let me hold him but gave a wide berth to Cal. "I did not do it for you," Garavel declared.

It didn't matter. I didn't need them all to get along. I needed them to be alive. "Thank you," I said, shaking Garavel's wide hand in both of mine while Cal pressed his nose to my cheek and breathed in.

"You're real," he sputtered, his voice full of the same tears in my eyes.

I clung to Cal while holding Garavel's hand. Now that I knew he was living, I took the time to notice the cuts on his cheeks and a bruise over his nose. Three deep gashes sliced across his chin and down his throat, but he couldn't stop smiling as he stared at me. "You look terrible," I said, laughing at the stupidity of it all.

He snickered as well and stared down at his naked form. "I never could pull off a tux. But you...you're beautiful even after walking out of a hurricane."

I kissed his sweet but lying lips, the tears of joy and fear mingling across our cheeks at the momentary touch of bliss. Cal cupped my cheek as he drew his tongue across my lips, tasting me. I opened my mouth, needing the same.

"I'm uncertain about settling down in this area. What are the schools like? How many invading Huns? Two thousand? Ten?"

At Ink's sarcastic entrance, I broke the kiss, but tapped Cal's cheek twice with my thumb before turning from him. My incubus didn't have a hair out of place or button popped, but his eyes had dulled with exhaustion and a wear I couldn't place. Rather than stand aloof from the joyful reunion, Ink slipped a hand to my waist. He didn't fight Cal for me and left us wrapped up in each other. But he held me too in his own way, reminding me I wasn't alone.

"I must return to my creator and warn him of the threat. If we don't stop this Rider, it will be...bad."

"Would you even say very, very bad?" Ink asked Garavel, but Cal groaned.

"He's right. This whatever White is...he wants to destroy the world."

"And here I thought you humans had that one on lock. He'll have to work hard to beat you at your own game," Ink said with a wry smile, but I could tell he was dancing away from something. Or worse, he was hiding something.

"I couldn't make a dent. You couldn't make a dent," Cal said to Garavel. "He nearly got to Layla." He squeezed me tighter before he turned to Ink. "What about you? Can you hurt him?"

"He's like you, isn't he?" I asked. "White, he said he was born out of fear and want. Just like you were born out of…"

Ink frowned deeply and I realized I was sharing a secret he didn't want known. But I had to understand what we were facing, what was coming to kill us. "In comparison to what White is, I am little more than a grain of sand on an entire continent. Though, in essence, we are the same in that he cannot be killed. Hurt…perhaps."

"Because you can't kill lust, you can't kill greed. It's always there, lurking in our souls, our minds. We need it to survive."

"You feed it because you're human," Ink said. "White is unbreakable as long as there is something to conquer."

"Here you all are." Daniel gasped as if he'd been out of breath. "I've been popping all over the damn place trying to get to you. Why was a part of my bone left outside the donut shop?" He aimed his accusation at Ink, who shrugged with all the innocence of a cartoon devil.

"Everyone loves donuts."

"You selfish, inconsiderate man-child. Can you think of anyone but yourself?"

For a beat Ink darted his gaze to me before he homed in on only Daniel. "You spit 'selfish' as if self-preservation was a curse and not a boon. Perhaps if you'd have had a bit more you wouldn't be in this" —

Ink waved his hand straight through Daniel's chest —
"powerless predicament."

"We can gather up all of Daniel's bits later." Cal
tried to mediate between them, causing Ink to snicker.

"You'll have to duel the worms for them."

"I don't know how anyone can stand your
pernicious tongue," Daniel fumed.

"Shall we ask our beloved?" Ink cocked his head at
me, all four men staring my way. Before, I'd have
blushed so hard my cheeks would have turned red. But
that night, hiding on a roof away from a creature trying
to bring about the apocalypse, all I could do was stare
back.

"Ramiel," Garavel whispered to himself. It drew the
attention off of Ink and his tongue's prowess. "He is a
celestial. He can stop Conquest. He will stop Conquest.
The creature has disobeyed his purpose and openly
declared war on the accord."

Garavel stood tall and spread his wings. Red beacon
lights danced among the white feathers as he strode for
the edge. A howl broke out from between the buildings,
causing Garavel to sneer. "We have our answer. I will
take you to my creator where we shall present the truth.
You can take your prize, then he and I will deal with
Conquest and the rest of the vermin."

I had nearly forgotten about the feathers in all of
this. Guilt struck me and I held tight to the locket in my
hand while glancing over at Daniel. He'd dropped his
gaze as if he too were thinking the same. End of the
world felt a lot bigger than bringing one person back
from the dead.

"Okay," I said, stepping toward Garavel. He
wrapped an arm around my waist and plucked me off
my feet. As I fell into his arms, he walked us to the edge.

"Hold a moment, sunshine." Ink touched Garavel on the arm. He then hauled up Cal the same way Garavel had me. "We're coming too."

Chapter Twenty-Six

Despite it being my second time, the plunge through the tunnel still unnerved me. I clung tighter to Garavel's shoulders, my face pressed to his chest until my feet hit stone. "You're safe," he promised, the smile of a saintly statue pinned across his cheeks.

I unbuckled my fingers from behind his neck and staggered back just as light struck through the darkness. Garavel raised his sword and I lifted my tender hands for a fight. An inch-tall flame flickered on the end of Ink's finger and he smiled.

"You took your time," he said, blowing out the candle on his hand.

"The wind was stronger than I expected," Garavel explained as if it wasn't going to take longer than the speed at which my incubus traveled.

"Cal?"

"Your moon-addled paramour is fine." Ink stepped back as Cal rose from the stone ground. He was still naked, which didn't seem to bother anyone else. I fought to keep my eyes level with his even as I wanted to leap into his arms.

"Did we land?" Daniel phased into the room by my side. He stared at Ink first, the two of them sneering at the other, then he looked to me. "Finally. I was getting real tired of falling every time I tried to find you."

Ink chuckled mercilessly at the idea while I held my hand out for him. Daniel stared at my fingers that were much less red than before. He was the only one who had seen the horrors they'd become. *Would he…?* I lost control as Daniel slipped his hand in mine. He pulled my fingers to his mouth. Even with the ghost controlling them, I couldn't touch his lips, but the chill caressed down my knuckles.

I leaned toward him and Daniel whispered, "We can find another way."

Slowly, I shook my head. Not in stopping Mr. White, not in saving him from death. Ramiel was our first and last hope. "I don't know why I don't keep sunscreen in here," I said, lifting my purse.

Daniel frowned. "Don't stay in there too long." I didn't need to hear the "or else."

"This place is weird," Cal said, staring up at the ceilings with pillars of limestone and salt dangling off of golden mosaics.

"It is one of the last bastions of my kind, a haven in the war," Garavel said, his voice dead as he glared at the werewolf trespassing in his territory. "You are the first to ever step paw here."

"I…guess I feel honored to walk around in an angel's broken basement," he tried to joke, but it crashed to the ground. Everyone was battered, worried and exhausted.

Garavel didn't approach the door, nor did Ink or Cal. We all stood where we had landed, trying to not make eye contact. Calling on a celestial felt like ordering an orbital nuclear strike on a clogged toilet, but we were out of options. Maybe if I was really nice and demure? That was something angels liked, right? My mother's lack of religion snapped back at me. What I knew about angels could fit onto the head of a pin.

"Are you ready?" I asked, raising my head and staring at Garavel.

His mouth dropped at me being the one to start this, but he nodded deeply. I took a step for him and the big door, when Cal touched my arm. Ink added his as well, both reaching for my hands as if they were about to whisk me away.

"While I would never question your magical wisdom," Ink said, causing everyone there to roll their eyes, "are you certain this path is wisest? People will not know to…"

Look away. What would happen if a phone or traffic cam caught the angel? Could the screen protect them or would even more eyeballs melt from the recording? "Give me another option," I pleaded, wishing he had one.

Ink sighed and turned away. His fingers slipped from my wrists down my palm. I tightened my grip and pulled him back. Surprise flared in his eyes as I kissed him, then the flames caught. Ink graced my kiss with his laugh, his hellfire chuckle knocking straight to my core. "Once this is finished, we will require an orgy of unfathomable debauchery."

What an incubus would consider debauchery sounded terrifying…and intriguing. "Sounds —"

The entire cavern shuddered. One of the stalactites cracked, the rock icicle plunging to the ground and shattering a small bench below it. Garavel snapped up higher and hefted his sword off his back.

"What in the devil is that?" Cal asked. "Earthquake?" Another tremor hit, this one with less force but louder. Its echo struck off the walls and ceiling.

Garavel walked away from the grand door to a section of the wall made of darker bricks than the rest. He raised his sword high and the blade began to glow with the phases of the moon. "The vermin have found a way in."

"Uh, vermin?" Cal said.

"He refers to werewolves."

"I got that. I'm just not a fan of being compared to disgusting rats."

"Rats are quite clean, really. They often bathe themselves," Daniel needlessly chimed in when an explosion burst from the other side of the wall. It sent a stalactite careening from the ceiling straight through his body.

"How are they breaking through all the defenses?" Garavel asked.

"Bombs. People don't often look into crazy off-the-grid compounds, even if they order a lot of fertilizer," Cal said gravely.

"We must speak with Ramiel now." Garavel dashed to my side and picked up my hand. Before he could open the magic door, he pointed his blade to Ink. "You, demon, you are capable of breaking stone?"

"On occasion."

"Obliterate that pillar there, but not the others. Use it as a blockade to slow them down. They will believe their fire has broken through fully and run into it. Which should give you..." Now he pointed his sword to Cal. Both glared at each other, Garavel's blade glowing brighter with the moons. "You should have an opening to attack unseen from the side."

Cal broke his death glare to look to me. It all sounded impressive, so I gave a little nod, but he wasn't looking to me for advice. He placed his hand above his heart and mouthed, "I love you," before shifting into the fur.

"What about me?" Daniel asked. "I could scout ahead." To back up his claim, he stuck his hand through the wall.

"No!" Garavel shouted so loudly that Daniel yanked it back.

Ink laughed at him a moment then sighed. "Amateurs." He sliced his claws clean through a pillar the width of a man, then moved to cut the other side.

"We don't want them to know this place is protected...though the stench of their fellow wolf will. Stand in the middle where their first line of sight will land. It will confuse the beasts so they'll attack you first."

Daniel nodded solemnly and moved to his spot while Ink raised a hand and laughed. "Using the ghost as bait. I like this one. Can we keep him?" As he asked, he shoved the pillar with his elbow and the slab tumbled to the ground.

I shook my head at Ink's nonchalance. Garavel handed me the same white blindfold of before. I began to lift it to my eyes, when Ink dashed for me.

"Wait a moment." He tugged on the buttons of his coat, slipped it off then guided it around me. The scent of brimstone and an amber cologne flooded through me. Ink brushed his thumb over my cheek, and he stared into my eyes. "So you don't get burned."

Some tiny part of my brain knew he was worried about himself. If I melted my brain from the angel, he went back to hell. But my heart wouldn't stop its delusional pounding. "I lo—"

The wall buckled. Ink spun around and dashed to the side, his demon skin crackling where the ancient dust landed. Garavel took my hand. "We have to go."

I held the blindfold up and felt him tying it in a hurry. "Do you have this?" I shouted to my guys. Garavel took my hand as I slipped into darkness. He pulled me toward the door, but I kept staring back, waiting for an answer.

"They are all nodding, Lady Witch. Let's get out of here."

I heard him opening the door to the angel's chambers, a haunting cry coming from the bricks themselves. Garavel didn't drop my hand for a moment, so I leaned with him to retrieve what felt like his sword. He walked me forward ten paces then turned around.

The sounds of stone rolling over stone were eclipsed by a great explosion behind. I spun around and took a step, only for Garavel's hand to land on my chest.

Howls erupted from the chamber along with the crack of shattered bricks hitting the wall. "Ink!" I shouted. "Cal?"

"We cannot help them," Garavel said. I tried to shove his hand away, but I was blind and his arm immovable.

A yelp shattered the air and all I could picture was Cal at my feet. I had reached out for them when the stone door slammed shut. In an instant, light burst around us. It warmed my bones inside and out, but I remembered the burn.

Sliding Ink's sleeves down, I bunched my fists away inside the jacket. Garavel held onto my arm as we walked toward the angel on his throne. Or so I guessed. I couldn't see anything, thank god.

"My creator." Garavel released me in order to fall to his knees. I heard the clang of his sword striking the stone, then felt a rush of air. Had he opened his wings to fully bow?

"You've brought death to my home, Garavel," Ramiel said. "And Azrael is long since retired to his home in hell."

"We have news, your greatness."

That was a new one. Just how bad of a situation had I walked into?

"We require your arm as well."

"I have not raised it in eons, Garavel." The voice shifted closer, followed by the sound of a dragging cape. Ramiel must have gotten off his throne.

"We've learned the answer to the question you put to us." Garavel too changed, his voice coming from straight ahead instead of near my feet. He reached behind and took my arm. "The realms' unraveling is the work of Conquest."

Ramiel chuckled once. "You must be mistaken. Conquest is nothing more than… A greater being than him must be at the heart."

"I saw with my own eyes. He ripped through the realms and plucked one of the primordial creatures to this land."

Silence fell. Ramiel was either shocked by that revelation or he had wandered off to get coffee. It was up to Garavel to keep going. "He blasphemed against the celestials. Considers himself above you, above everyone who gave him breath. He will bring about the destruction of every realm."

"So you came to me to obliterate the creature known as Conquest," Ramiel summed up.

I tightened at the tone in his voice. It had changed from bored ruler dealing with paperwork to a sharp note of discord. I couldn't say why, but I was glad Garavel was between us. The light increased, causing me to shut my eyes even behind the blindfold. My skin baked wherever it touched.

"My most loyal of soldiers," Ramiel said.

"We were all loyal." Garavel sounded like he'd been kicked at that instead of proud of the compliment. "We all guarded you with our lives. The others..."

"Yes, they sacrificed themselves — at your orders — before the gates of our citadel."

What? He'd sent his own soldiers to their deaths? What about the witches? What about Cal and Ink?

"A glorious end to that which I gave life," Ramiel continued without a shred of sympathy. I tried to pull my hand away from Garavel, but he cinched tighter to it. "Thank you for bringing this to my attention, Garavel. You may return to your post."

The light turned and I pulled in a gasp of air. Tears welled up behind the blindfold, smearing salt into my eyes, but I didn't dare move. Ramiel shifted, dragging his cape along the ground.

"My creator, I don't understand."

"As you said, you found the answer I sought. Your time amongst the mortals is over. Return to your deathless slumber."

He couldn't be serious.

"But Conquest, he will rip apart the realms. All that you and your siblings worked for, the gift you gave us, will be undone."

"Oh, Garavel." The light burned hotter than before and I heard a patronizing tap of a palm to a cheek. Suddenly, Ramiel's voice turned cold as ice. "Let him."

"My crea—" The hand that'd been holding mine was ripped away. Garavel gave a loud "Oof" as if he'd been struck in the stomach and I felt myself standing completely alone. I dipped to a knee and patted the ground while I heard the sound of feet dragging across the floor. *Garavel, hold on.*

Blind, I rummaged through my purse and uncapped my marker just as Garavel's body hit the wall. It struck with such force the entire room shook. Or maybe it was Cal and Ink in the fight of their lives.

"You swore an oath to me, stone *wardum*! To obey and give of yourself until your being is chipped to dust."

I kept one finger at the starting point while I drew a circle with the other, hoping to link them back up.

"Return to your place as ordered, or I shall deconstruct you and build anew," Ramiel thundered. The sound of someone sliding down the wall, then a gasp filled the air.

Please don't be dead.

Garavel coughed once and in a craggy voice asked, "What of your oath?"

"My siblings don't care about this realm or any other besides their own. Let them rot in heaven and hell."

I finished the line through the middle and slammed my hand in place. The same wall that had nearly stopped Mr. White erupted across the floor. But it didn't just form around my ward—it zipped from my hand until it struck the far wall, chasing the sound of Garavel's voice. At the loud slam, I stood up, ready to face whatever the angel would throw at us.

Ramiel didn't attack. He paced from the other side, separated from us both. I placed my hand on my wall and tried to walk down it in Garavel's direction. He wasn't talking. Had I hurt him?

"Garavel?" I called, hoping to run into him.

The air shifted like a thousand eyes were staring at me through the trees. I found my shoulders hunching up as I ducked lower and lower.

"Ah yes, the witchling. How could I forget your unhealthy attachment to them?" Ramiel said with a shallow chuckle.

I ignored the asshole and tried to find Garavel, when my support vanished. I flared my hand out, struggling to catch myself, but there was nothing to save me. My chest bounced on the stone floor first. I turned my chin to keep it from striking as well, and noticed a sliver of gray peeking in from the top of the blindfold.

Shit! Reaching behind, I tried to find the knot to tighten it.

"Such weak creatures in the end." Ramiel sighed.

The blindfold's fabric ripped at my hair, but I kept tugging on the knot's ends until it was secure. I looked up when boiling hot fingers sliced against my cheek. I yelped at the touch and the entire blindfold fell away.

With all the force in my body, I slammed my eyelids shut and tried to stare at the floor until the cool, smooth silk of Garavel's torn vestments curled under my chin. I couldn't look away no matter how hard I tried. Ramiel aimed my tearing eyes straight at him.

"You're nothing more than a handful of minerals and water. I could carve a thousand better beings from these stones who wouldn't burst into flames at the sight of me." He leaned closer. My entire face flushed like I'd shoved it into a hot oven. "Go on, human, give in to your inane curiosity and look upon the face of your creator."

No. My tears wouldn't stop, the salt stinging like bees. But if I gave in to the pain, if I even blinked... God, it was getting so bad. The heat burned hotter as my eyelids glowed red.

Don't do it. Fight it.

My lid began to slip, revealing an edge of deadly light electrifying off of something I couldn't understand. *Cal, Ink, Daniel...I'm so sorry.*

"Leave her alone!"

Ramiel dropped my chin. I collapsed to the ground, burying my face against the cool stone as he stomped toward Garavel.

"Do not show sympathy for them. You did once and look where it led."

Garavel didn't answer. I could only hear the thud of his sword falling to the ground. He'd already given up? No!

"I'm not a mage!" I shouted, trying to shake him awake.

"She is a witch. She is not like them," Garavel insisted.

I jerked my head to agree even if no one was looking, but my heart plummeted at Ramiel's laughter. "She is of them. A handful of powers doesn't stop her from being born of the same muck as the rest of the mages. She, as all witches, cavorts with mages, befriends them, beds them."

"Don't know if you heard there, buddy, but mages are long gone," I shouted even with my nose pressed to the ground.

"They helped us. They kept the realm safe," Garavel argued. "They still keep it safe."

"Are they? If Conquest has truly grown powerful enough to rip apart the threads, then it seems the witches are failing to uphold their end of the bargain."

They kept talking while ignoring me, treating me like a mouse that had scampered into a trap and couldn't escape. I knew the door was behind me, the sounds of muffled battle still carrying on. But I didn't know how to open it, or if I even could.

"My creator…"

"Are you not as tired of this prison as I am? Leave Conquest to his work. It seems poetic for the mages to be destroyed by their own creation. To know how we once felt. Stand down, Garavel, for the last time."

For the love of… "There. Are. No. Mages!" I shouted, slamming my hand to the ground with each word.

"Don't you know your own past, witch? Humans, all humans, were once mages. Arrogant, fiendish brutes who used our gifts to terrorize this world. They believed themselves better than their creators, so they strode across the land creating horrors in their image and unleashing them upon any who opposed them."

No. That…that didn't make any sense. "Garavel?" I called out to him, my heart racing. Did he think we were all monsters?

"If that's true, then why didn't you kill them?" I asked.

"Because they can't," Garavel whispered. "Only a demon can kill."

"That damnable accord," Ramiel cursed. "Were it not for that pact, I'd be free of this prison."

"Then leave." We didn't need him. We'd fight Mr. White on our own. "Fly out of here. Go to Antarctica. Or the Australian outback. Or the moon."

Ramiel snorted. "What do their elders teach them? This room is not the prison, witch. This realm is."

My heart dropped at how certainly he said those words. All of earth a prison for...for rebellious humans who had tried to take on their creators.

"I am its guardian to keep you damnable fools from infecting the proper realms. You witches, you were to be the conduits to keep such holes from forming. We left you your power as thanks for your service. But I see now how that was a mistake."

"So you're just going to let White rip away the realms? Turn us on the rest and attack them?"

A derisive laugh was his answer. "You humans are as toothless as a newborn babe. They will devour you, which they should have been allowed to in the beginning. But don't worry, witch. You do deserve a reward for your hard work."

I rather doubted he would hand me the two feathers and send me on my way. "For your service to the angels and the Accord of Realms, I shall gift you a quick death. Garavel?"

No! I craned my head toward him while keeping my eyes shut. "You don't have to do this," I begged.

"The witch does not understand."

"Please. What about your cat? What about ice cream? What about—?"

"Stop!" Garavel cried. I didn't feel him place a blade to my neck. Instead, I heard him toss it to the ground.

"I cannot harm her. She did as you asked. What of your promise? An angel's word is…"

"Do not quote my own mythos back to me," Ramiel thundered. "Very well, but after this you shall be decommissioned for insubordination."

"Don't you fucking dare!" I stormed as if I had any way to stop the angel.

It was Garavel who asked in a calm voice, "What of Layla? May I escort her out before you put an end to me?"

"Garavel, don't you let him. You're worth so much more than that!"

"To who?" Ramiel asked.

"To me!" I cursed back, all my heart in the statement.

He couldn't argue with me, even the angel seeing the truth. Garavel deserved to live in this world, even if it was a prison. We'd made good things in it. Bad things, yes, but amazing, wonderful things too.

"The battle is growing heated beyond my doors," Ramiel said. "Someone is in bitter pain. A pity you are not there to help."

I clenched my jaw, suddenly unable to hear anything but the wolf whimpers from beyond. They could be from the pack, but they could be Cal too.

"They're protecting you—a demon, a ghost of a human and a werewolf, no less. They're risking their lives for yours, angel. How is that worthless? How is that pitiable?"

He laughed again. "You think one good deed makes up for the atrocities of war? Atrocities you keep committing without end."

"They're trying. What are you doing?"

"You fear White in your soul, yet he would not exist were it not for the innate greed and lust that makes up humanity's soul. All four riders were made not by us, not by the care and delicate honing of a creator. No. They come from the hubris of mages alone, of feeding the monsters that turn around to eat you."

My skin was starting to ache as it peeled on my nose and forehead. *Fuck!* I bent lower, exposing the edge of my hand. It seared like I was touching a hot stove. A cry of pain must have slipped out as Garavel suddenly shouted my name.

"This could have been over so much quicker, Garavel. All you need do is pick up your sword. Instead, we will sit here and watch the witch slowly sear to her core."

Damn it!

"No, my creator, please. She does not deserve this."

"She deserves exactly what I give her, as do all who act out against me!"

A low chuckle rumbled in my throat. It started like a steam engine, picking up speed until I was full-body laughing on the floor. "I get it now. You're a self-centered parent who thinks because you made us, we have to do everything you say."

"That is precisely what you should do."

"No!" The week of confounding emotions against my own mother spilled from me. I hated her, I loved her, I never wanted to see her again and I missed her with all my heart. None of it made a damn lick of sense, and I screamed all of it at the angel. "The gift of life does not equal a return of servitude. Making us does not mean you own us! We are free to choose, to live as we want. We are not your slaves. We're your children."

"You're living life wrong," Ramiel shrieked. "You kill, you mutilate, you destroy and deceive without pause."

"We create. We love. Yeah, we fuck up. But we learn. We may fall but we get back up and try again. Sometimes..." Tears caught in my throat that I couldn't shake away. I turned to Garavel to say, "We even make ice cream."

He deserved better. The whole human race did, but I couldn't save all of us from this celestial prison. All I could do was try to help Garavel see what he was worth. "Your parents, your creators don't get to decide who you are. You do."

"I tire of this blather," Ramiel thundered. I felt his presence moving closer when fingers of hot pokers wrenched into my hair. He yanked me off the floor and clung to my cheeks. "Open your eyes, witch. End this already."

"No!" I tried to shake him off, but his touch sizzled against my skin. "Ink!" He couldn't enter. "Cal!" He was beyond my reach. "Daniel!" Every man I called was past the door, unable to save me. Every man I loved was fighting for his life while I died inside.

The slither of metal sliding over stone caused Ramiel to stop prying apart my eyelids. "Ah, good. If you finish this, then perhaps we can rethink decommissioning you."

No, no, no. Garavel placed his hand on my back. *Don't do this, you don't have to do this.* My lips couldn't stop trembling, the skin blistering from the heat. I tried to turn to look at him, to force him to see me, but Ramiel held me tight.

"I am sorry," Garavel whispered. He glided his palm from my back up to my neck, then behind my head.

I took a breath, knowing it wouldn't leave my lungs, when a force passed straight over my head.

"You..." Ramiel said. The unforgiving light flickered, dancing like the last flame of the bonfire. I turned to it and the world vanished into darkness.

Chapter Twenty-Seven

I kept my eyes closed.

Hands grabbed onto my shoulders and turned me around to face the sound of the door rolling apart, then they vanished. I stood helpless before the darkness, uncertain if I had been placed before the gates of the underworld. And still I kept my eyes closed.

"What's happening?" I asked, my voice weak and terrified. I couldn't fake strength anymore. My heart was bounding in my chest like a one-legged rabbit. "Garavel?" I looked over my shoulder just as the sound of a blade slicing into meat cut through my quick.

"The door is open." Garavel's voice boomed with command, but under the cold exterior I heard a vibrating string of pain. "You can go forward."

It could be a trick. For all I knew, Ramiel had killed him and was mimicking his voice. I stood firm, refusing to move. If I walked for the door, he could slam it shut on me.

"Layla? Please..." Garavel gasped beside my ear. I hadn't heard him move. He held my hand and I worked my fingers between his. There was no agonizing burn, only the cool palm of a man nearing his breaking point. "I have to leave." He scooped a hand around my waist and plucked me into the air. I could offer no resistance while we moved somewhere in the room.

As we landed, Garavel turned half away from me and I leaned with him as he touched something. After that, the door rattled closed. Still, I wouldn't risk it, keeping to the safety of darkness.

"You can open your eyes," he whispered.

I shook my head, the tears streaming. "Nu-uh," I mumbled.

"It is safe," Garavel pleaded. He could be right and telling the truth, but my heart wouldn't stop racing as my mind replayed one fact over and over. *Don't open your eyes.* I clung to that like a talisman against evil.

A hand graced over mine, warmer than Garavel's, the fingers nimbler and thinner. "My bond," Ink said. "You're not alone." He cupped my cheek, and in one swift jab, the pain of my blistered skin struck, wrenching my eyes open.

The tears watered my vision, the room nothing but shadows until I stared into the flickering dual flames of my incubus' eyes. I blubbered incoherently and leaped into his arms. Ink was slower to curl his arms around me, careful to not touch any but the part of my skin that'd been protected. Even then, my whole body was tender and about to crack.

"Layla?"

I lifted my head off of Ink to find Cal striding closer. His hair was stained red and matted. Blood splatter coated his chest and dripped down his neck, but he looked whole. "You're okay," I cried, reaching for him.

Cal took my hand, but he looked at me. "What the hell happened to you? Babe, does that hurt?"

I nodded, then shook my head, not knowing how I felt. Disillusioned didn't begin to cover it.

"Dan?" Cal called.

He too appeared before me, looking none the worse for wear save the shock of horror on his face. "Jesus Christ!" Daniel cursed, then he reached his hand out to my lips. His touch burned more than the blister and I reared back.

"Careful," Cal instructed. "You don't want to freeze the skin either."

Daniel took his advice and placed his finger an inch away. The ghost's cold touch became cool, then refreshing. "We were expecting angel assistance when the door opened."

"The wolves seemed to have the same thought. They tucked tail and ran," Ink added.

"Ramiel is…no longer of this realm," Garavel said.

I winced at the defeat in his voice. "You…you saved me." I turned to him, but Garavel wouldn't lift his gaze.

"Saved you from what?" Daniel asked.

"Not of this realm? The angel is no more? If he is returned to dust, then how shall we defeat Conquest and the pack of mangy mutts that chewed up my good shoes?"

I didn't have any answers. Ramiel had been our only option to stop White and that too was gone. I dropped my chin with the weight of my failure. It was Cal who lightly touched me until I stared into his eyes. "Doesn't matter," he declared.

"An exploded house and murder deer run amok says otherwise," Daniel chided.

Cal shook his head, focusing on me. "You're alive, you're... I hate that we sent you in there." The other two hung their heads as if they were to blame for what had happened.

"I hated that you were all fighting out here without me." We were a sorry bunch, teetering on an edge we barely understood.

Only Ink could shrug away the dour frowns. "Your wolf handled himself well, all things considered. The demi-angel knows how to lay out an ambush."

Garavel. He didn't acknowledge the compliment, or the fact he was probably the reason my guys were still alive. He stood next to the sealed door with a hand placed over the crack.

I reached for his hand. He didn't move, letting me trail my fingers down his forearm until I touched the dangling fingertips and pressed my palm to his. "We should get out of here," I said.

"We should get you to an ER first," Cal interrupted.

Great, more medical bills I couldn't afford. But as I took a breath, I knew he was right. This wasn't a simple sunburn I could sleep off.

"Garavel?" I wrapped my fingers around his hand, but he didn't return the touch. "Why don't you come with us?"

"Can your house support another, wolf?"

"That, uh..." Cal coughed and closed his eyes. "Layla, I don't know about..."

"He saved me by...by risking everything." I couldn't fathom an inch of the pain cutting through him, but I knew he shouldn't be abandoned.

"Okay," Cal said, nodding solemnly. "I suppose there's space in the attic."

Garavel folded his fingers around my hand. He tugged me closer by it and placed both our hands above his heart. "Lady Witch...Layla. You are kind to worry, but I can't go with you."

"I know you have bad blood with werewolves, but Cal isn't —"

Garavel finally raised his head and turned to me. Tears poured from his eyes, falling without end, but he held a smile on his lips. He raised his hand above my cheek without touching the burn. "Your heart is more beautiful than I could ever deserve."

"What will you do?" *Without him? Without me?*

"First I will...I will give his body peace where none can desecrate it."

"And then?"

Garavel didn't answer. He only stared through the door to where the dead body of his creator rested. A hand slipped around my waist and I looked back to find Ink tugging me away from the mourning angel. Once I was far enough, Garavel pulled his wings in and curled them around his body like a self-hug. My heart ached for the pain he was suffering, but I knew I couldn't help him unless he let me.

"We should go from this place before the wolves realize divine wrath isn't nipping at their heels." Ink wrapped both his hands around me, but he waited and looked to Cal.

"Take her straight to the hospital on the east side. I'll catch up later." Despite saying that, he cupped the back of my head and gazed at me with worry.

"I'll pop back to the house and look again for any recipes to help against angel burns," Daniel chimed in. Everyone was trying desperately to help.

I nodded, the pain on my cheeks and forehead growing too much to bear. All I wanted was to crawl into bed and forget this day happened.

"Wait," Garavel said. He reached inside the coat of his jacket and extracted two massive feathers unlike anything I'd ever seen. Up close, each strand looked like a fiberoptic cable that changed hue from the shaft to the tip. At a distance, the feather shimmered with a rainbow light, both delicate and stronger than steel in the same moment.

"Garavel..."

"You did as he asked, and an angel always keeps his word," he said, clasping both of my hands around the feathers. "Goodbye, Lady Witch."

"I'm sorry," I whispered to him as Ink pulled me away from the broken man who had shattered his life to save mine.

* * * *

"Layla, what are you doing?"

I paused in trying to tug my polo uniform over my head without touching any of my skin. It left me struggling to stare through the neck hole in the direction of my self-appointed nurse. For the past four days, Cal had damn near waited on me hand and foot, checking bandages, carrying me down the stairs, even sharing a cool bath with me. And it sucked balls that I was in so much pain I couldn't enjoy a second of it. I kept telling myself that in a few days when my face

Ellen Mint

didn't feel like Satan's sandpaper every time I sneezed, I'd put that huge, clawed tub to good use.

A girl could only take her boyfriend's massive erection against the top of her ass for so long before going insane. Was that what Ink felt like most days?

Before I could shimmy my face through the neck hole, Cal caught the top and pulled it off.

"I'm getting ready for work. My shift starts in...oh, shit."

"No," he declared, folding up my polo and placing it on the dresser. "You are going back to bed, after you take your ibuprofen."

"Look, you being all daddy knows best is brain melting and giving me ideas," I admitted aloud. Cal turned bright red and clasped his hands together like he was folding a shirt that wasn't there. His eyes dipped down from my still pinked-up face to take in my unburned décolletage and boobs partially bulging from the too small bra I didn't have the heart to throw out.

A low growl from deep in Cal's chest caused me to blush. That man was going to drive me up the wall before I healed. I pushed past him to pick up the shirt he'd expertly folded. "You and I both know the hospital visit let me miss one day of work, but two? I can't afford getting fired."

I had no idea what the nurse slathering me in burn ointment, wrapping the wounds and giving me forty-dollar aspirin tablets would cost me, but it wasn't gonna be good. Cal caught my elbow between his thumb and pinkie, stopping me from once again getting dressed. "Don't worry."

"What has our beloved in a flurry?" Ink popped in and reclined on the bed like a pin-up Lothario from the

314

seventies. All that was missing were the bear skin rug and mounds of chest hair. He beamed a smile at me, drawing his palm down his posed side. When he reached his hip, he stared past me to Cal and sighed. "Of course, her slavish duty to the lords of freight."

Rising off the bed, Ink clucked his tongue. "My bond, you need not concern yourself with the hustle and bustle of the grind." He swept me up into his arms and turned me about in a slow dance.

"I need to eat. You can't stop eating."

"I daresay I've been on quite the diet these past four days," Ink muttered to himself and my gaze dropped. "But" — he put on a smile and delicately pulled my hair out of the ointment slathered on my face—"your banking script has already been filled for the month."

"What? How? Cal, they would never approve time off, much less PTO. I'm not even full time."

He lightly crossed his arms and tipped his head to Ink. "We sent him in."

"What did you do?" It was one thing to get me out of my lease, but my boss... I was so fired.

"Do not worry so. We had a delightful conversation regarding the nature of his sexual peccadildos."

"Pretty sure it's peccadillo," Cal said.

"In his case it is not."

Both I and Cal full-body cringed at that nugget of information. "Thanks, Ink," I said, ordering my brain to not picture my manager surrounded by pink dildos. It wasn't working.

"You are most welcome, my bond." Ink twirled me on my toes, then he bowed deeply. As he rose, he took my hand and placed it to his lips. "May this provide you succor until you are of sound enough body that your body can create sounds of ecstasy from my talented fingers."

He kissed me on the knuckles once more, no doubt sealing in his pun, when he looked up from his debonair sweep. It wasn't fire burning in his eyes, or even annoyance that he was still denied his meal. For a brief flicker, I stared into worry on my demon's face. Ink tossed it aside as he rose to his full height then crashed an arm around Cal's shoulders.

"Shall we abscond to the market of many items?" he asked jovially.

"Yeah, I can drop you off." He seemed to know whatever that was about. But Ink was left to walk out the door alone as Cal stood and looked at me. "Get some sleep, Layla. Drink a ton of water. That'll help."

"I know, I know..." I gave in to their demands quickly. Truth was, I still felt like shit. When I stumbled, my knee struck the high mattress and I nearly face-planted onto the bed. Before I smeared the sheets with aloe and analgesic, Cal swept me up into his arms. He guided me into bed like I'd had too much to drink.

"I love you," Cal whispered, hovering his lips just above my forehead for an air kiss. It was stupid, but my heart flipped every time he did it.

He started to slip away, when I caught his hand. His eyes went wide and I tugged him closer. "I love you, too," I said as I pulled his lips to mine. Oh, that stung. But the heat of his gentle touch made the pain worth it.

Cal didn't say anything to that. He let go of my hand and walked to the door. Before leaving, he turned out the light. "Sleep already."

"Yes, nurse!" I called to him as he vanished out the door. I could hear him shouting for Ink to get in the truck, the two of them making a racket as they dashed down the stairs. Daniel was in his makeshift library, trying to find a way to protect us from one of the four riders of the apocalypse. All was quiet in the house, except the gentle tick of the clock slowly dragging me down to sleep.

Wait. Cal didn't have a clock in the bedroom.

I sat up fast, instantly regretting it, as I traced the sound to the window. "Garavel?" Flinging off the covers, I struggled to think of what to say to him. He didn't hover outside the window as before, but sat perched on the tiny balcony railing.

It wasn't easy popping open the old window, but when it went, I stuck my head out and said, "Sup."

Oh my god, what is wrong with me? Garavel's dour face lightened at my greeting. No doubt he was struggling to understand what I meant, or was worrying I had suffered brain damage in the fight.

"You…you're here. I didn't think you'd come back."

Garavel's smile twisted into a knot as he reached to the side and extended the tiny black kitten. "I didn't want her to go hungry," he said.

I reached out, taking the kitten in my arms. After the last few days, she already looked bigger. The fur atop her head was twisted like soft serve and she meowed at me. "Such a sweet baby," I cooed, brushing against her cheek.

"She likes to be scratched on her head, but not the belly. Never the belly." Garavel, the man of ebony who commanded the will of angels, looked stricken in terror from kitten ambushes. He held his hand up, as if to show me the scars from where the kitten had gotten him. "Running water is preferable to still, and she'll chew through all your woolen socks in a second."

Garavel held a single finger out, nearly reaching through the threshold to touch the kitten. She turned in my arms and bonked her nose against it.

"Why don't you come inside?" I asked.

He retracted his hand and gripped to the railing. I feared he'd fly off, but he stayed in place. "I don't know."

"Please?" I held out my hand, praying he'd take it. "You don't have to be alone."

His head shot up and he gasped. "I should be dust for what I did. I disobeyed my creator. I destroyed him. No demi-angel would ever betray their oath. What does that make me?"

He wanted me to hate him because no one was left alive to do it. The anger at life taking the wrong path, at fate being a fickle bitch and stealing his life away must have been pummeling through him. The need to whip or be whipped until it all made sense. I knew that one well.

"You're free." I held my hand out again, not about to give up.

Garavel stared at my fingers, then he raised his own palm. Slowly, he placed his atop mine and, one by one, he circled his fingers around mine. "I don't know what to do."

"I know." With barely any force, I pulled him in. Garavel slunk off the railing. He ducked his head down, struggling to slip into the bedroom. The wings caught on the sill, shedding feathers, but he kept at it until he stood beside me.

He placed his hand out and the kitten leaped into it. We both scratched her head, saying nothing. She began to purr, her tiny rumblings causing Garavel to smile.

He bent lower, bringing his nose to the kitten's face until he whispered, "I'm scared."

"I get that."

"I'm scared to be alone" — he raised his head and stared deep into my eyes — "without you. But you must fear me after what I did. I broke the contract, my oath. I am no better than a mage."

I drew my palm across his jaw, tracing the gentle curves of his face and the soft brow of the tender man who adored a kitten. "Garavel, you saved my life. I can never fear the gift you gave me, even at such a high cost."

Light broke in his eyes and a lopsided smile began to take form. Suddenly, he dropped to a knee, leaving me scrambling to support the kitten. "Lady Witch, allow me to swear fealty to you and your service."

I swept my palm across his vast shoulders and reached for the hand he held up to me in supplication. "No."

"No?" he whimpered as I helped raise him back up.

"I don't want a soldier. I don't want a servant to answer my every command."

He swallowed deep and blinked his heavy lids. "What do you want?"

"You. Free to live your life with me. Not in some rundown mansion, but here. Safe. Do you want that too?"

Garavel gasped in shock that anything could be so simple. "Yes." He leaned over me, his wings folding in to shield us both. The kitten scrambled up his shoulder and vanished into the white feathers. I clung onto Garavel's cheeks, holding him close. I could almost feel the pain broiling below his skin. I wished I were skilled enough to take it all away.

"Lady…Layla. May I kiss you?"

His request was so earnest, I nearly laughed. "Yes." I nodded. Garavel cupped the nape of my neck and he puckered his lips before mine. He started so gentle and soft, I didn't feel a strike of pain. Slowly, we melted together, the kiss seeming without end. He brushed his thumbs along the back of my jaw, holding me safe as he pulled back.

"That was…" Garavel's gaze softened and he breathed. "Home. There is much yet to do."

"I know." I braced myself on his forearms. Mr. White was out there scheming to rip apart the world. So was the wolf pack that was bruised but not beaten, and no doubt looking for a rematch. But we had each other.

"Where do we begin?"

A mewl answered before I could. The kitten leaped from between the feathers. She tucked and rolled, trying to chase her tail. Luckily the angel was quick to catch her.

I scratched her back and said, "First we need to give this kitten a name."

"But that is only for creators."

"You're her dad, which is like a creator, so…"

Garavel's eyes widened at the logic, but he picked up the tiny kitten and held her before his eyes. "Fiona," he declared. Little Fiona meowed at her new name and she leaped for the safety of the angel's feathers.

"I will fight for her, for this realm —" Garavel took my hand. "And I will fight for you. Because I choose to."

"Welcome to the coven."

Chapter Twenty-Eight

No one had stolen the flowers. I stared at the plastic daisies scattered in the vase. Every other year, someone had nicked them before I had a chance to get back to the graveyard. After being trapped in bed for a week, I was certain they'd be gone. Most of the burns had faded from a painful red to my normal freckled light brown, but I wore an aunty church hat to be safe. The brim hid my face in the shade. All I needed was a small veil to complete my black widow look.

Unlike Mother's Day, the cemetery was quiet, most of the mourners having left their loved ones' bones to rest while they went about their lives. I would have done the same if it weren't for Cal somehow picking up my shifts and his. As I bent over to pick up the flowers, a shadow passed overhead. To the people on the ground, it looked like a large bird, a vulture or an eagle, but I knew better.

We were all waiting on pins and needles for the next attack from White or the wolf pack. But life didn't stop even with the world hanging in the balance. In the distance, the roar of a riding lawn mower downed out the birdsong. I looked up as the groundskeeper came rolling by, caring not a whit for the other flowers he mowed down in the process. In the end, even the dead were business.

"It's still here."

I nearly jumped but kept my feet on the ground at Daniel's mournful voice winding behind my ear. "You're quieter than Fiona," I said.

He sighed. "Your kitten despises me."

"She just...she's getting used to you. We're all getting used to this." Magic, demons, angels, the earth being a prison about to end — all of it took getting used to. My mother alive and out there...

"I've found a bit more about the four horsemen, Conquest in particular. The first three surge in waves across the world, always falling back to obscurity before surging again. When Conquest marches with an army, he doesn't lead, but picks a champion. An old occult book theorized people like Attila, Genghis Khan, Qin Shi Huang or Alexander were all blessed by Conquest."

"I guess we know who his champion is now." Eric, the massive red wolf that wanted to kill me just to hurt Cal.

Daniel nodded solemnly. Every time I went to see him, he was hunched over a new book, flipping pages to find a new protection spell. Nothing could hold up against Mr. White.

"I'm worried about you," I said. He turned to me in confusion. "You keep researching at the rate you are, you're liable to work yourself to...uh."

"To death?" He snorted and clasped his hands behind his back. "That is one luxury I am well equipped to afford."

"But there's something else. Something that's bothering you." We had the feathers. All we needed were demon blood and a unicorn skin, then we had to figure out that piece of the other realms. We were one quarter of the way to bringing him back to life, yet Daniel didn't celebrate. He grew more sullen and detached from the others.

Snickering, he shook his head. "How is it that you can know me so well?"

"Well, you and Ink haven't been fighting like cats in a bag, so..."

Daniel tipped his chin at the acknowledgment, but didn't rise to the bait either. "I loved my mom. I love my mom. She didn't always make it easy, but I didn't either. I keep thinking back to the last time I saw her while alive. We fought, the same arguments without end. I was wasting my life. She was stifling me. I should go to community college. She didn't understand my artistic soul."

The cherry blossoms shook above our heads, scattering petals in the May breeze. They fell not around Daniel, but through him as he gazed across the cemetery. "They buried me last week."

"What? Why didn't you say anything?"

He shrugged.

"We should...should I visit? I could leave some or..." I reached into my purse and grazed the single picture I had of Daniel. It was as out of time as he was.

"I can feel them, hear them. When I was lost in that drainage ditch, I never felt a reason to return to my body. No one knew I was there, no one cared. But my mom, she's been visiting every day, leaving behind Pocky sticks...and crying."

My eyes welled up at the image of his eighty-year-old mother at last laying her son to rest and mourning the end of her hope. Daniel swallowed and his lips trembled as if he too were fighting back tears. "I've never seen her cry so much, so openly in front of me. I'm screaming across the chasm and she can't hear me."

"I...I don't know what to say." I fell dumb, having only been on the other side of a loved one grieving in a cemetery.

Daniel turned a rueful smile on me. "You don't need to say anything. Listening is enough."

"I want to help. To do whatever I can so you...so she can find peace."

He raised his palm and held it near my cheek. The cool of him didn't snap at my burned skin and I leaned closer, closing my eyes. "The compassion in your heart can only be measured in oceans. If I...when I determine what will help, I'll come straight to you."

"Is that a promise?"

"Always." Daniel skirted his fingers down my arm before he reached the end of my hand. "I should return home. There is a potion on the boil I'm certain the demon is failing to watch."

"Or he added peanut butter to it." God save us all from the day Ink discovered Nutella.

Daniel bowed his head to acknowledge my words, but he didn't laugh. None of us were in much of a jolly mood after the past week. We had escaped by the skin of our teeth, again. How many near misses could we take before one of us didn't come back?

He gave a little wave, then slowly faded away. I clung to the locket around my neck, reminding myself that he was a second away. Ink too would come running if I even caught a glimpse of a dog or a man in a white suit. Every night Cal held me close, enveloping me in his arms as if he could shield me from the worst about to come. And Garavel, my guardian angel, flew above me wherever I went. Whatever was coming, however horrific it could be, at least I knew in my heart that I had my guys at my side. And unlike my mother, they wouldn't abandon me.

I stared at the stone for a woman pretending to be dead one last time and realized I wasn't ever coming back here. As I walked away, I spotted a forgotten grave and placed the plastic flowers for a spinster who had lived into her nineties. Maybe that would brighten up her day wherever she was in the beyond.

"You're taking a big risk."

I jerked up, instantly spotting a silhouette under the old oak tree. Slowly, I rose off my haunches as a woman scratched her chin. A long blonde braid dangled off her shoulder and my heart constricted. "Being out in the open like this. It's easy for him to find you again."

I thought I'd forgotten it. That time would take the scratchy timbre, the hard end to sentences, the soft melody of the o's. But it came roaring back in a heartbeat as she stepped out of the shadows and into the sun.

When she tossed back her hood, the sun struck her golden hair and she smiled. "It's a lucky thing I found you first."

"Mom?"

Want to see more from this author? Here's a taster for you to enjoy!

Coven of Desire: Scales
Ellen Mint

Coming March 2023

Excerpt

"Mom?"

Fifteen years. For fifteen years, I'd stumbled alone in the dark. No mother to teach me how to drive, to show me what tampons to buy, to coo over my prom dress or embarrass me at graduation. I had faced every harsh sunrise alone, my family…my whole world ripped from me bit by bit.

"Hello, Layl—"

I ran to her and buried my face in my lost mother. Instead of her soft belly cushioning my tears, it was her shoulder that caught me. Uncertain hands patted my back, and as I crushed tighter against her, she returned the hug. I'd never thought I'd feel those arms again.

Never imagined I'd hear her voice calling to me.

The scents of jasmine and burnt wiring plunged a rosy spear of nostalgia through my heart and I sobbed. I'd broken her bottle of perfume my first week in the foster home. It'd shattered on the sink. Even with glass shards slicing up my fingers, I'd tried desperately to mop it up so I wouldn't lose it. So I wouldn't lose her.

Nimble fingers tugged through my hair, parting the twists as she cupped the nape of my neck. A tingle I'd always thought came from my imagination pulsed at her touch. Now I knew it to be magic, my mother casting a spell to calm me as if I were a child in a panic after a nightmare.

"You..."

My arms fell off of her. She'd left. She didn't just leave—she had made certain I wouldn't follow. That I couldn't follow. I staggered back, punch drunk from the emotions roiling in my heart. Wrinkles had built near her eyes and her cheeks sagged, but it was my mom. Looking at her, the years I'd spent building over the scar of her death ripped away.

"You left."

She smiled dolefully. "I know. I didn't have a choice, but that's in the past. What matters is what happens next."

"In the past?" In the fifteen years of mourning her, my grief callous had hardened over a node of rage. Seeing her broke it open.

"Do you have any idea what I've been through because I didn't have a...?" My lips wobbled, tears spilling over at the word 'mom.'

"Laylee." She sighed with my old pet name. I shivered, both in anger and...relief to hear it again. "What matters is you've done it, gained your powers and your..." She jerked her head to my purse. On instinct, I slapped a hand over it to protect my spell book, but that only made my mother smile with pride.

"Though, I'm concerned."

So am I.

"It was quick thinking of you to amplify the realm creature, but you should have been much stronger fighting against the man in white."

What? "You! You were there. You were there at the house, the monster ball. And you didn't say anything!"

My mom shrugged, and her blonde braid slipped off her shoulder. The woman, the face behind the mask in the crowd—it had been her and I'd walked on past. I hadn't even once looked back to her. She could have been killed because of me, and I'd never have known.

"Lucky for you, I was. I saved your life. If you'd been hit by that abomination's spell, it'd have cast you through every realm into depths I can't even imagine." She crossed her arms as if she expected gratitude—like she'd brought my lunch to school after I'd left it on the table.

I clenched my fist, rolling the power inside of me down my forearm, over the back of my hand and into my palm. It ebbed with each pulse, sinking my nails deeper as I fought to keep from screaming. "You leave. You left me alone for fifteen years."

"Layla, now is not the time."

"You abandoned me!" I shrieked and opened my fist. Fire sprung forth, dousing the green-tan grass in flames. My mother pursed her lips and raised her hand.

Even though I knew she had to be a witch, seeing wind erupt from her movements floored me. She had magic, same as me. She was the only person who knew what I'd face, and she had left me in the dark instead.

"Honestly, this is not the place to be—"

"How long have you watched me? How long have you stood by the sidelines refusing to help me?" I clung to my temples, my body shaking. My mind rewound through my past. Every time I'd feared for my life, had my mother been there? Even back before my powers, before Ink and the book? When I'd been kicked out of the system with nothing to my name but the clothes in my backpack, where was she? When I'd slept in a rat-infested apartment because it was all I could afford, had my mother known?

"There's a lot you don't understand, yet. Look…" My mother reached out to wrap her arm over my shoulders, but I ducked and ran away.

"I understand perfectly well. I know you faked your death, that you killed an innocent woman—"

"She was going to die anyway," my mother interrupted.

It sure as hell hadn't looked that way in my vision, but I gritted my jaw and kept going. "And you left me. You left me alone."

"Layla. That isn't what—"

I dodged her again, both of my palms up. Power crackled between us, the air tasting like lightning right before the strike. "And the second you find me, when you come back into my life, it's just to tell me I'm not good enough?"

"It's not that you aren't…" She groaned and pinched her nose. "Didi's better at this."

I gulped at the mention of my dead auntie. Just as I'd accepted my mom was never coming back, death had snatched Didi away, too. Did my mother know that as well and still refuse to come back?

"Please, let me explain why I—"

"No. No, I'm not… I can't deal with… Ink!" I closed my eyes tight, picturing my incubus from his jet-black waves, to his come-hither smirk and down his sinful body. My mind zeroed in on the new tattoo on his chest of a heart made of chains. As I pictured it, hands swept across my waist and my cheek pressed against a pec.

"You rang?" Ink asked.

I clasped my hands around the back of his neck. Ink jerked as if surprised, then he tenderly swept his arms around me. "My bond, are you suffering yet from the angel's malady?"

"Who's this?" my mother demanded, her hands raised to cast a spell at the man holding me safe.

"I was about to inquire the same. An enthusiastic grave robber perhaps?"

I cast a single eye back to my mother, the other buried in the darkness of Ink's chest. "She's no one," I said. "Take me home."

Ink wasn't stupid. He stared at the woman with my face but paler and less voluptuous features. Still, he caressed his palm over my back as he said, "While I am not one to call a lie a lie, perhaps it would be in—"

I turned tighter in his grip and gasped out, "Please."

He bent closer, his lips almost caressing my forehead. "Of course." Ink swept me up in his arms and the realms parted. My skin tingled in a way it never had before as Ink took a step out of the cemetery and back to our home.

Just before he did, my mother cried out, "Layla," one last time.

About the Author

Ellen Mint adores the adorkable heroes who charm with their shy smiles and heroines that pack a punch. She has a needy black lab named after Granny Weatherwax from Discworld. Sadly, her dog is more of a Magrat.

When she's not writing imposing incubi or saucy aliens, she does silly things like make a tiny library full of her books. Her background is in genetics and she married a food scientist so the two of them nerd out over things like gut bacteria. She also loves gaming, particularly some of the bigger RPG titles. If you want to get her talking for hours, just bring up Dragon Age.

Ellen loves to hear from readers. You can find her contact information, website details and author profile page at https://www.totallybound.com

Home of Erotic Romance

Sign up for our newsletter and find out about all our romance book releases, eBook sales and promotions, sneak peeks and FREE romance books!